Silent Judgment

Also by Zaire Crown

Games Women Play

The Game Never Ends

Silence

Silent Judgment

ZAIRE CROWN

www.kensingtonbooks.com

Chapter One

The call came at three thirty in the morning.

And I had just spent the last two and a half hours whooping Kierra. That angry dick tried to screw her through the mattress and had eventually fallen asleep in it.

Would've just said fuck whoever was trying to disturb my post-nut nod when my fuck buddy heard the buzzing on the nightstand. But this was the Big Phone. The one I couldn't ignore.

That text was what put my naked ass into some sweats, my bare feet into some boots, and had me in my Ram 1500 headed to the worst neighborhood on the eastside of Detroit at four o'clock in the morning. Pissed off and still half asleep. I carried a 10mm Glock G20 on my lap along with an AR-15 on the back seat. I pulled into the Citgo in the area of Mack and Conners, still recalling that I didn't have much luck with eastside gas stations—damn near got robbed and killed at one not far from here.

Prime and his boys were already there. Two old-school Chevys and a new Trackhawk Jeep had the Rolls-Royce wedged in at the pumps. The white exotic had traded paint with the gray Cutlass, trying to fight its way out. I parked by the service mart, jumped out the pickup I was leasing in Kierra's name. A chilly April wind snaked up my pantleg and made me regret not slipping on boxers.

Prime had cut his dreads off about a year back—I guess the hair was a reminder of his struggle years, a point in his timeline he was eager to erase. At six-foot-seven, he no longer resembled a broke-ass 2 Chainz: a mink hood covered a clean shaved head, buffalo-horn Cartiers covered his face, expensive denim covered his legs, and limited-edition Jordan 11s covered his feet. He met me with a crew of seven at his back. His greeting equaled the night's chill.

"This bitch must be crazy. You lucky this my hood. If it wasn't for the juice you got with me, niggas would've been feasting."

I just let him have that, didn't bother to explain that he was the lucky one. Prime might have seen her face once or twice in the newspaper but had no idea of who the woman in that car really was. More importantly, he didn't know who she was connected to. If anything had happened to her, this hood he was so proud of would've suffered something biblical. I'm talking about five to six acres of nothing but smoke and ash.

Prime and his boys parted to let me through. I got a couple of glares, was able to pick up on the hostile energy. This would be a problem soon. Dark clouds that forecast a pending storm.

The white paint and chrome of the Rolls-Royce Ghost shimmered like something ethereal under the gas station's pavilion lights. I approached the driver's door and softly tapped on the window. The rich lady was slumped in her seat with her chin touching her chest. She raised her head and stared as if it took a few seconds to bring me into focus. Once recognition kicked in, I received a disgusted frown; then she closed her eyes against me. Her head rolled to the right, and she returned to the stupor of whatever drugs momentarily claimed her.

I walked around to the passenger door and let myself in. When I claimed the seat, she momentarily snapped awake. She looked as if locking the doors only occurred to her then. She screamed at me to get out.

I leaned back and gave her an apologetic refusal. I used my forearms to deflect the blows that I knew were coming next. After half a dozen attempts to punch my face, she exhausted herself, then slumped back in her seat.

She looked broken—and it pained me to see it, because I had played some small part in the breaking. Her eyes were puffy and swollen. She looked to have aged five years in the few months since I had seen her last. Still beautiful, just damaged. Mascara tears streaked her face, the makeup hastily applied only for effect.

She wore an ankle-length white spotted sable coat along with what appeared to be every piece of jewelry that she owned. She was a walking eight-figure lick, had on more jewels than an ancient Persian king. There were maybe thirty diamond necklaces on her chest, forearms sleeved in bracelets, three to four rings shared each finger.

And just to insure the worst possible outcome, she was naked under the mink.

Her head drifted with her eyes closed before she snapped back to reality. She turned to me and seemed to be surprised that I was still there. I smelled brown liquor wafting through her pores, but I couldn't guess whether it was powder or pills that glazed her gray-green eyes.

She had perched between her lips a half-smoked blunt she fished from the ashtray. I assisted with my own lighter after she made several failed attempts to put fire to it.

"This ain't some fake-ass cry for attention. I know the devil is watching. I figured he might send somebody—didn't think it would be your snake ass—" She spoke the rest of the insult while blowing smoke, which made it difficult for me.

She leaned forward a bit in her seat and turned her shoulder away from me. "You came to pull the knife out my back. Or you gone be a real nigga this time and at least look me in the eye when you stab me in the front?"

I assumed the question was rhetorical. I just sat there inhaling the scent of rich bespoke leather mingled with high-grade Kush.

There was more pain and regret swimming through me than I let be revealed in my stare.

The woman put on a smile that wasn't meant to appear genuine. "Go ahead. Ask me how my day went."

I accepted the blunt when she offered it. I made a *gimme* motion with my hand.

"First, I finessed a Texas billionaire out of a thirty percent stake in his oil refinery. Then, I closed a deal that will bring almost seventeen thousand new jobs to the city, and boost my personal network another seventy million. After that, I went to St. Jude Hospital and pulled the plug on my baby girl."

I cringed as if punched in the stomach. Her daughter's cancer battle had been kept out the news, but I had been kept abreast through my sources. Glioblastoma. I wasn't a doctor, only knew it was something in the brain that was aggressive. The failed attempt at surgery had dropped Tanisha into a coma. The girl was just six years old.

After two quick puffs, I passed her the weed back. She needed that shit way more than me.

I looked at the woman, admiring the strength it must've taken for her to make the hardest decision a mother could possibly face. But also seeing that the decision had bankrupt all the strength she had left.

There was no condolence I could offer that felt adequate. As much as she hated me, and had every right to, the need for human contact overrode the resentment. She permitted me to put my hand on top of hers.

I sent Prime a text telling him that he and his boys could go. I had her now, and wasn't shit going to happen to her while she was with me. And for a while, we sat and smoked in silence.

Eventually the rich lady let me take her home. I transferred Tuesday to the passenger seat. I drove her and the Rolls-Royce back out to Farmington Hills.

I pulled into the gated grounds of her seventeen-million-dollar estate. Some might find it hard to believe that this same woman, who owned and ran one of the biggest export companies in the country, who had single-handedly revitalized entire areas in the inner city on the legitimate side, who had taken down cartel bosses on the criminal side, not ten years ago was a stripper robbing dope boys just to make ends meet. She was a bossy bitch who had climbed her way up from nothing.

I had once helped to protect her and her family. I felt the loss of her daughter, not like it were my own, but empathized only because I had a child I couldn't be with.

I parked the Ghost beneath the portico of a modern castle. Her home was a Tudor-inspired masterpiece with turrets and parapets. Landscape lighting bathed the limestone façade. Large, vaulted windows offered sneak peeks at the luxury within.

I offered my shoulder to lean on as I walked her to the front door. The big man met us at the entrance. He charged towards me with his face twisted in fury.

"Watch out. I got her." He scooped his friend and benefactor up into his arms like a child after throwing me a *Fuck you!* glare. DelRay had every right to be pissed at me, too. Which was probably the only reason he didn't get fucked-up. He used to bounce for her when Tuesday owned her strip club, and after a brief stint as an arms dealer, was now her protector and confidant. He was six-nine and 400 pounds but still didn't want it with me.

I typed into my phone and let DelRay read the unsent text. I explained if he really had her, I wouldn't have gotten the call and then had to call in the favor with Prime to make sure she was secure.

I followed DelRay as he carried her through a foyer that could hold my entire house, up a split staircase with marble balustrades to a second-floor suite. He laid Tuesday down with a gentleness that came from pure love. He removed her mink and tucked her into bed like a child. I watched this tender moment between friends, awed and envious.

"Get yo' bitch ass out of here!" DelRay said to me after turning away from a massive canopy bed with velvet drapery. He emphasized his comment with a dismissive wave of the hand.

The Shango warrior in me wanted to test myself against one of the few people who was bigger than me, but the guilt kept my hands unfisted. I turned and was ready to slink out of the room before I noticed Tuesday flagging for my attention in the reflection of a mirrored vanity.

I approached her bed, head down, shoulders stooped. I already knew what she was about to ask me and already knew I couldn't do a damn thing to help her.

"You know where he's at."

I shook my head, because I genuinely didn't.

"Fuck you. You helped him steal from me."

Tuesday had come to me during a crisis point in her life: she was broke, on the run, and under pressure from the Mexican cartels. She had hired me to protect her, never knowing that me and her husband already had a previous arrangement. So when her husband took something from her, it looked like I played a role in it. When in truth, I was just as fucked-up as she was. .

I didn't waste my time or cellular data trying to text her my side of the story. I knew it wouldn't matter.

"You don't have a fucking clue of who he really is or what he's connected to. All the ghost stories and rumors they spread about The Invisible Man are mostly bullshit. But the truth is a helluva lot worse.

"And now he's got his arm so far up your goddamn back that your breath smells like hand sanitizer." I didn't like being compared to a puppet but couldn't fake the wounded pride because it wasn't untrue.

But as much as I felt her pain, I couldn't help her find her husband. If I had the voice, I would explain that me and dude didn't text back and forth, wasn't hitting up Pistons games together with seats on the hardwood. About a year ago, he had given me a phone, and I was expected to obey the orders from the other end.

The texts might come from him or from some faceless henchman. Might come from someone seated across the street, or from somebody in Japan.

I had to stay in line for right now. I had been taught since I could walk how to fight, kill, and survive by any means, but the man she had married was probably the only man in the world I genuinely feared.

And not for what he could do to me, because I had no fear of dying. But I had loved ones to consider. And his reach was such that he could get to them anytime he wanted.

I could only apologize with my eyes as she cursed and screamed at me. Tuesday was talking too fast for me to make out the words, but I could easily infer that she wanted me to get the fuck out.

Chapter Two

It took damn near a hundred dollars to get back to the city by cab, and then I had to pick my truck up from Prime before I made it home. A few months back, I had bought myself a low-key crib in the area of West 6 Mile and Asbury Park. I had no connections to this hood, which was exactly why I made the move. This was an area that had gone to shit during Detroit's economic decline, but had been recently revitalized thanks to subsidies and home ownership grants provided by Abel Incorporated. Ironically, the same rich lady who I had refused to help was the very one responsible for helping me own a $140,000 home for a fraction of the price.

While I had gotten the house for pennies on the dollar, the renovations done to the interior were what had dealt the heaviest blow to my pockets. Thanks to corporate sponsorship, the community was on the upswing, but my line of work had me taking no chances when it came to security. Motion-sensor lights and doorbell cameras might have been enough for the neighbors. On the outside, my home looked just as mundane as any other on the block, but any person foolish enough to try to break in would get a huge surprise.

After I backed my Ram into the driveway, I let myself in through the side door, expecting full well for Kierra to still be up. She was stretched across my bed, nibbling on the tines of a plastic fork while watching the morning news. I collapsed next to her, lying head to foot. My face said, *Damn, straight up?* at seeing that she was in a pair of my Jordan hoop shorts with no bra, and more than likely no panties underneath.

She rolled her eyes in response to me. "They smell like yo' balls." Those were my workout shorts, pulled from my dirty clothes hamper. I didn't bother to comment on the fact that her nasty ass had sniffed them and still put them on anyway.

"I thought you might be hungry." Passing through the kitchen, I had seen the plate of bacon, eggs, and grits left for me in the microwave. I blinked my thanks. But I had no appetite, just wanted to rest my eyes for the next few hours.

While I usually went for plus-sized girls, Kierra had the tall and thin frame of a runway model with the face to match. Her lips were so thick and full that they made you think of nothing other than the erotic promises of her mouth. Kierra also had an oral fixation—always had to be biting, chewing, or sucking on something. Usually me.

But outside of the fact of being a grade-A soul snatcher, Kierra was cool enough to be one of the few people who knew where I stayed. She played her position, didn't ask too many questions, and she had all her own shit.

I had a 62-inch Vizio set up in my room. Kierra switched on the closed-captioning, assuming I wanted to follow along with the news story, even though I gave less than a few fucks. Lately the media cycle had been dominated by the latest police killing of another unarmed teen, complete with all the prepackaged generic outrage and calls for social justice. The twist being that this time it was a white kid killed by a Black cop.

I rolled onto my side and tried to get a three-hour nap. Later that morning, I had moves to shoot that I needed to be fresh for. The Big Phone had interrupted my sleep. I called it the Big

Phone not due to the actual size of the device, but who was represented on the other end.

I was drifting off when I felt fingers undoing the drawstrings of my sweats. I knew it was coming, and she ignored me even after I shook my head. She pulled my beast free and inhaled me while I was still soft.

When we met, she had jokingly introduced herself as "Givenya Moorehead." I eventually changed her nickname to "The Android," because I swear this chick never eats, sleeps, or gets tired. Kierra is like a dick-sucking machine. She don't even need you to be into it.

I was too tired to fuck and too tired to fight her off me. My beast stiffened without my consent, and Kierra attacked him hungrily with those monster lips and a suction that resembled a plunger unclogging a stopped toilet.

And even though it was the best head I ever had, she still couldn't take my mind off of Quianna. My hazel-eyed baby momma was somewhere raising my one-year-old son without me. The fault was totally my own. I had driven her away before learning that she was carrying my seed. My connections on the other end of the Big Phone had the means to find her, but I didn't want to know. It was safest for all of us if I kept my distance for the time being. Just until I got these dangerous muthafuckas off my back.

Eventually Kierra's throat felt good enough to take my thoughts away from my preoccupation with Quianna. Kierra worked my stick with both hands, jacked me into her mouth. She rubbed the dick all over face, then sucked the balls with care. Each time she gave me head, I felt as if she were auditioning for something. Like there were hidden cameras in the room that I didn't know about, and she was trying to win a contract with Vivid Video.

I found a little bit of energy from somewhere that I was willing to expend on her. I pulled her up and let her straddle me. The advantage to having Kierra was that she was lightweight and extremely flexible. Plus when she rides the dick, she can go absolutely buck, while the thicker girls can only bounce or just grind back and forth.

She threw that wet on me in circles, twists, and reverse spins. I met her with upward thrusts that soon had her mouthing nonsensical shit I couldn't make out. I always loved watching the faces a woman makes from the pleasure and pain my ten-inch beast provides. I could always tell that Kierra was close to her nut when she closed her eyes and started biting her lips.

I had another few rounds in me but wasn't looking to prolong things. I started chasing mine with short, quick jackrabbit pumps. I got off five strokes after her. We weren't four hours removed from our last session, so I reached a not particularly strong, but satisfactory finish.

But that sudden burst of energy left right along with my semen. I was dozing off before she even had a chance to climb off of me.

Chapter Three

My post-coital nap hardly lasted fifty minutes before I was up and out the door again—this time wearing drawers.

From my newly revitalized neighborhood, I drove to an area of Schoolcraft Road that was still in the struggle. The only thriving business was a liquor store that anchored the two main cross streets. The livable dwellings were losing three-to-one to scorched shells and empty plots filled with bulk trash.

I parked near the corner of Robson Street and watched the block's outlier: the huge brick Colonial was well-tended and would easily list for half a million in the suburbs. I didn't have to wait twenty minutes before the burgundy Tahoe pulled from the driveway, looking country as hell with too many chrome accents and big thirty-inch rims. The product of another young nigga with more money than discretion.

Thirty seconds after he bent the corner, I was out the door of my pickup. I took the alley and approached his house from the rear. I vaulted a seven-foot privacy fence with a single hop.

The backyard was as well-maintained as the house. A thick velveteen lawn with fresh mower tracks and manicured hedges, a stone barbecue pit, an aluminum tool shed.

And three large cane corsos. One tan and two dark gray that might have been litter mates. All running towards me with a head full of steam. These were real killers, too. They didn't bark or make some aggressive show of intimidation. They came straight in for the attack on the intruder.

What happened next would probably piss off the people at PETA.

The first one to reach me got it the worst. She tried to snap at my leg but only got a mouthful of Levi denim and started to shake. I felt guilty about the hammer punch I dropped on the top of her skull. She let out a loud yelp, then staggered away, dizzied.

The second one leaped at my chest but got caught midair. I continued his upward path with the same power that allowed me to clean-and-jerk 360 when I was still locked up. I launched the eighty-pound canine maybe twelve feet high. It flipped wildly, head over tail, until it disappeared on the other side of the privacy fence. I guessed its landing was less graceful than a feline.

The third one did the most damage, managing to lock onto my left hand. My first instinct was to punch the shit out of him with my right, but guilt still gnawed at me. Instead I snatched off my Louie belt and looped it around his neck. I didn't strangle him, just applied enough pressure to squeeze out all the fight. When I released him, he slumped into the grass as if ready for his afternoon nap.

This was my fault, bad recon. I should've known he had dogs before coming in and planned accordingly. This was a rush job, something handed to me in haste with an extremely tight window to pull off. I had only been watching the house for two days when I usually took a longer time to do a scouting report.

I crept towards the back of the house, sure I was on camera but not giving a fuck. I knew other than doorbell monitors, there wasn't a home security system. So I launched an aluminum deck chair straight through the glass in a sliding patio door.

I wasn't expecting any more surprises. I knew nobody was home but still moved like I didn't have time to waste.

The interior wasn't what I expected for a man in his twenties.

Spacious and clean with gleaming hardwood floors. Antique mahogany tables and floral-printed drapery that matched the living room set. Like he had gotten the furniture from his grandmother. But I tore all that shit up looking for the work. I ripped open the couches and pulled all the clothes out the closets. I snatched out cabinet drawers to dump the contents on the floor. I was about as bad as the police during a raid.

In the master bedroom upstairs, I helped myself to a busted-down Audemars Piguet and a nice pinky ring I found on the dresser. When I flipped over the king-sized mattress, there was a Mossberg pump-action 12-gauge under the bed that also got accepted as a donation. The closet was filled with retro Adidas and tracksuits, but I didn't find a safe. Dude was clearly getting to a decent bag, but if he had a stash, it wasn't there.

The second upstairs bedroom was barely furnished and gave me flashbacks of being in the joint. No carpet, dresser, nor drapery. The windows were covered with interior bars. The twin-sized bed had chains attached to the footrest. I got a creepy vibe.

This was starting to look like a dry run, and I was trying to imagine what the motivation might be for sending me on it. My business relationship with Dirty Red was still tentative, and neither of us quite trusted the other yet. But until then, his targets had always been on point and our dealings mutually beneficial.

I hit the basement stairs, trying to be as light as I could be on my toes. The casement windows were painted over, leaving the basement nearly pitch dark even at eleven in the morning on a cloudless spring day. I didn't bother searching for a light switch. A Glock G20 came off my waistband at the same time a small LED flashlight came from the cargo pocket of my sweats. I rested my left wrist on top of my right. A tool in each hand. I sank into the blackness, swinging my arms in whatever direction I turned. My left would spotlight the potential threat before my right would blow it away.

Even before reaching the bottom of the stairs, I smelled bull-shit weed and felt the tremulous vibrations of a subwoofer. I shined my LED on an anterior room with a rusted washer and dryer set and gardening equipment. Old boxes were stacked waist-high, containing something that reeked of mildew.

A small door served another room that was revealed to me due to the light shining from underneath. The music and weed came from in there. I also sensed the presence of at least two people. I doubted somebody was smoking alone.

I didn't come in expecting drama, but I stay ready so I don't have to get ready.

I kicked in the door using surprise as my advantage. My disadvantage is that I'm big, heavy, and never quite sure of how much noise I'm making. If they had heard me going through the house upstairs, they could be waiting on the other side of the door with weapons raised and ready.

But it was clear these fools weren't expecting company at all. Two sets of eyes exploded out of their sockets like I was from another planet.

The smell of feet and sweaty ass crack overpowered the bullshit weed. There was a blanket on the floor and three people on top of it. These fools didn't hear me upstairs because they were busy down here running a train on some dope fiend.

A slender brown female was on her hands and knees with a male positioned at either end. Dude hitting her from the back froze mid-stroke and just stared at me like he'd been caught by his mother. The sight of my Glock made his boy at the top end pull back, tuck his dick, then raise his hands in surrender.

The fiend didn't seem to notice my intrusion, or the fact that both partners had pulled out. She kept on throwing it back and working her neck, fucking and sucking the air. Either these niggas weren't working with shit, or she was so high she was on autopilot.

The one getting the head got yanked up from his knees and pushed down on the sofa. Another young skinny dreadhead with face tattoos. He yanked up his too-tight jeans from around his thighs and sat there obediently.

But his boy was giving off that hostile energy, like he was thinking about trying me. About three feet from him, a vinyl Pistons Starters jacket was draped across the back of a folding chair set at a rickety card table. He was still on his knees when he dove for it.

I kicked the chair over and away from him. While my foot was still in midair, I changed the direction of my leg and put my heel to his face. He flopped backwards against the wall cupping his bloodied nose, tears glistening in his eyes. I'm not a black belt, but I know a little bit. I still had the .40, so he was lucky I didn't just shoot his ass.

I went over to retrieve the Pistons jacket and the pistol I knew was inside it. There was a small .25-caliber pistol in the front pocket. I gave him a *Nigga please!* look. Even if he had gotten to it, this weak muthafucka wasn't gonna do shit but make me mad.

I typed something into my phone and held up the screen to the one seated on the couch. He looked from my phone back to me like he didn't know what I was doing. It was always a bitch putting people up on how I communicated. I went across the top of his head with the G20, then pushed the screen closer to his face. There was an undelivered text on my phone that read: *Where da work at?* If I had to ask again, I was going to put one of these big-ass 10mm slugs through his kneecap. I didn't have patience for this whole game where he pretended to play stupid until I beat it out of him. I pointed the business end at him to let him know this.

That pistol slap seemed to help reduce the learning curve. Young Dog looked to me wide-eyed, holding his head. Pointed to a small door at the rear of the room.

As he stood, his boy that I kicked said something to him that was probably a warning. He was just at the edge of my periphery, so I couldn't read his lips, but could see if he made a sudden move.

I wasn't with no surprises, so I made Young Dog go and pull that door open while I followed with my pistol. It opened on a storage closet that was lined with shelves, but only the top two were in use. The fourth had bill stacks lined up in neat rows. The fifth had a row of white bricks wrapped in clear plastic.

Chapter Four

The stash held six kilos and what looked to be about $140,000 in cash. I would count up later to find out the actual amount. It wasn't quite the lick I expected but still pretty decent. The dope and money got swept from the shelves into a garbage bag that I brought down from the kitchen.

I typically bring duct tape with me in situations like this but honestly didn't expect anybody to be home. So instead I had the two dudes seated side by side on the couch with their wrists tied up with jumper cables I found in the anterior room. The girl was docile, either by nature or as an effect of the drugs, but was lucid enough to cover her nakedness with a blanket.

It was only in taking a serious look at her that I noticed she was a lot younger than I thought previously. It may have been the adult act I caught them in that caused me to assume she was much older. She had dark brown eyes ringed with heavy bags; even though they were vacant and glazed over from the whatever she was on, they revealed her youth. I guessed her shy of seventeen years old.

Meanwhile, both of these fools were clearly in their late twenties. That foul shit made me want to pistol-whip them until I put them both in comas.

What pissed me off even more was that I noticed needle marks in her arms and didn't think they came from insulin. A ringlet of bruised skin surrounded her ankles. Anyone who had ever been in prison and had to wear shackles was familiar with those markings. I thought back to the room upstairs with the barred windows and the chains.

I had got what I came for and was in a rush to be out, but that annoying little voice started whispering to me. The one that occasionally tried to convince you to put your nose in some shit you knew wasn't your business. Some people called it conscience. But it was dangerous in my line of work, because it typically went contrary to your survival instincts.

I approached the girl, who sat on the floor cross-legged, hunched over like a whipped dog. I tried for her attention and nearly had to shake her before I got it. I asked a two-word question with my iPhone: *U okay?*

Dude I kicked in the face jumped up like I didn't have any right to be engaging her. He glared at me and took a step in my direction. I shot him a look that shut that shit down. He retook his seat on the couch, still cupping his broken nose.

When the girl didn't answer me, I pulled her to her feet and through my phone tried to ask if she needed help. I got that I was an unlikely ally, but I didn't like the look of what was happening here. But she had no responses, verbal or otherwise. She only stared through me as if I were made of glass.

My intention was to drop her off at Henry Ford Hospital's emergency entrance. I wasn't going inside and wasn't signing shit. I figured somebody there would get her the help she needed. From the looks of her, the girl needed food, fluids, and about thirty-six hours of undisturbed sleep. After a chemical detox, staff could get in touch with her family and help to enroll her in a drug treatment program.

I tossed the garbage bag over my right shoulder and grabbed her wrist with my left. But when I tried to pull her along, she went crazy. The girl started screaming, pulling away, even fighting with me. We were halfway to the steps when I finally let her go. She clawed my arm hard enough to leave deep scratches. I had to check myself, because I damn near slapped the shit out of her on reflex.

At that point, I'm like *fuck it*. She was clearly where she wanted to be. A better man probably would've forced her to come along, or at the very least called and left an anonymous tip with the police.

But I'm a goon, not a citizen, and damn sure not a hero. I took the cash and dope I hit for and got the fuck out of there.

Chapter Five

Leaving the young girl behind ceased to bother me by the time I reached my car. I was more upset at myself for trying to play Captain Save 'Em in the first place. In the past, every time I've led with my emotions, the shit has gone bad. T'wanda and Quianna were the proof of this.

I dropped the cash off at home with Kierra and left her to count up for me. She had earned that much of my trust, and I often wondered if I were being gullible again. I told her to text me the number when she finished.

I took the six bricks with me over to the area of Joy Road and Cascade to Dirty Red. He was barely twenty-one, but already getting to a big bag.

When I hit a lick for some dope, I gave it to him to sell. Sometimes Red put me up on the lick himself. And even though this arrangement was allowing us to make good money together, we still didn't quite like each other. Probably never would.

My business partner had actually started out as an op. About a year ago, I had to take a look at him and his crew because I had mistakenly thought they killed my boy Doc. What I learned was that he and I were both being squeezed by the same dirty cop. I eliminated that threat for both of us in exchange for a twenty-percent stake in his business.

His spot on Cascade was a big five-bedroom Venetian surrounded by an eight-foot security fence—almost a palace when compared to the boarded-over and burned-out shells that shared the block. Whenever I looked at the malignancy of blight that had overrun my city, I was stabbed by a feeling of guilt. My own actions had played a part in Detroit being kicked out of the Urban Renewal Project. Even with the corrupt politicians looking to siphon off their share, minority business owners still would have seen billions to improve the city.

This was a playhouse for a bunch of young niggas with way too much money and not enough sense. The living room furniture was a mismatched collection of scavenged pieces. The only thing that looked purchased was the 85-inch 4K television mounted on the wall. There was no dinette set or anything to mark the dining room as a formal place to eat together as a family. They decided to fill that space with an expensive pool table with cream carpet and balls trimmed in gold, even though I doubted that any of the youngsters could shoot for real.

Dirty Red was chubby, light-skinned, and wore enough red to announce his affiliation, even if you weren't smart enough to guess it by his name. He still wore the chain that had been passed to him by the man who served as a mentor to both of us: a heavy Figueroa-style link with the Detroit signature old-English D crusted in diamonds. He sat on the living room sofa, playing *Call of Duty* on a huge television while something skunky and loud passed between him and his girl. They were sending a clear message by not offering me the blunt, one to which I took no offense.

I had already stacked the bricks on top of the pool table in the dining room. Dirty Red only offered a disinterested glance. He didn't even bother to pause his game. "What I'm supposed to do with that?"

I knew Dirty Red primarily dealt in heroin, but I also knew he had the connections to move the cocaine easily. This was just his opening gambit in our chess match. I just sat back and waited for him to come with the bullshit.

I leaned against the wall, watching him and his girlfriend shoot their way through some post-apocalyptic urban battlefield. I could tell by the way Red handled the controller that the two fingers on his left hand hadn't healed one hundred percent. There was still animosity over me breaking them.

About a year ago, during the height of our beef, the Joy Road Boys had shot up my mother's house, and a bullet had come through the wall, striking a civilian. The girl was only five years old. She had needed multiple surgeries, but had lost one of her kidneys and a portion of her small intestine. She had even briefly fallen into a coma. Two fingers and twenty percent of Dirty Red's business was what I had charged for the collateral damage of that drive-by. I usually took lives and those of family members, too, so I felt the price was cheap.

His girl died onscreen and cursed as she stood. She was a brown-skinned cutie wearing red hair and about 20,000 dollars' worth of surgical enhancements. She strutted off to the bathroom in white stretch pants that were damn near see-through. I watched her overly inflated ass jiggle and wanted Red to see me staring.

"Curtis Jackson, nigga?" I knew me eye-fucking his girl would help to speed along the negotiations, but I only looked at him like he was crazy. Each brick had a street value of about thirty-five to forty grand, and he was offering fifty for all six. He was trying to stick more dick to me than I wanted to stick to his girl.

"Sixty-five, and that's love. The shit was free to you, so it's all profit." People always tried to make that argument when dealing with scammers and thieves. But regardless of how I came up on something, that doesn't diminish its value. Plus worrying about my profit margin was too much like counting another man's pockets. A violation of street ethics.

I wasn't expecting showroom prices for a stolen Bentley, but he damn sure wasn't going to play me like it was a Hyundai. I gave Red an irritated glare to let him know that his next offer had better be reasonable.

Dirty Red placed a call to an older fiend, who came through to test the quality. Unc sniffed a line and had tried to keep his face neutral in the moment. Red had obviously coached him. Then he pulled Red aside to whisper something in his ear.

The fiend couldn't have known that they were trying to pull this farce on the one person it would never work against. My expertise in reading body language allowed me to detect the exact moment that coke kicked him like a mule—I watched his spine straighten a little and his eyes briefly swim out of focus. On top of that, I'd been forced to read lips since I was seven years old. Even from a distance, I deciphered his mouth forming the words: "That shit on point, bro. At least an eight out of ten."

So when Red offered me 80,000, I pushed him up to one-twenty for wasting my time with the bullshit. For a minute, he played butt-hurt and pretended like was going to let me walk away, but I knew better. Even if he sold them brick for brick without breaking them down, he was still going to do another 120 grand in profit. He couldn't lose.

Half was paid upfront with the other half due after the flip. So I walked out of there with my pants sagging, sixty racks weighing my pockets.

I made sure to give Red's girl a smile before I left. Neither she nor her man appeared to appreciate it. It was *fuck you* glares all around.

Chapter Six

I dropped the cash off at home for Kierra to put with the rest of my stash. Her final tally was 132,000, bringing my total to 182—two forty-two once Dirty Red pays the balance on the cocaine. I definitely get to my bands out here, but won't pretend that my days typically go like this.

I was out the door again with a few of the bands in my pocket. I pulled up to meet her at a Family Dollar on Wyoming Street and West 7 Mile. The lot was half full, and I slotted my pickup next a Chevy Traverse that desperately needed a wash.

The driver slipped out her seat right into my passengers wearing nurse's scrubs and large-framed sunglasses. She removed them and turned to me with almond-shaped eyes that looked tired and irritated. Trisha was still a stunner with the dark circles.

"I told you the last time we wasn't gone keep doing this."

I just pulled my money out to speed this along. I wasn't in the mood for the same lecture that was starting to come standard with these transactions.

She pulled the pill bottle from her purse. A 120-count of Percocet in thirty-milligram tablets. She didn't accept my money or hand me the bottle when I reached for it. I sighed a little bit, because I knew the bullshit was coming.

"You know if you take too much of this, it causes mood swings, fainting spells, seizures."

I nodded, already knowing all this and not giving a fuck.

A couple of months ago, I'd gotten shot and had my homegirl here to thank for pulling the slug out of me. To help me handle the pain, she had even been G enough to steal me a little something from the hospital pharmacy. Her problem was that she had only expected that to be a one-time deal. But as long as I was still in pain, we were still in business.

She gave me a long, irritated glare before snatching the cash from my fingers and tossing the pill bottle at me.

I wasn't trying to see my friend lose her job, so I only used her when all my other plugs were dry. Plus I always paid her three times the street value for the script. This did little for her enthusiasm.

I tried something that had worked a few times in the past. I put on a playful smile and tried to rub her thigh.

This half-Black/half-Asian dimepiece had once been a member of the BANDS Society. This was a group formed by my baby momma filled with the baddest dancers in Detroit. They had done it all, from stripping, tricking, to pulling scams. Back then, Trisha had called herself Chun Li and was an absolute demon with the head—the only person I'd met who had Kierra beat. I had only got to sample her once and was still thirsty for another taste. But Trisha wasn't fucking with that life anymore, had wisely used her time in the game as a stepping stone to pay off her loans for nursing school.

Chun Li pushed my hand off her thigh, wasn't going for it this time. I couldn't tell if it was that fourteen-hour shift at Sinai Grace or if she was just tired of my shit.

I used my phone to tell her that I would break these into thirds and then only take them when the pain was unbearable. I told her I would slow-roll the bottle and make it last a few months.

She looked from the lies on my screen to the truth in my eyes. She rolled her brown ones away from me and pushed out of my passenger seat without comment.

Before she even backed the dirty Traverse out of her parking spot, I downed two whole Percs and chased them with a swig of Red Bull.

Chapter Seven

I was about to make it three-for-three for pulling up on people who weren't particularly thrilled to see me—and that made me consider how few they were that truly would be.

When I hit the block of Monica, Kiyuana was outside in the front yard, chasing after a little boy close to her own age. She looked clean and well-fed. Kiyuana was in barrettes and braids. A white shirt with a denim collar matched the blue of the romper she wore over it.

A lot of home renovations on my old street. Most of the old brick multi-family flats that had sat abandoned for decades were under construction by the avalanche of new white faces starting to invade many Detroit hoods. I had been warned of this by the dirty sergeant who also wanted her stake in the buying frenzy. The corner house had been unoccupied for so long that the rusted old Plymouth Duster the previous owners left parked out front had weeds sprouting from under the body. I didn't expect it to be there much longer, but couldn't imagine my block without it.

But by the time I parked my truck, Kiyuana's mother had appeared in the doorway and quickly summoned both children into the house. I didn't like it, but I understood. Her mother would never forgive me for what happened, as much as I would never forgive myself.

I walked up the porch steps, and as usual, she guarded the front door to lower flat as opposed to just standing in it. I know better than most that ninety percent of communication is nonverbal. The message she sent with her body clogging the doorway with crossed arms was clearly intended to let me know that this was her home now, and I was not welcome. It didn't matter that it had once been my home, too.

Quianna had taken over the two-family flat once owned by our mother Mrs. P, and Quianna had either turned over the property to her as a consolation or was merely allowing her to rent it.

I imagined it had to be purely for sentimental reasons that she was choosing to live here. Even without my help, she was doing enough for herself to own a much nicer house in a much nicer neighborhood. This was proven by a new Cadillac XT-6 in the driveway. Staying here may just be her way of feeling closer to the woman we both had once been in love with.

The chick living in Quianna's old upstairs flat sat on the porch with her man and two of their three kids. She was mediocre but thick and had given me a sneaky choosing signal the last two times I came this way. I didn't feed into it, because I had already been the cause of too much drama at this address.

Quianna had used a portion of her money to improve the property, at least from what could be seen from the outside. There was brick and tuck work, along with shingles covering a new roof. New windows all the way around and not just replacements for the front ones that had gotten shot out during my beef with the Joy Road Boys.

Kiyuana appeared in one of those front windows just long enough to give me a quick wave before vanishing behind the curtains. She had most likely been warned by her mother to never engage me, but even six-year-olds were determined to choose their own friends. This was her older daughter by a different nigga. The one we shared together I had never been able to hold, wasn't even allowed to be in the presence of.

I met my baby momma at the door, along with the perpetual frown that seemed to be etched into her face. She did not care for our once-a-month visits, even if she did, on some unvoiced level, appreciate the efforts.

I gave her the money in a paper bag just so the neighbors wouldn't be in our business. This was one of the few things she and I agreed on when it came to the drop-off. She would have to take it in the house to count up, but there was twenty in the bag. The past few months were light, and I just wanted to make up for that.

She was still one of the most beautiful women in the world. Still had that flawless Hershey-bar dark chocolate skin, and those large, expressive eyes that made you think of a Disney princess. The conservative tan skirt, the matching jacket, and the white blouse underneath was all loose-fitting, but still couldn't conceal those curves. She was wearing her natural hair color: gelled down with styled edges and pulled into a silky black ponytail that flowed to the center of her back.

She had changed her life, done a total 180 in the past year.

Lexy accepted the bag on behalf of our daughter, then gave me the look that it was time to go. The exchanges were typically done quickly and without pleasantries.

After the shit I went through with my old man, I never thought I would be one of those men out here with a child, and not be in their life. I'm not a deadbeat-ass nigga. In this case, the choice had not been mine.

But I did understand, and respected the decision.

Chapter Eight

I crossed the bridge on East Jefferson Ave. telling myself the knot in my stomach was just hunger but knowing better. I always felt a twinge of anxiety whenever the Big Phone rang. My anxiety ten-Xed whenever I was asked to meet in person.

Belle Isle is a small island park that rests in the Detroit River between the coasts of the city and Windsor, Ontario. The island is only one-point-five square miles but equipped with an aquarium, a zoo, a golf course, and a beach, in addition to plenty of picnic areas.

I was summoned there but was given no particular place to meet. I parked along the strip on Sunset Drive, knowing that someone would ultimately find me. I looked across the river to the Canadian skyline while I devoured a breast and thigh from KFC—the same greasy food that had been indigestible to me when I first came home.

I had just stepped out of my Ram 1500 to drop my trash in the receptacle when a blue Dodge Pacifica took the next open spot.

I was surprised to see him stepping out of something so low-key. He was dressed the same in a Polo shirt, designer jeans, and the original Dream Team Jordans. I was used to a more mafioso sort of vibe—10,000-dollar suit, 100,000-dollar watch. I can't believe this nigga actually got on a Timex.

There was an empty picnic table and small grill in the grass about twenty feet away from where we parked. He asked with his hands if it was okay for us to sit there. It was seventy-five and sunny, so I agreed. Plus I didn't want the temptation of being alone with him without witnesses.

It was only on rare occasions that I met with one of his go-betweens face-to-face. While he never sent the same person twice, for my convenience, he always made sure that the person was proficient in American Sign Language.

This was only the third time the man himself had permitted me into his presence. This was a muthafucka who never did business in person, never let anyone see his face. For over twenty-five years, he'd been a Midwest kingpin whose name struck fear in the hardest gangsters, without any of them even knowing what he looked like. Even the people within his organization don't quite know who they are working for. He had mastered the power of anonymity, and it was the secret to his longevity. It had also earned him the moniker: The Invisible Man.

I sat across from him at the table. I knew he was at least in his forties based solely on his reputation, but his appearance was of a man ten to twelve years younger. Dark skin, six-foot-three, eyes as white as his teeth. He had the glow of a brother who'd just come from the joint, even though he'd never had so much as a traffic ticket.

Despite the casual dress, his demeanor was businesslike as usual. Without exchanging pleasantries, he asked me about the situation with the rich lady. His hand formations were crisp, and he didn't mouth the words as he went. He used facial expressions to emphasize certain points and not exaggerated movements. I could tell he had learned to sign early in life and had adapted it as a second language.

I told him the information that I was sure he was already aware of. How the last several months had momentarily broken one of the strongest women I knew. I didn't think going there last night had been her attempt at suicide by gang. It was more self-flagellation for not being able to protect her daughters, both of them. I told him about how I used Prime and his boys to secure her until I arrived, and how I took her home. What I didn't tell was how Tuesday had begged me to help her find him. Considering who this dude was and the reach he had, he might've already known.

Thirteen months ago, I'd come home from prison looking to solve, then avenge, my best friend's murder. I'd only expected enemies in the form of rival gangs and conniving hoodrats. I never imagined the trail would lead to a crew of drug-dealing cops and a corrupt politician secretly in the pocket of the extremely powerful and mysterious individual sitting across from me. The Invisible Man didn't even exist to me until I got a strange visit one night while serving forty-five days in the detention center. My drama in the streets had reverberated all the way to city hall, costing Detroit billions in free stimulus money. A huge slice of that was supposed to be headed for his vault. The result left me in his debt.

We talked about Tuesday a while longer, and I closely studied his demeanor. One would never guess that the child she lost to cancer was the natural daughter they shared. He wore no pain or regret on his face. I couldn't tell if he was heartless or just as broken with a much better poker face.

Then he abruptly changed the subject when he asked if I'd heard of Amelia Chess. The name seemed vaguely familiar, so I screwed my face up as I scoured my weed-compromised memory for the connection.

He jumped in before I gave myself an aneurysm and explained that Amelia Chess was a talk-show host who was currently in hot water. I nodded as the story started to come back to me. Amelia Chess was one of those Black conservatives who seemed to hate their own people. When a white teen got killed by Black officers, she made some comments so inflammatory that even her racist right-wing producers thought were over the line.

A woman I never met got fired from a show I never watched. I asked what the fuck this had to do with me.

He mouthed this part, either for clarity or discretion. He looked around cautiously before he started. "A friend called in a favor. Amelia fears for her life and needs a capable man with a specific skillset serve as her bodyguard."

I was shaking my head before he could finish the statement. The last time I played bodyguard was for his wife, and that ended horribly.

"Like I said, a friend called in a favor, and I'm doing the same." I looked at him skeptically. I couldn't imagine nobody who had that type of juice with him. This nigga didn't do friends.

"This is not an order. It really would be a good lookout, though. My appreciation would be reflected in me wiping out the rest of the negative balance."

That raised my eyebrows, just as he suspected it would.

Chapter Nine

It was a short drive from Belle Isle. The high-rise condominium sat right off East Jefferson, overlooking the riverfront. I tried to imagine what it must cost a month to live in a place like this. My former best friend Doc had once hustled his way into a building like this before his fall off and eventual death.

The man had told me I would be expected, and this appeared to be the case. The instant I hit the front gate, a stout woman in the security booth immediately raised the arm to let my pickup through without asking a single question or for proof of my identity.

I walked through a lobby adorned with a thirty-foot glass waterfall flowing into a koi pond surrounded by miniature bonsai trees. A huge masterpiece of three-dimensional art dangled from the ceiling: twisted copper ribbons of the same length hung spinning from individual cables, but only when all twelve ribbons were turned at just the right angle was a woman's face revealed. The entrance alone was enough to let you know big money lived there. Shit had me looking and feeling out of place in my dirty sweatpants and work boots.

I rode the elevator up nineteen floors. The doors parted and placed me eye-to-eye with a sour-faced dude in Cartier frames. He matched my height at six-foot-five and was close to my build. He had definitely curled a dumbbell or two in his life—even under a fine-tailored suit, I could see the cut of his physique. He directed me to follow him with a subtle head nod.

I didn't expect the elevator to open up directly into the penthouse. My escort led me into the living room, then paused me with a hand. Overstuffed gray furniture and a massive grand piano sat atop hardwood floors polished to a high shine. A fireplace centered the room, mounted on a circular stone hearth. Beyond this, floor-to-ceiling windows offered 180-degree views of the riverfront and downtown skyline.

Seated at the huge concert Steinway was a round boy around fifteen years old in equally round glasses with a box-style fade. As he fingered the keys, I could feel the vibration of the chords but could discern nothing of what he played or his level of talent.

Big Fella in the suit disappeared into an anterior room, then returned moments later with his employer. Amelia Chess was casual in a floral-printed summer dress and open-toed heels. The second gentleman accompanying her also wore a suit but was nowhere as imposing as the first, whom I already judged to be my competition.

I had seen Amelia Chess a few times on television, and perhaps it was her political stance or the vitriol with which she excoriated the first Black president that made me think so little of her appearance. While it was obvious that media outlets would only want someone who was camera-friendly to serve as on-air talent, it was seeing her in person and in a natural setting that fucked me up. At forty-plus, this chick was aged like rare tequila. Naturally curly hair just barely scraped her shoulders. She was a brown-skinned stunner, even without makeup or studio lighting.

She approached me with none of the caution I typically received from women who didn't know me. I accepted the hand she extended but did not return the plastic smile that probably had $30,000 worth of dental work.

The smaller dude with her looked me up and down, clearly less impressed by me. I didn't know if it was just my lack of swag in the dirty sweatpants or if there was something particular about my face he didn't like. "Miss Chess would like to know what exactly are your qualifications."

If this bitch was asking for a résumé, I had no paperwork I could provide. My name was made in the streets. I kept no evidence of all the work I'd put in, because it was enough to put me in the Fed for a thousand years.

Dude seemed annoyed by my experience or lack thereof. "I don't know who recommended this person, but it's a clear choice." He nodded to my competition. "Spencer has eleven years' experience. Special Forces with three tours in Iraq, he's served on protection details for three senators, even celebs like Oprah and Angelina Jolie."

I watched dude swell with pride as his accolades were listed. He was bossed up in a tailored gray suit, navy blue shirt that matched expensive leather shoes. Like me, I could tell his size wasn't just for show. Even before learning he was Special Forces, I judged by the way he moved this guy knew a little something.

I stood face-to-face with him, looking the polar opposite in my wrinkled T-shirt and hiking boots with no socks. I stared long and hard at him before I slapped the Cartier glasses off his face, then dared him to do something about it.

He was heated, and I could tell he wanted to swing on me. But he looked over to Amelia and her partner and attempted to keep himself tempered.

"You two are not about to brawl in my house," Amelia screamed.

"Another reason why this was a mistake," her partner chimed.

I allowed Big Fella to usher me to the elevator, after he picked his glasses up off the floor. He made sure not to put his hands on me, though.

We stood face-to-face at the elevator, just as we had the moment before when the door opened. He said, "Brotha, she saved your life back there."

I just favored him with a smirk, because we were about to find out right then who saved who. I snatched his ass in the elevator with me just as the doors were closing.

From the perspective of Amelia Chess and her partner, the doors were hardly closed for a second, and when they reopened, her bodyguard was lying face down. Both of them stared at me wide-eyed when I re-entered the condo, stepped over his unconscious body. I pressed the lobby and let the doors close on him again.

She cried, "What the hell did you do to him?"

I needed to use my phone to explain that there was a difference between people who had become soldiers at eighteen versus those who had been born into it. I had been raised in what could only be described as a radical Black cult. I had been trained to fight since I could walk, which was why what happened in the elevator took almost no time at all.

The moment I pulled him inside, he put everything he had into a huge right hand, just as I anticipated. Slapping a man always fucked with his pride and had been a little psychological warfare on my part—anger should never be brought into a fight. He wanted to knock the shit out of me, and that actually played into my hands.

So I weaved to avoid that right and responded with a quick hammer punch to the throat. This wasn't hard enough to do damage, but even a light shot to the throat would stun a person, trigger that choke reflex. After that, an elbow strike from the left caught his chin and ended it. His eyes scrolled upward, and he was asleep before he hit the floor.

The ability to fuck people up didn't necessarily include the ability to prevent people from getting fucked-up. The TV host just stared at me like I was a savage, but her partner seemed impressed.

I pulled out my phone to let them know my expectations. And of course, my fee.

Chapter Ten

I slipped into the guest bathroom, massaging the stiffness in my right shoulder. I was reaching for my Percs the moment I pushed the door closed.

I stripped off my hoodie and shirt in front of the mirror to inspect the healed wound. My Muay Thai was still crisp, but that bullet I took a year ago had diminished my speed. And the pain was a bitch. Even that brief demonstration had ignited the fire in my shoulder and back.

Amelia wanted me to start right away, and I pretty much had to, since I retired her other bodyguard. I still had shit to take care of in the streets, but that would have to wait. This job had come down from Sebastian Caine, which made it the priority.

I sent words to Kierra, not detailing anything, just letting her know not to expect me for a while. She liked the text without return questions or comments. Part of me really did appreciate the fact that she didn't press me about anything I was doing; the flipside was that it made me question how much could she really care about me. Quianna had stayed on me, and even though there was manipulation, I felt that at least some of it had come from genuine concern. I was asking for distance and emotional support at the same time, and only on my terms. I'm a goon, not a psychologist, but I do know the definition of hypocrisy.

I slipped the bottle back in my pocket as I left the bathroom. I had chewed up two more of the pills that I had promised my connect would last me for months. At my current pace, I would run through them in two weeks.

I met Amelia and the man I then learned was her manager standing in the living room. His name was Cameron, a thin man whose tailored lavender suit and mannerisms shouted his orientation. I had no problem with that, but I needed to know who exactly had a problem with his client.

Amelia abruptly cut in before he responded to excuse her son from the room. The four-eyed boy with the nineties fade had stopped playing the moment the elevator doors opened on the bodyguard stretched on the floor. At that point, he only sat at the piano, fingering no keys, just watching me with eyes both cautious and curious. At his mother's behest, he left the instrument and scrambled up a spiral staircase that I could only imagine led to his room.

"For me, death threats are just par for the course," Amelia explained. "I've even gotten into the habit of reposting some of the more creative ones—"

Cameron chimed in. "Like that guy from Florida who said he was going to cover you with honey, lock you in a trunk with three starving raccoons, then drive the car off a bridge."

She shrugged. "And to be honest, I just thought that was cruel, having those innocent raccoons drown with me."

"And of course, PETA and all the animal-rights groups would find some way to make that your fault, probably picket outside your funeral."

I stopped them, gestured with my hands to let them know that I could only focus on one pair of lips at a time. These Percs were kicking in. Plus, if I wanted comedy, I could've caught Katt Williams downtown at the Fox Theatre. The twirling motion with my finger signaled them to speed this along.

She pulled her phone and showed me a string of texts that didn't seem like nothing to me. Someone called her a *house nigga* and a *sell-out* and indicated in a few that her tongue needed to be cut out—opinions I, frankly, agreed with. I didn't see the urgency of the threat when considering what she had just told me to be par for the course.

"This is my personal number," she stressed with narrowed eyes. "One I changed four times in the last three months. It's one thing for some lefty extremist to twit something out or leave something on my Facebook page. I'm a public figure—I can handle that. But there has always been a veil between Amelia Chess TV journalist and Amelia the person. Someone is piercing that veil."

The texts came from a Texas phone number that I knew to be fake. For some reason, that area code was a popular choice for scammers. I returned Amelia's phone along with a look on my face that told her I needed more.

She explained, "Shortly after the *incident,*" and said the word with an eye roll that clearly indicated she thought it was bullshit. "I started being followed. Then some stranger approached my son at his school. Where's the security? With all the mass shootings, and as much as I'm paying for tuition, I should sue their asses."

The problem was that she had said some shit that pissed off pretty much every Black person in America. So getting to the bottom of who wants you dead isn't going to be easy when the answer is: EVERYBODY.

Her manager tried to discreetly slip me a check. I shook my head. Cash only. I don't do bank accounts, credit cards, or picture IDs. I couldn't tell you my social security number even if I wanted to. As fucked as he was, I do thank my father for unplugging me from the matrix. Because of him, I barely even exist on paper.

I had only done protection work as a favor to my baby momma when Quianna and her girls in the BANDS Society had needed me and for the same rich lady who came to the hood half-naked wearing ten million dollars in jewelry. I was the first to admit this really wasn't my thing. I am more of an offensive weapon, but for now, I would be stuck playing defense.

Chapter Eleven

The manager was more leery about hiring me on than Amelia. I expected the pushback to come from her, considering that being her bodyguard meant staying close to her for the foreseeable future. She would essentially be moving a total stranger into her home. Not to mention the fact that I still had no résumé to offer other than that brief display of my skill. But she was surprisingly receptive of me.

Her only concern was an understandable one, and the very same question I had to face when Tuesday hired me as her bodyguard. Amelia was hesitant, almost too embarrassed to ask if my disability might hinder me some way in protecting her and her son.

I only responded with my phone that she had nothing to worry about. I didn't go into detail or explain that I had been totally deaf since age seven and that I had learned to hone my other senses to such a heightened degree that they made up for my hearing. I could've done more to put her mind at ease, but fuck her. I would guard her life, not her feelings.

I was given a spare bedroom that sat right off the kitchen. Moderately spaced, a queen-sized bed with its own full bath. I had nothing to offer the dresser drawers, because my only clothes were on my back.

I made Cameron give me a tour of the entire condo just to understand the layout. Two floors divided the 7500 square feet. The spacious foyer-slash-living room dominated the first floor with bleached hardwood opposing a thirty-foot ceiling. One had to pass through a small chef's kitchen to reach the room on loan to me. A spiral staircase led to the second floor that housed two larger bedrooms and a home office.

The boy's name was Antwon, and his room was surprisingly well-organized for a fifteen-year-old. The full-sized bed was made in the military style—the same way we had to make ours in the church I grew up in. Not a crumb or speck littered his carpet, and nothing sat on his desk besides a fancy computer with three monitors. Thick paperback tomes stuffed his bookshelf with spines labeled: C++, PYTHON, and ASSEMBLY LANGUAGE. The adjoining wall was covered with Retro Jordans and Air Max 95s, reminding me of the display at Foot Action.

Amelia wasn't too enthused about me entering her boudoir, so I gave her a *bitch, please!* look to kill whatever she was thinking. The room that belonged to the lady of the house was just as immaculate. A king-sized bed was draped in purple satin, a makeup table with a mirrored vanity. I briefly scanned a walk-in closet that would give my shopaholic baby's momma an orgasm: there wasn't a single high-end designer for whom she didn't have shoes, boots, bags, and belts.

My quick security assessment of the condo concluded three points of entry: the elevator that opened directly into the foyer, a door in the living room that led to the hall, and another in the kitchen that accessed a service stairwell. A sliding-glass door served the balcony, but we were nineteen floors up, so I didn't prioritize that as a potential weakness.

I rode the elevator down to the lobby and took the service stairs back up, surveying the building floor by floor. I learned from Amelia that tenants paid five figures a month on lowest levels, so I expected comparable security for the price. I saw cameras mounted every four feet and electric doors controlled by biometrics. More cameras covered the exterior of the building, and walking the perimeter, I didn't even find a garbage chute that one could slip in undetected. A private firm patrolled the grounds made up of bonded guards who were mostly ex- and off-duty police.

Hours later, I watched dusk descend on the city through those thirty-foot penthouse windows. From here, it was easy to forget that the malignancy of blight that infested the inner city even existed. The setting sun painted the sky in a thousand crimson shades and made silhouettes of the Renaissance building and downtown skyline. The night eventually brought twinkling light to those structures: the casinos, the sports venues, and the Ambassador Bridge. My gangster-ass city had taken off her bonnet and stretch pants. She was made up in false lashes, wearing an evening dress with high heels, ready to prey upon unsuspecting tourists and gullible suburbanites.

Cameron seemed hesitant to leave at the end of the night. It was obvious to me that he was purposely lingering around. Amelia peeped it, too, and had to assure him several times that she was safe being alone with me. He shuffled slowly towards the elevator, throwing several wary glances back to me.

Amelia offered me a slice of a vegan lasagna. I would've expected her to leave that to a personal chef, but in watching her cook, I could tell she was proficient and took a measure of pride in it.

She made several efforts after I declined her lasagna, even conceded to cook me something else of my choosing. Through my phone, I told her I was fasting. She served Antwon at the dining room table while I contented myself with a bottled water.

Amelia and her son retired to their rooms shortly after eating, and I retired to mine after making one final walk-through. I double-checked the entry doors to the penthouse as well as the elevator, which couldn't be accessed without a security code. I checked the windows, even though none could be unlocked from the outside, and muthafuckas still hadn't grown wings, as far as I knew.

I showered and slipped into bed, but it was my own restless mind that disturbed my sleep more than the unfamiliar mattress. I watched compilation videos of Amelia Chess's show on YouTube. Told myself it was purely client research.

The woman on my phone resembled my kind and generous host only in appearance. From her soapbox positioned far to the political right, she talked about Black men as if we were some shiftless, ignorant, gold-teeth-wearing subspecies whose only saving grace was that we kept the prisons full. Her own Black sisters she reduced to loud, hypermasculine, bridge-card recipients; bitter baby mommas with ten kids by ten men, who sold their souls on OnlyFans. She excoriated the first Black president as the king of all socialists and spoke with a vitriol that would make you think her and Barack had fucked around once and he left her for a white chick. Her critique of Black culture was scathing, and while reading her discourse via closed-caption, I didn't realize my hands had curled into fists.

Meanwhile, the Republican Party was praised as a shining beacon of hope, with Trump being its white knight. She regurgitated the party line from the cult of Individualism and Meritocracy: that anyone could make it in America, regardless of their ethnicity or class. Let her tell it, Racism was a brief event that happened centuries past and in no way connected to modern whites or the Black experience. It was just the default cry of "Cheater!" for the sorry-ass niggas who were losing a perfectly fair game.

After two and a half hours of this, I couldn't take any more of that shit. I killed my phone and dropped it on the nightstand.

I tried to deduce why would the man on the Big Phone want me to take this job. And what would be the punishment for walking away.

I didn't think there was any way I would be able to protect Amelia Chess.

Shit, I was this close to killing the bitch my damn self.

Chapter Twelve

Waking up was the only proof that I eventually got to sleep. Shook off that momentary confusion that comes with spending the night in an unfamiliar place.

I had to slip on the same dirty sweats and boots from yesterday. Some time that day, I would have to swing by the house and grab a few 'fits. Wondering how many was born from the unpleasant realization that I had no idea of how long I would be stuck in this job.

The scent of breakfast reached me even before I opened the door to my room. When I came into the kitchen, Amelia was standing over the stove. Wearing yoga pants and sports bra, looking like she'd already gotten in her morning workout.

To my eyes, this little bitch was sexy as hell—I couldn't even deny that. But it was all that rhetoric that kept my beast in a perpetual sleep state. Even though ten inches of hard black dick might be exactly what she needed to take her off that White-Makes-Right bullshit.

She offered to make me an omelet identical to the twins she prepared for herself and Antwon. I passed, because I knew she probably made that shit with some type of non-dairy artificial eggs.

I opted for cereal and immediately regretted it upon seeing only bland choices designed to be high in fiber and low in sugar. Even Amelia seemed surprised at finding a box of Honey Nut Cheerios stuffed behind the others. She cut her eyes at Antwon, and he had a face like she'd just found his porn stash.

"Cecilia and I are going to talk about her inability to stick to the shopping list," Amelia said calmly. "If this happens again, she'll be fired. And I'm going to make you do it."

I watched Antwon's eyes drop to his plate. Already figured that Cecilia was their housekeeper.

She wasn't my goddamned mother, so Amelia couldn't stop me pouring myself a hefty bowl before stuffing the remainder of the box in the trash. Antwon absently stabbed at his omelet, watching me enviously as I shoveled spoonfuls of sweet cereal into my mouth.

After breakfast, Amelia gave me my first assignment. She wanted me to drive Antwon to school. I looked at that bitch like she was crazy. I reminded her that I was there to protect her from people with guns. I'm a goon, not a chauffeur, and damn sure not a babysitter.

I wasn't feeling this shit, and every part of me wanted to tell her to kiss my entire ass. I hated that I was in a position where I had to weigh all my decisions against the repercussions of offending The Invisible Man.

I argued against leaving her alone, being that she, not Antwon, was my primary charge. Amelia countered that I myself had signed off on the penthouse being perfectly secure. She foresaw no problems occurring in the twenty minutes it took to get to his school and back. She persisted that they were only vulnerable coming and going. I didn't disagree with that. My argument centered around not wanting to be treated like Morgan Freeman in *Driving Miss Daisy*.

The only perk was that she gave me the key fob to a brand-new Mercedes-Benz AMG S63 sedan. I stood in the underground parking garage, staring as the overhead lights gleamed against its glossy black paint, thinking she didn't even know me like that. I wouldn't have trusted a complete stranger with my Benz.

To Antwon's credit, he sat in the front passenger seat and didn't try to play me like I was just the help. I was nervous around most young people, as much as they were around me. It was as if they could sense the love of violence in my aura.

"I saw the camera footage of what happened in the elevator." Antwon made certain to look at me when he spoke.

But the nervousness I sensed in Antwon didn't seem to come from me. His eyes did go buck at seeing that demo I put down on dude, but that felt to me more like fascination than fear.

"Did your father teach you to fight like that?"

The question seemed oddly specific. I thought for a moment before I nodded. My old man didn't teach me directly but was responsible for it. I didn't text Antwon the details, because time didn't permit an elaborate explanation about the UOTA and how I'd been trained since childhood to be a soldier.

"My mom tried to sign me up for karate lessons, but it didn't work out," he shared. "I was fine with solo training but hated having to spar. I would get so nervous having to face another person that I would start throwing up—I'm talking *Exorcist*, projectile vomiting. The other kids started calling me *Pukeahontis.*" My own training in the church involved us being paired up and having to fight one-on-one. There were a few people who just didn't have the stomach for it.

"You can probably imagine how proud my mom was when the sensei booted me from class. Then sent her a hefty dry-cleaning bill for all the size five-X uniforms."

People were often more comfortable telling things to a mute they would be too embarrassed to confess to a talker, but I didn't sense something deeper than just catharsis at work. Antwon spoke about his experience with a self-depreciating humor that I guessed he'd long adapted as a coping mechanism—laugh with those who laughed at you to dampen the sting. Kids were cruel, but sometimes very clever. I tried to keep my face neutral, but that *Pukeahontis* shit had me cracking up inside.

I chose to pivot, thought we'd spend the rest of the ride talking about the things he actually enjoyed doing. The books on his shelf left no doubt that he was into computers big time. My twelve years in prison left me feeling like a Neanderthal when it came to tech. I used my phone to set him up with what was basically an underhand pitch, then let him knock that out the park.

His pupils widened and his energy changed when he talked about coding and programming. He claimed he was making good money doing something called crypto-mining. I tried to lipread while watching the road, but even with working ears, ninety percent of what he said would've been lost on me. He went on and on about it in a way that proved he was passionate.

But I saw that enthusiasm wane as I pulled into the drop-off lane at his school. "How much would it take to get you to floor this mutha, and head straight to the Mexico border? If you have an offshore account, I could have the money wired to you instantly."

I shook my head to let him know that wasn't going to happen. I typed some comment in my phone about not speaking Spanish, as well as the penalty I would suffer not returning his mother's car.

Before he got out the car, I apologized for getting him busted but warned him he needed to find a better hiding spot for his cereal.

"I once saw a special on *Dateline* about the South American cartels smuggling drugs out of Medellín. They would purposely allow one of their shipments to get hit just to placate law enforcement. Cops would be so busy patting themselves on the back that they would totally ignore the fifty shipments that made it through." Antwon winked at me. "Now she won't even look for the Cinnamon Toast Crunch and Frosted Flakes I keep under the sink."

I had to dap him up when pushed out the car, but when he joined a group of friends on the sidewalk, I saw one of them push the back of his head. Another one put his hands into the front of his shirt in imitation of a fat stomach.

Antwon just wore that same plastic smile he wore when he told me about karate class.

Chapter Thirteen

I didn't pull off until Antwon disappeared into the building, walking with his group of friends. His school, like most of those that survived the rash of closings in 2008, had been rebranded as a leadership academy. Even without that playful little head slap, one could tell at a glance that Antwon was not the leader of his group. He was the Omega dog in the pack—the lowest man on the totem pole. The fat kid who had to be funny to fit in. It was his job to provide the jokes, or be the joke if he ran out of material. Half court jester, half whipping boy.

While in the unloading line, I got lingering stares and few smiles from the young mothers looking for a stepdaddy. I immediately returned to the penthouse, wishing I had more time to play in Amelia's Benz.

I smelled it before the elevator doors fully opened. I walked in the condo and was blasted in the face by the scent of skunky weed.

Amelia was on the couch with her feet tucked under her thighs. She wore one of those plush-ass bathrobes, the kind you stole from expensive hotels. A thin blunt burned between her index and middle fingers, rolled in some type of tan leaf that I wasn't up on.

She had her laptop open, facing away from me. Amelia glared long and hard, deeply engrossed in whatever she was reading or watching.

She didn't notice my presence until my hand entered her field of vision. I was only trying to return the keys to the Benz. She jumped a bit, snapped her laptop shut. I tapped my chest to say, *My bad*. I didn't mean to startle her. I made no effort to sneak up on her, but I can't ever be too sure of how much noise I'm making or not making.

"No, I was just distracted." She waved her hand. "Considering the situation, it would behoove me to be more aware of my surroundings."

I told her this was her home. If she couldn't let her guard down here, what was the point of living in this glass tower? She was probably dropping every month what I cashed out for on my own house.

"And I imagine this didn't help." She held up the smoky blunt. "Oh, I'm sorry. This helps with my anxiety. I can put it out if it bothers you."

With facial expressions and hand gestures, I informed her she was good. I smoke my damn self, which is why I could tell that shit definitely had the aroma of some top-tier dispensary Kush. I was more surprised that she fucked with the trees. I thought her hyper-conservative ass would be calling for the death penalty if the police pulled you over and found a roach in your ashtray. She didn't offer me any, and I wouldn't have accepted if she had. Blowing with her just felt unprofessional. She took another puff; smoke rolled like lazy fog from her mouth to her nostrils.

She obviously took a shower before her morning session. Under the weed, I could smell body wash and those dozen other things Black women did to make themselves smell sweet and delicious. Amelia seemed a little too comfortable around me, because she was in no hurry to get dressed. She didn't flash me, kept the belt tied and the front tightly closed, but I saw enough skin on her chest and upper thighs to deduce she was totally naked under the bathrobe.

It was enough to make my beast briefly crack an eye before drifting back to sleep.

"Antwon didn't give you any problems, did he? He'll sometimes do anything to try to get out of going to school."

I imagined he would. I didn't tell her that he tried to bribe me to take him to Mexico.

"Were his *friends* out there?" She used finger quotes because she was clearly aware of her son's status within the group. "Last month, I had to go to his school for a meeting. The principal believes Antwon's been hacking into the school records, changing students' grades. Of course, Antwon is too good to ever leave proof so they can't discipline him.

"So I go in his room the next day and find his stash spot. Not cereal. A small pouch tucked behind his dresser. There was almost sixty thousand dollars in it."

So Antwon was a little bit more than just comic relief.

"What happened to the good old days when a mother went snooping and only found a dirty magazine? I blame his father. He was just too damn soft on him."

The boy was obviously smart, and clearly had some hustle about himself. He just needed a little confidence.

I could sympathize with Antwon, because when I left the church as a teen and came to the city looking for my mother, I was just as socially awkward. I was good in a fight but couldn't quite figure people out. My former friend Doc had manipulated me for my talents, and I had allowed it for the sake of fitting in.

The conversation about her son eventually exhausted itself. I turned the discussion back to her and the job I was there to do. Using my phone, I asked Amelia who in her life would want to do her harm. I wasn't concerned about Twitter beefs and social media. I was focused on people who could actually get close enough to put a knife in her back.

Amelia claimed to have no enemies within her circle, and I instantly called *Bullshit!* She's a successful Black woman with a big-ass mouth and strong opinions. I figured there were at least four people in her family who secretly, if not publicly, hated her fucking guts.

I asked about past relationships, any disgruntled exes. I even asked about Antwon's father. Typically, when a women was murdered, her lovers were the prime suspects. Having myself murdered an ex, I knew this better than most.

Amelia confessed to having broken a few hearts, as well as having hers broken a few times. But those relationships had not ended with the type of animosity that triggered crimes of passion. According to her, the breakup with the baby's father had been the most bitter, but only because a child was involved.

While she swore they were now in an amiable place, I still planned to go take a look at the dude. Men can hold grudges for a long time—I had waited twelve years to take revenge on T'wanda.

We wrapped that up, but eventually, we were going to have a real conversation about how I came to be there. It's not like I found this job on Indeed. I was ordered to take it. And my boss wasn't the type of man who did favors for just anybody.

Chapter Fourteen

Amelia eventually got dressed to go out, but chose a cashmere overcoat—despite the mild temperature—a head scarf, and big stylish sunglasses. Looking conspicuously inconspicuous. It was like holding up a huge sign that read: DON'T PAY ME ANY ATTENTION.

We reached the Benz, and she stood by the back door like we were gonna be on that *Driving Miss Daisy* shit. I let that bitch know with a look that we wasn't doing that. Made her get up front with me. Moments later, we pulled out the underground parking garage looking like equals.

At first I took her to run a few mundane errands like picking up a prescription for Antwon and dropping off her dry cleaning. I stayed in my mirrors, constantly scanning traffic for any vehicle that might be directly or indirectly tailing us.

The kid in me was almost hoping for a car chase. I wanted to have a reason to open this Benz all the way up. It boasted 791 horses, and I wanted them to have a chance to run. I loved driving Amelia's car, but didn't see an S63 in my future. Along with all those horses, it also boasted a 275,000-dollar sticker price.

I asked Amelia for her baby daddy's whereabouts, and at first she was hesitant. Despite all that mature separation shit she was talking about, that nigga was still about to have a discussion. How that discussion went was totally up to him.

I knew that ninety percent of the violence that was perpetrated against women came at the hands of a current or former lover. It might be a case of domestic violence gone too far; it might be a jilted partner on some If-I-can't-have-you, can't-nobody-have-you type of shit; it might be a cold and calculated husband who offs his chick for the insurance money so him and his side piece could live it up in Costa Rica.

Amelia told me about a house on Detroit's westside, but ten o'clock on a Tuesday would put him at work. According to her, dude had spent seventeen years working for the city. Had started out as a regular garbage man, but climbed his way up into a supervisor's position.

She claimed that he got off work at four, and would be home by five. I let her know that we wasn't waiting that long. I had to do more pressing in order for Amelia to give me the address to his job.

Fifteen minutes later, we were pulling onto the grounds for the Department of Public Works. An empty guard shack and open fence proved how concerned they were about security. To the right were several gas pumps used only by municipal vehicles. To the left was a parking lot, and a long T-shaped building with only one floor connected to a series of garages. Huge salt domes could be seen rising above it from the rear. A fleet of white garbage trucks were slotted before a brick wall. A larger fleet of white Ford pickups with the city's logo on the door surrounded the building.

I parked the Benz in an empty handicap spot and had Amelia place the call.

She sighed, "I'm telling you, Terrence doesn't have anything to do with whoever is threatening me."

I let her see in my face that I planned to make that decision, only after me and that nigga had words. I didn't have to see to know that she rolled her eyes behind those big sunglasses. Our staring match came with a battle of wills. I undid my seat belt, slouched a bit, and began to calmly tap my fingers on the wheel. Amelia eventually figured out that we weren't going anywhere until she placed that call.

She reluctantly pulled up her phone and I used her lips to follow her side of the conversation. She explained that she was aware that he was at work, and that she would never just show up at his job if it weren't important. If he could just come outside for five minutes and talk to her, she would be appreciative.

But I could tell from her responses that his questions only centered on Antwon. Once he learned there was no emergency involving his son, he pretty much told her to fuck off. Amelia was trying to negotiate for his time, from five minutes down to two. I held up my phone so she could see what I typed: *Tell dat nigga he don't want me to come in and get him.*

Apparently his role as assistant senior supervisor kept him too busy, even for a two-minute conversation. He was responsible for coordinating the entire solid waste division, which included almost fifty drivers, twenty-three open-bed trucks, and eighteen other pieces of heavy machinery, all currently throughout the city in operation.

That seemed to be enough for Amelia. She put down the phone with a face that was some mixture of defeat and relief.

Her expression immediately changed when she saw the look on my face when I killed the engine and jumped out the car.

Chapter Fifteen

Amelia was walking quickly on my heels as I hurried to the entrance to the building. I snatched open a set of glass double doors, found myself in a long hallway with walls of fascia brick. It was filled with memos and signs that read: WE APPRECIATE ALL YOU DO and YOU'RE A ROCK STAR—psychological bullshit to convince the employees that they were unsung heroes and not just the niggas who handled our garbage. I went to the right, just because it looked to be more offices in that direction.

Amelia tried to pull at my arm several times, but I snatched away from her. I warned her it would go this way if she didn't get him to come out.

The building was centered by a small courtyard, and through it I saw a large glass office with four desks and three people inside. When I burst through the door, both men and the female took in my size with wide eyes and open mouths. They had on powder-blue work shirts with name tags stitched on the chest.

The heavyset female wore a shaved head and was the first to approach me. "Excuse me, sir, can we help you?"

I made a face to let her know she could not, and she really didn't want to try. That made her retreat a step back.

The dark-skinned nigga with the heavy build had T. JENKINS on his shirt, and I saw enough of Antwon's inheritance to know that T stood for Terrence. His eyes ping-ponged from me to Amelia, who appeared in the doorway behind me, and back. I made the *come here* motion with my finger.

The other male was a skinny dude with an uncombed afro, looking like Huey from *The Boondocks*. He apparently felt cartoon tough, too, because he walked up on me boldly.

"I don't know what this is, but y'all can't just come in here like this." I could tell by his energy he was supervisor, someone used to being in authority and obeyed within these walls. "If y'all don't leave right now, I'm a have to—"

I put my hand on his shoulder just to let him feel the weight of it, the strength, and its destructive potential. It was enough to kill the rest of that threat. After that, he stood there frozen, a portrait of fear and compliance. I guided him to a chair, made him sit.

Terrence approached Amelia. "Why in the fuck would you bring yo' ass up in here?"

I stepped in the middle of them to block his path when he got within three feet of her. That one motion let him know what my role was here. He looked me up and down like, *Who the fuck you supposed to be?* I looked him up and down like, *Don't fuck around and find out.*

Just then, a security guard appeared in the doorway. A 280-pound flashlight cop who wasn't about to do shit but get beat down with his own baton.

I gave Terrence a look that told him to calm this fool down. Or else I was about to make it very unsanitary inside the department of sanitation.

Terrence pulled rank as a supervisor to diffuse the situation. He dismissed the security guard. He apologized to his coworkers, citing family issues, then excused us from the room. He led us from that big glass office, which was the dispatch room, to a smaller, more private room that was his personal office.

The moment the door was shut, he turned on Amelia. "On top of everything else, you wanna see me lose my job, too." He gestured towards me. "And gone come up here with this ol' I-put-creatine-in-my-Apple-Jacks-lookin'-ass nigga."

"I just hired Silence to be my personal security." Amelia seemed genuinely apologetic. "Look, I didn't want to do this here. And definitely not like this."

I stepped forward and tapped my chest to let him know I did. I wanted to do this here, and just like this.

He met my eyes for a moment, then turned back to her. "My son not hurt or dead. So what the hell couldn't wait 'til I got off work, or at least my lunch break?"

She explained, "I hired a bodyguard because someone has been making threats on my life."

He sputtered, "Duh, what else is new? People been making threats on your life since you decided to go from Oprah to Auntie Ruckus."

"People are calling my personal phone. And—" Amelia took a breath, clearly hesitant to tell the next part. "Someone approached Antwon at school."

She spoke over him before he could erupt. "But he's fine. They tightened security at his school, and we have protection at home."

Terrence looked me up and down, assessing me. I watched his eyes zero in on my dirty sweatpants and old boots. He didn't seem impressed. "I meant, yeah he big—his momma definitely got a caesarean scar, and they gone have to kill about five sheep to make this nigga a shearling." I was starting to see where Antwon got his sense of humor from. "But other than that, what can he—"

Before he could finish the statement, I grabbed his arm, twisted it, and slammed his head down the desk. I applied a little pressure to the arm to show him how easy I could break the bone. Terrence looked at me wide-eyed. He spoke words I couldn't make out through his clenched teeth.

Chapter Sixteen

I had Terrence's head pressed against his wooden desk, his arm in a chicken wing.

Amelia was screaming at me, tugging at my arm. I pulled my phone and shot her a quick one-handed text: *I thought he wanted a demonstration of my skills.*

What this little slick-talking-ass nigga didn't understand was that when he told her no outside, he had also told me no. And people don't tell me no. Unless it's screaming in terror like, *No!! No!! No!!*

I would've been down to have a gentleman's conversation had he just came outside and kicked with us when we asked. But, I personally love when people choose to do shit the hard way.

I typed the questions into my phone, made Amelia read them to him and then repeat his answers to me. I told her to make sure he understood that the pain would increase to the degree that I thought he was lying.

I assumed Amelia was screaming at me by the look on her face. "Let him go. I already told you that Terrence doesn't have anything to do with this. He's the father of my child."

I let her see in my face how few fucks I gave about that. Experience has taught me that it was usually the ones closest to you. My former best friend had been robbed by his own sister, then killed by his own son. I had killed one of my former lovers and had been nearly killed by another. I considered for a second that I might be projecting some of my own shit into their situation.

Amelia relayed my first question: "He wants to know if you hired anybody to hurt me?"

I saw his lips move, but his face was planted against the desk in a way that only gave me a view of his profile. I needed to see his entire mouth in order to understand what he spoke.

Amelia translated: "He said 'no.' What reason would he have to?" I could tell he'd said a lot more than that, probably threw in some slick-ass jokes, but she was giving me the summarized version.

I typed that he might still be salty because he lost a bad bitch who was on TV, getting to a big bag while he was stuck playing in the garbage.

For some reason, Amelia seemed hesitant to relay that message from my phone. Her eyes shifted away from me, and I could sense her embarrassment.

After a moment, she said to me, "I promise you, that's not the case." Terrence was talking at the same time, some shit I couldn't make out. Amelia finally confessed, "Our thing was over a long time ago. He was the one who broke it off."

With that, I decided to let him go. Terrence stood erect, glared at me while working the soreness out of his shoulder. "Strong-ass, even-my-beard-can-curl-two-twenty-five-lookin'-ass nigga. If-a-cane-corso-was-a-person-lookin' ass."

I couldn't lie. That last one was actually pretty good.

I was still trying to process how this fat, bug-eyed muthafucka had managed to scoop a chick like Amelia. And had been the one to dump her.

She said to him: "I know you're still upset about how things turned out in court. We could've avoided all of that. I never wanted to put Antwon through it."

Terrence reached into his desk drawer, and I was ready to strike just in case he pulled up a pistol. He pulled out a Blow Pop from an industrial-sized bag, snatched off the wrapper, and threw it into his mouth. He and his son seemed to share the same coping mechanism. "I didn't want it either, but I ain't mad it happened. I would rather my son see me in there fighting for him than to think I would just sit back and let you poison him with all that pro-Trump, anti-everything bullshit."

"I'm keeping to my promise. I do not push my political views on our son, don't even discuss politics in the house."

He pulled the sucker out his mouth to speak. "Funny, how he *ours* all of a sudden."

"You only fought me because you lack the vision to see that Antwon is far too gifted to let his life unfold haphazardly."

"Yeah, but we both know it was a fight I couldn't win. Even my lawyer said it was like playing Spades against with two uncles and a cousin."

Amelia looked remorseful. "I know you can't see it now, and probably never will, but all of this is actually for Antwon. He's going to be seated at the table. He'll have opportunities like you wouldn't believe."

"Yeah, 'cause under me, he was gone turn out to be one of them niggas standing outside the liquor store begging for change. Or better yet, just a garbage man like his loser-ass daddy."

She sighed. "You know that's not what I meant."

"That's where you got it wrong. I know a lot more than you think I do. I can remember the Amelia Fordham who grew up on Linwood in a house full of roaches. Who went to school to be a real journalist, was gonna peek behind the curtain and expose to her people all the corruption and bullshit that was keeping them down."

He took a long, slow slurp off his sucker, and I could tell by how he held the stick between his fingers, Terrence was using them as a replacement for cigarettes—opting for diabetes versus lung cancer.

"But somewhere along the line, you realized controversy gets more shine than activism. Changed your name from Fordham to Chess, just like you changed your stance from liberal to conversative. You sold your soul for the likes and retweets. You became a whore for the industry, and you would lay down and bust it open for them honkies just to stay relevant."

I personally thought he had just fucked her up, and would've said *Damn!* if I had the voice. But Amelia was cool as ice water.

"Don't think I forgot about those days on Linwood, shaking roaches out the cereal box. The path I'm on, and the one I'm laying out for Antwon is for that little girl, and a bunch of other kids who look like her.

"The reason I switched up was because I did get that peek behind the curtain. And you wouldn't believe the games that are being played. I changed my name to Chess because if a pawn moves far enough up the board, it can become anything it wants, even a Queen.

"You call me a whore for the industry, and that's nothing, I've been called worse. The difference between me and you, is that I'll be that and more for my son."

"You keep telling yourself it's all for Antwon. And just like that other shit you say, if you repeat often and loud enough, you convince yourself it's the truth.

"The only muthafuckas I hire to do my dirty work is the ones you see out there picking up bulk trash. And I damn sure wouldn't pay somebody to do harm to my own seed."

He'd chewed the candy down to the gum, spit the stick into a nearby waste can. "Now I gotta get back to work. So you can take this ol' Magilla Gorilla, I-eat-oranges-with-the-peel-still-on lookin'-ass nigga and cut a path up out of here."

Chapter Seventeen

We left, but not before he took a few parting shots. Said I look like the bad guy in every Tyler Perry movie.

It was clear that there were issues that lingered between the two of them, but in the end, I was convinced Terrence wasn't behind some plot against Amelia. He seemed to have about the right level of hostility for a man who was still sick that he'd lost his son in some bitter custody fight. He hated his baby momma, like ninety percent of the niggas out here. But it wasn't that Rae Carruth type of hate.

The instant we got back to the car, Amelia fired up the rest of her blunt. After two puffs, she looked to me apologetic, then cracked the passenger window. "I know you said at the house that this doesn't bother you, but that wasn't in a confined space."

I texted Amelia to let her know she was still good. This was her car, and as much as she paid for it, she had every right to smoke this bitch out if she wanted to. So she sat next to me baking herself while I navigated the big Benz out of the Department of Public Works's parking lot.

She directed me to Times Square, not the New York landmark, but a men's clothing store on the city's westside in the area of Livernois and 7 Mile Road. It was Black-owned, just like every other store in this district. Detroit was fashion famous for three-piece suits in bright pastel colors with the gators to match. Times Square was the one of those places where the real ballers came to get fly for the weekend cabarets.

Amelia clearly wasn't feeling me in dirty sweatpants and scuffed-up Timberlands. I couldn't be mad that someone on her level didn't want a muthafucka working for her who looked like he was supposed to be on the side of the road holding up cardboard.

It wasn't a huge shop, and there were only a few customers, so I didn't feel the need to be in Amelia's back pocket. We perused the shelves on either side of the store, touching fabric and admiring the different fashions. I saw a suede overcoat and a Dobbs-style brimmed hat that I would rock the shit out of when I was stepping out on my bossy vibe.

I was treated to a crispy white button-up, gray slacks in pin-stripe with the matching vest—not the most expensive brand in the store, but far from the cheapest. Amelia tried to pick out a tie for me, but I texted to let her know I wasn't going full-on monkey suit. I left my collar undone but did accept some shiny-ass patent leather loafers in a 13-E wide.

I got dressed in the changing room, impressed at how well Amelia had done to pick out my size. My build was far from average. They had a tailor on site, but everything already hung on me damn near perfect. I had only needed a slight alteration in the shirt, because it was a little snug around the pits.

Minutes later, I was in the mirror checking myself out, and thinking I should have a lot more hoes, when from the corner of my eye, I saw someone approach Amelia. She was on the opposite side of the store, checking out a houndstooth jacket, possibly for Antwon since I damn sure wasn't going to wear it.

A couple, who had been arguing over a paisley suit, suddenly turned their attention on my client. The chick was pushing about 300 pounds, light-skinned in a burgundy bonnet, carrying a Gucci bag that even my untrained eye could tell was a knockoff. Her man had some size, too, about five-ten and 260, rocking a bubble vest with a plaid flannel underneath.

The woman approached Amelia, flagging for her attention. "Hey you, lady. Ain't you somebody famous?"

Amelia tried to ignore her, just continued a careful examination of the houndstooth jacket as if sharing my disability.

But the woman was persistent, put herself right in Amelia's ear. "I done seen you somewhere before. You be on TV? One of them shows by Tyler Perry?"

"I'm sorry, you've clearly mistaken me for someone else." Amelia offered that with a painted smile. I didn't think for a moment her weak-ass disguise of sunglasses and a head scarf was really going to fool anybody.

No sooner than I had that thought, her man stepped in on cue: "Bae, this that bitch from the news. The one who be talking all that crazy shit about Black people being lazy and ignorant."

Recognition widened Big Girl's eyes. "That's right. They on yo' ass right now 'cause of what you said 'bout that white boy."

"Them muthafuckas kneeled on George Floyd's neck for ten minutes, and this bitch on TV sayin' the officers ain't do nothing wrong."

I stood closer to the action just in case Amelia needed me to have her back. But I learned Amelia was pretty good at defending herself, in her own way.

She was calm in her rebuttal. "You can rewatch every one of my shows, and you'll never hear me say that the officers didn't do anything wrong. I simply stated that police are in a unique position to have to respond to perceived threats in real time. It is easy for us, who are so far removed from the situation, to use hindsight and say what they should've or shouldn't have done."

"But you always take they side, tho," the woman said, with wildly swinging arms. "Just like when they was giving out the pandemic money. You swore every Black person with a PPP loan was just gone blow it on jewelry and liquor."

Amelia raised an eyebrow. "And how wrong was I about that? How many people do you know received a fraudulent loan? And out of them, how many actually had the foresight to at least start a legitimate business once they got the money? I saw a whole lot of Black people out here buying Dodge Chargers and Challengers, partying with the biggest bottles of D'ussé.

"Meanwhile, real small-business owners, the actual people for whom those funds were targeted, many of them lost out. That mom-and-pop shop down the street, and many Black-owned stores just like the one we're standing in, had to close their doors. Not only because their own people stole what had been rightfully allotted for them, but then their own people didn't even use the funds when they had it to support Black businesses."

I read that off of Amelia's lips, and that shit raised my eyebrows. I saw the couple struggling to formulate a proper comeback.

Dude finally said, "See, you just one of them sellout-ass Uncle Tom muthafuckas who gone always point the finger at Black people while ignoring what them honkies do."

I fisted my hands just in case this got physical, but Amelia wasn't just skilled at debate, but diplomacy as well.

"We all have our perceptions and opinions—only I get paid to share mine publicly. And I fully understand that, among African Americans, my opinions aren't always popular.

"Now, I'm okay with having an open discussion where there is a free exchange of ideas. But if you're just gonna resort to childish name-calling or use this as an opportunity to take personal shots, then I'll return to my shopping and wish you a good day."

Amelia turned her back on them as if they were suddenly inconsequential. Dude was heated he'd lost their verbal exchange, but Big Girl was the one with the hostile energy. She wanted to drag Amelia's narrow ass all through the store like a rag doll. And as much as part of me wanted to see that, I gave her a look like,

Don't even think. I wasn't one for hitting women in my personal life, but I am a professional goon. I'd hate to have to fuck up her and her man.

But Big Girl clearly decided to call my bluff. She reached into her bag for something, but I put my hand on hers and froze it before she could pull out what I thought was for sure a gun.

Her man tried to grab me, and that was always a mistake by unskilled fighters. If you were close enough to grab me, that meant you were close enough to get hit.

With my free arm, I gave him two short but quick elbow shots. One to the solar plexus and another to the throat. He was hunched over, coughing and choking, while I twisted his girl's arm behind her back.

She didn't carry a pistol but a small Taser. I fed that to my pocket.

The commotion brought the owner of Times Square from behind the register. He was elderly, late sixties or early seventies, but clearly had taken care of himself. And of course, was immaculately dressed in an olive-colored three-piece suit, tailored to fit.

I was about to send the couple out of his door the way Uncle Phil used to do Jazz when he spoke to them. "Look, I appreciate you all's business, but anybody with a problem with her is not welcome in my store."

He nodded to Amelia. "I'm not a Republican, and damn sure don't agree with half the things she says. But I will defend to my death her right to say it."

"And another thing about Amelia Chess is that she definitely walks her talk. Back during the lockdown of 2020, I was about to lose this place."

Amelia apparently knew what he was about to say and tried to cut him off, but the old man spoke over her. "This young lady right here, the one you all calling 'sellout' and 'Uncle Tom,' wrote me a personal check for sixty thousand dollars and ain't ask for a red cent in return."

I turned to Amelia, who stood there looking more embarrassed by his testimony than any insult launched at her.

The owner's gnarled hands had probably spent over half a century cutting and sowing fabric. He ran that over a short afro that was more salt than pepper. His wrinkled lips trembled with emotion as his eyes became moist. He castigated the young couple with a wagging finger. "So think about that before you go judging people. 'Cause what you see on the news ain't always the whole story."

Chapter Eighteen

I stepped into Times Square looking like a broke thug; I stepped out the store looking like a James Bond movie henchman. All I needed was the shoulder strap for my pistol. My baby momma had treated me to a shopping spree when I first came home from prison. Amelia didn't drop twenty stacks on me, though, just enough for two more outfits in black and navy blue.

I apologized to the old man for having to use violence in his store. Luckily, it was over quickly and led to no damage. He let the couple go without choosing to involve police.

At the car, Amelia stood by the back passenger door as if waiting for me to open it for her. She read the look on my face as I brushed past her.

"I was just playing, damn." She smiled, then joined me in the front seat.

That playful mood waned the closer it got to noon. Amelia had a lunch meeting with her producers. Two bigwigs from the company that owned the network that owned her show had flown up from Atlanta. She sat in the passenger seat, hands folded in her lap, nervously tapping her fingers. I slowly peeped that this was the reason she had needed the blunt earlier.

Joe Louis Southern Kitchen sat right off of Woodward Avenue and East Grand Boulevard in Detroit's New Center Area. Another part of the city that had seen investment dollars, so the white people felt safe here. I parked in the car and walked in at Amelia's side.

The interior was a blending of ultra-modern décor with boxing memorabilia from the 1930s. The space was filled with small tables that sat four. Framed photos of Motown's own Brown Bomber lined the walls, while highlights from some of his legendary bouts played on flatscreen televisions. Vintage gloves, heavy and speed bags hung on display. The dopest part by far was the kitchen actually being a reconstruction of his childhood home, complete with an entire exterior façade, rear patio, and wooden fence. This sat across from a cocktail bar.

Her manager Cameron was already there, seated in the rear with the two execs. I didn't quite know what to do with myself. I wanted to stay close to my client but didn't want to be all in their business, either.

I seated myself at an empty table that was two away. I asked no permission and didn't care if it had been reserved for someone else. The waiter hurried over to me, looking like he was about to ask me to move until my size and twisted mug registered with him. He instead did the smart thing: put on a phony smile and sat a menu in front of me.

Joe Louis Southern Kitchen was one of those breakfast/lunch/brunch places that didn't stay open past four o'clock. I absently glanced over menu items like the Golden Gloves French Toast and Knockout Catfish Arcadian while using my peripheral vision to scan the other diners. I was looking for anybody who seemed out of place. Took notes of the few customers who had carry permits. I peered through the windows at the front entrance to see if there was anyone on the street, just lingering there giving us undue attention.

I didn't intend to order, but the smell coming out of the kitchen, combined with seeing everybody around me eating, had me ready to fuck some shit up. I felt we were safe, so I didn't think a meal would distract me that much. I ordered something called The Heavyweight: a fluffy three-egg omelet, infused with spicy beef sausage, bacon, pork sausage, sauteed spinach, mushrooms, onions, and cheese.

While I waited for my food, I couldn't help but throw glances to Amelia and her party. The two producers were dressed like stuffed suits. A white middle-aged blonde woman was in a light sweater and loose khakis, while a man close to the same age that might have been from the Middle East had his round body stuffed in a no-name golf shirt and jeans he should've retired twenty pounds ago.

The conversation started off light but slowly escalated in intensity, so much so that when served, no one at the table hardly touched their food. I could've read lips to put me up on exactly what was being said, but I don't just make a habit of being nosy like that. Instead, I just focused on the energy coming from them. Amelia and the foreign dude did most of the talking, while her manager and the blonde chick only occasionally sprinkled comments. The exchange got so heated that at one point, Amelia snatched off her sunglasses and spoke with animated hand gestures, even smacked the table several times while driving home a point.

The meeting broke up before my meal arrived, but I still left the waiter a tip. The producers were the first to leave, and they departed with none of the informal banter that had been exchanged at the greeting. The manager inched closer to me, discreetly slid me a thick envelope that I knew was my fee.

I had to sprint to catch up to Amelia, who had already stormed out the door. I met her at the car. Even though I still made her sit up front, I did hold the door open for her.

It was a weak consolation, but the best I could offer in the moment. I knew her temporary suspension had just become permanent.

Chapter Nineteen

Amelia was short on conversation as we pulled away from the restaurant. I sensed enough trepidation in her before the meeting to know she had anticipated a negative outcome, but I imagined she had hoped for a lighter punishment. She didn't seem to want to talk about it, and since she clearly wasn't looking for me to push the conversation, we rode in a thick bubble of tension.

People might assume I'm comfortable with awkward silences, but it's just the opposite. I'm comfortable with confrontational tension, and extremely comfortable with actual violence. But I was unsure what to do in situations where I felt I was supposed to provide some sort of comfort.

But it was the inbred Black nationalist in me that kept me from making an attempt. That part of me was like, *Fuck you, bitch, you get what you deserve.* Them white folks had given her a soapbox that she could stand upon to bash her own people, and then as soon as she crossed the line, they kicked that box right out from under her.

Last night, I watched the broadcast that wound up getting her ass in all this trouble. In North Carolina, there was another police shooting of an unarmed teen. Only in this case, the two offending officers were Black, and the victim was white. Amelia thought she would use this moment to call out Black Lives Matter and all the liberal activists who would typically take to the streets with calls to defund the police. She then tried to take it a step further by using this incident as a way to eliminate race as a motivating factor for every single police shooting in the past sixty years. Amelia only did what they usually do on the right: support the officers and try to blame the victim.

Amelia didn't do her research or simply missed the memo, because the victim in this case was not just ordinary white, but Jewish. That turned her hot take into something radioactive. So when the Anti-Defamation League and all the other organizations started baring their fangs, Amelia's bosses served up her head on a platter, garnished with spinach and an apple in her mouth.

My old dude was a die-hard conspiracy theorist. So much so that books like *Behold a Pale Horse* by Robert Greyeagle and *The Unseen Hand* by A. Ralph Epperson were required reading in the UOTA. I'd been told since I was a kid that there was supposed to be a hidden cabal of Jews that secretly ruled the world. Although I did just recently find out that there are secret societies with that level of power, I never found any real proof of the Jewish conspiracy. But I did know one thing for sure, and two things for certain: any public figure who offended the chosen people by omission or commission suffered a swift and immediate downfall. Ask Arsenio Hall, Kanye West, and Kyrie Irving.

I could feel the heat coming off of Amelia as we headed back towards her condo. Her hands no longer sat on her lap, tapping with nervous energy. They were fisted and tightly clutching the hem of her cashmere coat as if ready to do destructive work.

I was still just trying to figure out what my response should be. A pat on the shoulder felt too supportive; my tongue and middle finger felt too petty. I opted for the median of those two extremes, which was to do nothing. I made no effort to burst the bubble, but instead just drowned in the tension.

We took Woodward Avenue south, headed towards downtown. It was my intent to connect with Jefferson Avenue and take that back to Amelia's building.

That was until I looked into the rearview mirror and realized that we were being followed.

Chapter Twenty

It was two vehicles, which was why I didn't notice the tail right away. A white Ford panel van without logos or decals. The second car was a late model Ford Taurus, dark gray with tinted windows.

The white van would trail me, staying about 200 feet back, and would stay on me for two to three miles before turning left off of Woodward. Then a block later, the Taurus would turn right onto Woodward and pick me up for a few miles. They didn't ride my bumper like a cop running my plate, always stayed in the lane to the left or right of me. Whenever I changed lanes and put myself directly in front of them, the driver would wait for about the distance of one traffic light, then merge into an adjacent lane. In an effort to not be so blatant, the Taurus even sped up and passed me a few times.

They were good enough to know what they were doing, more than likely had been trained, and it was only my own training that allowed me to peep them. I was sure they'd been on me since we left the restaurant, maybe even since the clothing store. But not since we left the apartment. I would've noticed them sooner.

I thought about flooring this bitch, and showing them weak-ass Fords what this AMG could do. And I probably would've if we were in the hood. But this was downtown in a Detroit that city officials were desperately trying to rebrand from our once-infamous title of murder capital. Not only had downtown been fitted with casinos, hotels, and new sports venues; there was a heavy police presence—couldn't go three blocks without seeing a squad car.

The other problem was that downtown was constructed like a weird maze with too many narrow one-way streets, too many de-tours or entire streets shut down due to construction, too many streets that curved and weaved only to lead to dead ends. Traffic was nearly stop-and-go at any given time of day. So fucked-up that many native Detroiters avoided driving downtown as a rule.

Even with a superior engine, I wouldn't be able to shake them. And I damn sure wouldn't be able to shake the police if they intervened.

So I just continued to head for the condo and didn't see any reason not to. If they could find out where she was having lunch, I was sure they already knew, or could easily find out where she lived. The way they coordinated that tail proved these were not amateurs.

I kept on Woodward southbound, past the Fox Theatre, and through the heart of downtown. And swung around the clogged arteries of Lafayette Street to Griswold. By the time I reached the coastline on Jefferson Avenue, both the van and the Taurus had turned off. They stopped their pursuit because at that point, it was obvious we were headed to her home.

Amelia sat next to me in the passenger seat, totally oblivious. She was still fuming, eyes still hidden behind the big sunglasses, and her hands still looked as they were about to tear a split in her cashmere coat. I made it safely onto the grounds of her building, which were still secure, and her condo was still a vault.

I also saw no reason to tell her we had been followed.

Chapter Twenty-one

The rest of the afternoon was uneventful. At three, I went to grab Antwon from school and used my pickup simply because it was less conspicuous than the Benz.

Antwon hurried to my truck, hopped into the passenger seat. There was a huge brown stain covering the front of his uniform shirt. His hair was wet, and I could see where he'd tried to wash most of it from his box fade. It was clear that his day had gone about as well as his mother's. People typically didn't spill chocolate milk over the top of their own heads. He didn't address it, and I wasn't the one to press. I just drove while scanning my mirrors for a white Ford van or a gray Taurus.

Once I was sure we didn't have a tail on us, I stopped at a Coney Island.

Coney Island was a Detroit staple, as much as the old English D and the high crime rate. They specialized in all sorts of comfort food, with the chili, or Coney, dog being the classic. There were probably two or three of these small carry-out restaurants in every hood, but all under different ownership. Because of this, there was a huge variation in menu selection, price, and most of all, quality. All Coneys were not created equal. But damn near every person in the 313 had their favorite. If you're ever in the mood to start some shit, just ask two Detroiters which is the best Coney Island in the city, then step back. 'Cause they might fuck around and come to blows.

I treated Antwon to a Coney dog and fries, figured he could use the pick-me-up after the day he had. It probably wasn't necessary to warn him not to tell his mother, but I still let him read a message off my phone that snitches get stitches.

I pulled back into traffic, still in my mirrors every few seconds. Being followed had me back on my paranoid shit. I took a long, circuitous route back to the building.

I hit a couple of corners when from my peripheral I peeped Antwon flagging for my attention in between bites of chili dog. "So what's up playboy, you gone smash Amelia, or what?"

I damn near spit Sprite in his face. Made him repeat that shit to make sure I heard him right.

He repeated it for me slowly and word-for-word, like I had a learning disability, as well.

"I'm just saying bro, it ain't gotta be weird. I won't be mad if you end up clapping her cakes. I could tell she'd let you smash. Now I ain't saying Amelia is a slut-bag, I'm just saying you ain't gone have to work too hard for it. It's a layup."

I made the throat-slit motion, let him know we not about to do this. Not about to chop it up with a fifteen-year-old about fucking his mother.

Antwon's energy immediately changed the moment we reached the condo. He went straight to his room and spent most of the evening behind his closed door. He emerged only for practice between five thirty and six, but after spending that half hour at the piano, shot right back to his room and locked the door.

Amelia's mood remained unchanged in the wake of her meeting. She smoked a little more before Antwon got home, then spent half an hour seated on the floor cross-legged, looking like she was meditating. Around six, she prepared dinner, and the only conversation I got was her asking if I wanted one of the nonbeef patties she was slapping between her palms. I declined with a rigorous shake of the head.

Even the conversation between mother and son was scarce, and the little there was felt strained. Their brief interactions were cold and formal. They sat to dinner, and Antwon wasn't even treated to a veggie burger, just a plate of steamed vegetables that he attacked like a man doing a job versus someone enjoying a meal. He scraped that shit in under four minutes and was asking to be excused before he could wipe his mouth. Found his way back to his room and remained there.

I didn't know if this was just a particularly fucked-up day or if this was their normal. Either way, it was like watching two people share a space versus a real family.

Amelia finished dinner alone, then washed the dishes wearing the face of someone in deep contemplation. On the way to her room, she walked past the chair I was sitting in and dragged across my shoulder. It wasn't as formal as a pat, but not as sensual as a rub. I told myself it was just appreciation for a day's work and nothing more.

Before retiring to my room, I did a perimeter walk and was extra thorough. I checked the elevator, the locks on both doors to the hall. I even checked the patio door as if somebody was going to scale those nineteen floors like a mountain climber.

I was too active in the mind, so I decided on a late-night work-out just to fatigue myself. I did 500 burpees and 1000 crunches, then regretted that the instant I was done. The old injury in my back stung with an intensity I hadn't felt in months. I swallowed two Percocet.

After I took a shower, I again thought about that touch on the shoulder while I lotioned up. Was ol' girl trying to shoot her shot? I thought about Amelia's reaction if I just walked into her room, still butt-ass naked. A part of me guessed that she would be with the shit. The smarter part of me decided not to find out.

The pills quieted the pain in my back enough to find sleep, but only for a few hours. I rolled over and checked my phone. It was 1:37 in the morning.

My stomach issued a painful reminder that pride was less filling than the veggie burger I refused. I left my room to find the entire first floor pitch black and perfectly still.

I crept into the kitchen for a light snack with actual carbs and sugar. I was only expecting to raid one of Antwon's stashes.

I wasn't expecting to come face-to-face with an intruder.

Chapter Twenty-two

What first presented itself as a fleeting shadow creeping through the kitchen into the dining room, suddenly turned towards me and attacked. I found myself blocking blows, not from a phantom, but from a black silhouette with substance.

And definite skill. The intruder was an aggressive but restrained martial artist. Punches and kicks came with equal amounts of power and speed. The roundhouse had the grace of a ballerina and perfect form. Had I not got my forearm up in time to block, it probably would've taken my head off my shoulders.

I retaliated with a right jab and caught nothing but air. I took two shots to the short ribs and a front kick to the sternum for my trouble.

I stumbled back into the stove, then switched my fighting style from boxing to Muay Thai. My opponent stopped for a moment, then went into a fighting stance that mirrored my own. I thought it might just be to be comical or mock me.

But it was not. My Muay Thai was skillfully countered by my black-clad foe. In return, I received elbows and knees to sensitive areas of my anatomy. Punches to the head, kicks to the shins. I was on the losing end each time we exchanged blows. I was being outclassed by a superior fighter—something that had never happened to me since my earliest days training in the UOTA.

We clinched and the advantage of height and weight went to me versus my smaller opponent. I picked up his slight frame and used every ounce of strength in my muscular 270-pound frame to hurl him into the other room.

But this nigga clearly had feline DNA, because he fell backwards into a handstand, then flipped up onto his feet. Plus he had an incredibly light step, because the floor communicated no vibrations of his movements. He was like a real shadow.

He charged again, stunned me with an open palm to the throat, then punished my kidneys and ribs. As I folded, he bounced my head off the granite countertop, then finished with a spinning back fist.

I stood on rubbery legs, gagging with a hand on my throat and tasting blood in my mouth. I was getting my ass kicked and not liking the feeling. My opponent stood across from me in perfect black against the darkened kitchen. Nothing of his face could be seen. It was as if he was wearing a head-to-toe body stocking. He could've been laughing, could've been mocking me, could've been talking cash shit, too. And in my mind, he was.

There was a butcher's block of large kitchen knives on the counter near me, and out of desperation, I snatched one. I faced off with him again holding a curved meat cleaver.

I slashed twice, carving an X in the air, but missed my speedy foe. With lightning reflexes, he spun to put his back to me, threw an elbow back into my already tenderized ribs, took control of my knife hand. He tossed his back into mine, giving me a reverse head butt that sent mine back against a heavy cast-iron skillet hanging from a rack. He banged my wrist against the stove until I broke my grip on the cleaver.

This dude was quicker than me and much more skilled, but made the potentially fatal mistake that so many had before him. He fucked around and got too close to me. I wrapped him from behind in a bearhug. I picked him up, slammed him belly-flat to the ground, and pinned him there. He tried to scramble and crawl to get free but he was flattened under my 270 pounds.

In the middle of the kitchen floor, I locked his arms over his head in a way that didn't allow him to use his hands, and this was how Amelia found us. The lights switched on, momentarily burning my dark-adapted eyes. Amelia and her son stood in the doorway, both wide-eyed, obviously drawn by the sound of the commotion.

I kept both arms pinned with one arm while I tried to snatch off the mask. It didn't have eyes or mouth holes but was clearly made of some thin, breathable material that allowed him to see. Only I couldn't get it off, because it seemed to be attached to his outfit like one large body stocking. I reached for the meat cleaver to cut it open. I had to see this muthafucka's face before I snapped his neck. The only person who had ever gotten the best of me in a one-on-one fight.

He was still face down, twisting and squirming while I cut open the back of the mask. His dreadlocks were well-treated, oiled and twisted down into tight Bantu knots. I grabbed a fistful of those black braids and turned him over to see his face.

Her face.

He was a *she*.

Chapter Twenty-three

I was still trying to process the fact that I'd just gotten my ass kicked by a girl. I turned her onto her stomach and sat with my shins pinning her shoulders. She was lean and muscular, which was why I'd first mistaken her for a man. She had the squared, angular physique of an Olympic swimmer, but her face was round and feminine.

After those first few minutes of thrashing against me, she was surprisingly subdued. She lay on the kitchen floor and looked up at me calmly with those brown eyes. She revealed neither frustration nor fear.

Amelia pulled her phone, presumably to call the police, but I stopped her with a waving hand. That wasn't the type of justice I dealt in. Plus I needed to ask our uninvited guest a few questions first. Like how she'd gotten into the condo, and more importantly, where'd she learned to fight like that.

I asked Amelia for something I could tie up the girl with. Amelia voiced sensible objections, still persistent that we should call the authorities. These got overruled by my stern glare. Even while Amelia debated me, Antwon disappeared from the doorway and returned minutes later with an extension cord and one for a USB that was twenty feet long. His mother was still bitching me out while I thanked youngin' for the assist. I bound the intruder's ankles and wrists.

My interrogations can be bloody, and extremely loud. Hardly the type of conversation to be held over tea and biscuits.

But before I could get her someplace where I could make her scream, I had to figure out a way to get her out of the building unseen. Would help if I knew how she'd gotten in and followed the same path. There were cameras in the elevator, the hall, and the lobby.

But according to Antwon, the emergency service stairwell at the rear of the building was used only in case of fire, and the cameras covering it were not being fed to a live monitor. The cameras were only activated by a motion sensor, and then the footage was downloaded to a special server in the security office.

He explained: "Now, unless there's an actual fire, the security desk considers that footage low priority and won't review it for at least thirty-six hours. That's plenty of time for someone who knows what they're doing to send a virus to the server and corrupt the data."

That revelation earned the teen a threatening glance from his mother. Antwon had tipped his hand. Amelia, as well as I, figured he had just shared his own secret escape route out of the building.

I typed the obvious question and held my screen for Antwon: "What about the other cameras, in the hall and the parking garage?"

"Those are on a live feed, but—" He threw a guilty glance to his mother. "They can be hacked remotely, again by somebody who knows what they're doing." Antwon gave Amelia a look that was basically asking for permission.

"Boy, just do it. And don't act like you haven't before."

I thought Antwon might need the desktop in his room, but he pulled out his phone. and his thumbs started working at lightning speed.

For whatever reason, he tried to explain to me what he was doing, but I'm only built for punching and kicking on shit. Plus, I just did twelve years in the joint, so this tech shit was still lost on me. Antwon was hard enough to understand, staring down into his phone and speaking quickly in the terminologies of his craft. He claimed he didn't need to take the whole building, just the electronic eyes covering our route; however, he noted that there could be some issue with rewriting the time stamp on the video. I just waited for the little nigga to give the nod that we were good to go.

I thought it would be smart to do a dry run first. So just in case something went wrong and security found me somewhere I wasn't supposed to be, I could always play the deaf card. Remember, most people think deaf means dumb. I'd taken advantage a time or two in my life.

I took to the hall and reached the emergency stairwell. I took a breath before I pushed the door open, fearful that flashing lights and a high-pitched siren would wake the entire building. Antwon had remotely disabled the alarm. And just as the boy said, the emergency stairwell was never used at a decent hour, so it was perfect at three in the morning.

There were a few cameras down in the underground parking garage, but Antwon had them under his control. I strolled past those boldly, knowing that he would either digitally delete my image or simply loop past footage for those watching the monitors.

I went back upstairs and had to fireman-carry my captive down nineteen flights. She had fought like a demon earlier but was surprisingly docile going down. Even restrained, she didn't thrash and squirm. I got her to my Ram, then slammed her down into the pickup bed. She looked at me like we were going for ice cream.

I couldn't leave Amelia and Antwon alone at the condo since the place was clearly compromised. I hustled her and her son into the cab of my Bighorn, even though her Benz was slotted a few cars away. I pulled out the underground parking garage hitting corners hard, purposely tossing my captive around in the back.

I drove cautiously once I hit the streets. Detroit's affluent riverfront was heavily policed, and a Black man out driving at three thirty in the morning would get pulled over just because. The girl tied up in the rear of my truck would be a bitch to explain. I turned off East Jefferson with intentions of taking smaller surface streets to I-75 to get the fuck away from downtown. The rich lady from the gas station was the only person pouring money into the city's neglected interior. I would feel safer once I got back to the hood.

I turned on Mt. Elliot and made a quick left at Lafayette, and saw through my rearview the gray Taurus mimic the same route. The pursuer slammed into me from behind.

We were all pitched forward in our seats, and the wheel momentarily got away from me. I swerved left, sending half my pickup over the curb for a grass center island. To the right, I bowled over a few orange cones that had briefly funneled traffic to a single lane.

Clearly the tough bitch sliding around my covered cab wasn't working alone. I started to worry over the type of numbers I was facing. I knew she was at least part of a duo. But could it be a team or a whole damn battalion?

Chapter Twenty-four

I learned from my previous car chases where I was stuck driving some weak shit. My Ram 1500 came off the assembly line running a 5.7-liter Hemi. I stepped down hard, putting some distance between us and the trailing vehicle. I read panicked utterances from Amelia's lips. I cranked my speed up to seventy, blowing through intersections and past signs posted with thirty-five miles per hour.

I-375 was fast approaching, but between us was a gauntlet of road construction. More orange than a Syracuse home game. Barrels, signs, and stripped gates that cordoned off entire sectors of freeway. The avenues were no better. Our governor had gotten elected with the battle-cry, *Fix the damn roads!* and even the Trump supporters who had plotted to kidnap her would have to agree that she was keeping her campaign promise, even though it was frustrating the hell out of daily commuters. It seemed at any given point street repair had half of Detroit bottlenecked.

Even with my beefed-up Hemi, I couldn't lose the Ford. In my mirrors, I saw the driver was keeping pace about ten feet behind me. His arm came out his window holding something that I couldn't identify in the dark and distance. The muzzle flashes proved it was something fully automatic. My back window became an opaque screen of weblike cracks. Bullets sheared off the driver's-side mirror.

I turned to Amelia and Antwon, motioned for them to get down. The chubby boy did his best to stuff himself into the foot space between the front and rear seats. I had to forcibly push her head down before his panicking mother got the message.

In that split second of dealing with her, I took my eyes off the road. A raised crosswalk that doubled as a speed bump appeared in my headlights. I hit it so hard that my Ram momentarily got air. I bounced high enough in my seat to hit my head on the ceiling, and the landing tested my suspension. I lost the wheel again. I took out two orange barrels on my way into the work zone for street repair.

This side of the road was unpaved, which made regaining control even more difficult. My tires sprayed gravel as I fishtailed left to right. Luckily no workmen were out at this hour, but they'd left their equipment on site. Ironically, I flattened a sign warning reckless drivers that killing a worker was a 7500-dollar fine and punishable with up to fifteen years in prison. The tar kettle was a trailer connected to a huge gravel hauler; I narrowly missed that, traded paint with the city dump truck.

My pursuer took the speed bump at the same rate and landed with more grace. He raced me along the paved side of the street and prevented me from crossing back over to where my tires would find traction. He occasionally sent a short spray of bullets over the hood of his car but seemed more content to let the obstacles kill me. A less-skilled driver would have already skidded into the massive asphalt roller or spun out and buckled his vehicle against one of the adult elms that decorated the Lafayette curbside.

In my haste, I nearly forgot about my own pistol. Busting this .40 a couple times made the driver of the Taurus back his ass up, especially when I sent one through his windshield. After he retreated a few feet, I was able to escape the construction zone and get back to the paved side of the road.

The freeway service drive was less than a quarter mile away. I was eager to hit the freeway, where my stronger motor gave me the clear advantage. I'll open this bitch up and watch the Malibu shrink to nothing in my rearview.

I bent a right on Chrysler Drive so sharp that I was nearly on two wheels. But as I approached I-375, I realized I had a problem. The on-ramp was barricaded with an orange gate and a reflective sign that read: OUT OF SERVICE. More construction had the service drive closed. I went backwards into the Michigan U-turn that would swing me across the bridge to the other side of the service drive.

It was nut-check time, wanted to test how far these niggas would go to get their target. I raced past a DO NOT ENTER sign that warned of one-way traffic. I entered the exit ramp and sped down the Walter P. Chrysler Freeway in the wrong direction.

Amelia was screaming at me, slapping my shoulder as if I hadn't done this on purpose. With a look, I told her to calm the fuck down, I had this. Then I tried to convince myself of the same.

Through my rearview, I saw the silver Malibu take the exit a few hundred feet back. A lady in a white Traverse had hit the ramp right after me and nearly met the Ford head-on. My pursuer won that game of Chicken, because the Traverse swerved hard to the right. It jumped the shoulder, skidded up the embankment, spun out amidst a cloud of dust and flying grass.

I stomped down on the gas pedal, floated the odometer needle past ninety, and watched the silver car get little in my rearview.

Luckily there wasn't much oncoming traffic with three hours before most people's morning commute. The few drivers headed towards downtown quickly darted out the path of the asshole in the black Ram who was clearly suicidal. Those flashing headlights were most likely accompanied by blaring horns and a few obscene words.

With at least half a mile between me and my pursuer, I started looking for an on-ramp that I could use for an exit. I'd hit the surface streets, bend a couple of corners, and lose his ass in the hood.

Only the next available on-ramp was barricaded due to construction. So for the time being, I was stuck going north on southbound I-75 dodging oncoming traffic.

Governor Whitmer's "Fix the Damn Roads" initiative had even extended to many freeway overpasses. Some of these old cap and pile relics, built in the aftermath of World War II, had been totally demolished to receive a much-needed upgrade in style and structure to either cable-stay or tied-arch bridges. Because of this, there were sections of the freeway reduced to one lane, primarily where workmen were in the process of tearing down or rebuilding the support columns. While orange barrels sufficed on the surface streets, here they had used concrete dividers to funnel traffic safely by the freeway crews for fear a drunk or inattentive driver might lose control and plow through the construction site doing ninety miles per hour. The same speed I was going as I entered one of those restricted lane areas.

I could only imagine the signs I sped by warned of reduced lane width and a sharp traffic shift ahead. Of course I couldn't read any of them, because they were facing drivers with the sense to be driving in the right direction.

The concrete barriers closed in to a few feet on either side of my truck. The next half a mile, it would be so tight that even a motorcycle couldn't squeeze by me.

Then, after a deep rounded turn that would take me from the Chrysler Freeway to the Lodge, I was blinded by bright headlights. I had to suddenly stand on my brake pedal. Facing me was a huge Peterbilt rounding that bend from the other way. It was a log-bearing semi carrying about 75,000 pounds and coming at sixty-five miles per hour.

Fully loaded, my Ram 1500 barely topped 5,000 pounds, and I was coming at him still doing about seventy. With no way to move out of his way or avoid a head-on collision.

I imagine that the truck driver gave his horn a long, continuous blast. A warning that our inevitable confrontation would not favor my smaller pickup.

Chapter Twenty-five

The grill of the Peterbilt was bearing down on me like the sheer face of a mountain. It couldn't have been good for the transmission the way I went from drive to reverse without coming to a complete stop. I was at least going in the direction of traffic, even if facing the wrong way.

The NHTSA legally requires that a trucker be able to bring his rig to a complete stop within 250 feet, regardless of the speed. However, so many other things come into play when figuring the braking distance of a tractor/trailer. Things like being on a flat surface in ideal road conditions, the weight of the load, but most importantly, the reaction time of a driver who is assumed to be well-rested and sober.

Consider that old buddy was pulling a flatbed stacked with fifty-foot maple logs in excess of 70,000 pounds, that the roads were still slick from last night's passing shower, that he was coming down a ramp, and that the driver might be tired or drunk. He could need anywhere from 600 to 1,000 feet to come to a complete stop.

And the driver was either inexperienced or buzzed off something. He jumped on his air brakes, sending the truck into skid, and started to jackknife. From the front, I saw the rear of his trailer swing out to the left. It bumped the concrete divider, the back tandem tires rolled up and over the barrier. The truck was still sliding down the ramp towards me while the undercarriage of the trailer hung halfway over the guardrail.

This caused the load to jostle and shift until the weight snapped one of the tie-down straps. Some of those huge fifty-foot logs started to roll off the flatbed. Because the trailer hung half over the railing, a few of them spilled over the edge and would have killed any freeway drivers going southbound on 75. Two hopped off the flatbed and skidded down the ramp towards me like massive maple torpedoes.

I backed my way through the construction gauntlet doing seventy. Even using my backup camera, taking some of the steeper turns at that speed was tricky. I scraped the concrete divider on the rear passenger side and ruined the Ram's glossy black paint. The lease and insurance paperwork was in Kierra's name, and baby was gone be pissed when she saw the damages.

The gray Taurus appeared in my rearview. We approached each other fast. He was trapped in that single lane of traffic with no way to pass or avoid me. I mashed the gas, ran the speedometer up to ninety. Kierra was about to be beyond pissed as I prepared to ram my tailgate into the front end of that car hard enough to push the engine into the driver's lap.

The driver fired a few more shots at me, but when I got within twenty feet, he screeched to such an abrupt stop that it smoked his tires. He sped away from me in reverse, mimicking my very move against the semi.

The driver clearly knew something. He slipped through a S-turn doing ninety, and even with the reduced lane width, didn't scratch his car on either side.

Me, on the other hand, was scraping the shit out the truck, trying to stay ahead of the semi and the falling lumber. One log jumped the concrete barrier, entered the construction zone, and took out the scaffolding for the bridge columns under repair. The other log was a huge javelin still headed towards me.

The driver of the gray car did some foul shit. Once he put enough space between us, the Taurus came to a stop. Through my mirror, I watched another lean, dark silhouette spring out the open door, then hurdle the concrete divider with athletic grace. The appearance was identical to the stocking-clad girl currently sliding around the bed of my pickup, although the sex of the driver was unknown.

But the intent was well-known, even to a deaf-mute with no formal education. The stalled Ford was being used as a blockade to cut off my retreat. The massive tree trunk was closing in on me, being followed by the out-of-control semitruck. I was trapped.

If we were immediately crushed by two tons of untreated lumber, 70,000 pounds of metal would surely finish the job.

Chapter Twenty-six

My first impulse was to just floor it, try to get up to one hundred in reverse and bulldoze the stalled Ford. There was some power behind my Hemi, and if I built up sufficient speed, I should've been able to push the smaller Taurus back out the way it came in. Looking through my shattered back window, I judged there was only about an eighth of a mile between the silver car and where the lane reduction had begun. If I hit that bitch with enough force, I would be able to get back through while maintaining the speed I needed to stay ahead of the logs. This was provided that no other car entered the work zone.

The problem was that the collision would most likely destroy my rear end and kill the captive tied up in the truck bed. Sympathy didn't add a single gram to the scale. The girl's life only weighed in my decision because she had information that I needed.

What happened next was the child of desperation more than inspiration. I didn't recall any *a-ha* moment where I was illuminated with this idea. It was totally instinctive. Had my conscious mind had time to intervene, I would've immediately dismissed the thought as reckless and crazy.

I simultaneously reduced my speed as I eased the truck closer to the right divider. I scraped the concrete twice before a slight bend in the lane allowed me to catch the perfect angle to roll up the wall. I fought to get my passenger's-side tires atop the temporary divider. My driver's side was still on the ground, putting my truck on a forty-five-degree slant.

The divider was about three feet high, and it took a helluva lot of skill and concentration to skate my tires along the top without slipping off. It wouldn't be easy for the average driver to pull this off going forward, but luckily, I'd started training in the art of defensive and tactical driving at just eight years old. Without the perfect coordination of speed and wheel control, I would've slipped off to destroy the undercarriage, or worse, oversteer and tip the whole truck over.

This allowed me to clear enough lane space for the first log to slide by me, albeit close enough to scrape the paint off the driver's side and send splinters through the open window.

The giant log raced by me to spear the stalled Malibu. The force buckled the front end like an accordion, and the momentum carried the car backwards several hundred feet.

The Taurus cleared the construction with just enough space. I scraped the side of the truck again, nearly lost control when my passenger tires hit the street again. I spun the truck into a 180-degree turn and sped away in the right direction, back towards downtown.

The semi was coming down through the construction zone like a bowling ball thrown wildly down a lane. It scraped the temporary divider on one side, then drifted to the other. The front drive tire exploded, and sparks flew as the metal rim met the asphalt. The truck swerved hard, the cab burst through the concrete barrier into the work area, where it crashed into a front end loader.

I couldn't tell you if the semitruck driver survived, because I didn't wait around. I hauled down 375, used the same exit ramp I had just come down the wrong way, then used the surface streets to get the fuck away before police, fire, and news crews arrived on scene.

If only it were that easy to escape the feeling in the pit of my stomach. Something told me the night was about to get a lot crazier.

Chapter Twenty-seven

It wasn't that I wanted to take Amelia back to my place; home just happened to be the safest place I could think of. I kept one would-be assassin tied up in the bed of my pickup truck. At least one more ran around loose out there, most likely plotting a second attempt.

I had spent hundreds of thousands in renovations, but not in the way of extra rooms, screened-in patios, or swimming pools. On the outside, my house looked just as unassuming as every other three-bedroom, one-and-one-half-bath in the area appraised at about 90,000. In fact, the upgrades I'd made would certainly depreciate the value. None of it had been cosmetic.

I had borrowed and improved on a theme I had seen the first time doing business with DelRay—the fat nigga playing right hand to the rich lady from the gas station. DelRay had enjoyed a short stint as Detroit's number-one arms dealer after stumbling upon an underground cache of illegal weapons. I'd gone to his spot to cop some heat for this beef I had with these Joy Road Boys. I had stepped into a house that should belong to somebody's grandmother only to find myself locked in an urban fortress.

I led Amelia and her son through my security barriers. Antwon scanned around with eyes widened by amazement. I imagined his mother was out of earshot when he said, "It's like you a superhero for real. This is a low-budget Batcave. And you the broke Bruce Wayne."

The temperature dropped ten degrees when I introduced Kierra to my client. Although she was a street chick, Kierra watched the news enough to be up on Amelia's journalistic career and the controversy that ultimately got her cancelled. Kierra didn't even pretend to be courteous. She just looked Amelia up and down with visible disgust.

Kierra's expression worsened when she peeked out the window and saw the truck. The Ram was leased in her name. The back window was busted out, the side-view mirrors were sheared off, and the body was peppered with bullet holes. This was just the visible damage: I was sure the suspension and parts of the underbody were probably fucked-up, too. I gave her an apologetic look that said *My bad,* but also a stern one that warned this wasn't the time to bitch at me about it.

Kierra really wasn't happy about me leaving Amelia and her son there for her to babysit. I wasn't really worried about anybody getting to them while inside my house. I just needed Kierra to keep an eye on them just in case.

I took the girl, still tied up in the back of my truck, to an abandoned rec center not far from my house. I still had questions that I intended to get the answers to, and planned to ask forcefully. My house had been beefed up for security purposes, but I had done nothing in terms of soundproofing. I didn't want the girl's screams to get me kicked out the block club association.

I opened the tailgate, dragged her out by the ankles, and let her drop to the ground. Despite being knocked around back there during the car chase and shootout, she looked calm and content. I snatched her by the neck and ushered her into the building through a rear entrance.

This was a crumbling structure that should've been demolished years ago, set in the middle of a field overrun with chest-high weeds and cordgrass. Recreation centers were community staples back in the '70s and '80s, where teens and young adults could participate in various after-school programs from organized sports to learning skilled trades. Of course this was back when parents forced you to go outside and play, before PlayStation and the internet turned all the kids into phone-obsessed, smart-mouthed shut-ins with a thousand different social anxieties.

I dropped her like a sack of potatoes in the remains of a basketball gym. The metal bleachers had long since been stolen by scrappers. Shattered backboards faced each other with bent, rusted rims. A warped hardwood court already had weeds sprouting up between the planks.

I dropped her into a chair that was situated at the far end of the court. The squeaky old office chair was scavenged from the illegal dumping done outside the building. The seat and backrest were wrapped in faded gray upholstery stained with blood splatter from my previous visits.

I retrieved a bowling bag that I kept stashed nearby. I unzipped it and made a show of unpacking my tools: a ball-ping hammer, pliers, industrial-sized bolt-cutters, an acetylene blow torch.

She watched me unfazed, even let out a yawn that wasn't genuine. I'd seen too many times the smug indifference of someone who thought their resolve was unbreakable. Their expression was never quite the same once the interrogation began.

I loaded the first question on my phone. I wanted to know who hired her, hoping my own suspicions were wrong.

When she didn't respond, I slapped her across the face with about fifty percent of my functional strength. The force whipped her head around and sent slob from her mouth. Once those brown eyes refocused on me, there was no trace of the fear or rage that a slap like that should've triggered. Her eyes were smiling at me even before her lips curled into a mocking smirk.

My next blow erased that look right off her face. It was a

straight right to the sternum that stole her wind. After a few coughs, I watched her gasp like a fish out of water for a few seconds. I momentarily pierced that veneer of self-control. There was something closer to anger in her glare while she sucked air in greedy gulps. But once she was fully oxygenated, she returned to a place of calm indifference.

I thrust my screen in her face again, let her see in my face that this was only going to get worse for her. Her response was to close her eyes to me. Her shoulders rose and fell from deep, controlled breaths.

I worked her over like a heavy bag, alternating left and right hooks. She absorbed each blow with a grimace. She would occasionally glare at me, baring her teeth like something rabid. Then she would close her eyes and refocus on her breathing.

The ensuing battle was one of mind versus muscle. I worked her body over, mostly focusing on her midsection while she tried to use the discipline of meditation to mitigate the pain. I intended to inflict more pain than she could tolerate. I felt like I'd already lost to her once in Amelia's kitchen, so I was more determined to win here.

I was pulling my punches but not by much. Many women didn't have the same bone density as men. At any point, I could've broken a rib and sent it into her lung. I wasn't practicing chivalry; I just didn't want to kill her right away.

Still, I was hitting her so hard that she would probably piss and shit blood for the next few weeks. Repeated blows would do permanent damage to her liver and kidneys.

It's important to note that I'm not some sadistic perv who gets off on hurting women. In my professional capacity, I'm an equal opportunity ass whipper. I'd only killed one female for personal reasons, and it was the hardest thing I'd ever done. I'm a goon, not a gentleman.

She was tough, easily one of the toughest women I'd ever met. Most men would've tapped out by now. She was still absorbing my body shots, albeit with a lot less meditative calm, but still not talking.

I stopped, breathing heavy from my own effort. She stared at me, breathing deeply herself. Her eyes didn't shine with victory, because she knew this was just an interlude.

It was time to turn up the heat, and I meant that literally.

I got down to one knee and pushed her legs open. I gazed up at her from the position of her gynecologist, but the expression on my face assured her that she would find my exam extremely unpleasant.

I grabbed the acetylene torch and my lighter, engaged both until I had a blue flame.

She was a G, and I respected that. She was by far the toughest opponent I'd ever met, physically and mentally. But there was no level of meditative calm that would steel her against me putting fire on some very sensitive areas of her anatomy.

She told me everything I wanted to know, what I already knew. I was just hoping like hell I was wrong.

Chapter Twenty-eight

"You were not what I expected of an elder chief's son."

The Bantu knots; the thin, muscular frame that had led me to mistake her for a man in Amelia's kitchen; even in reading her lips, I judged the rhythm and speech patterns to be authentic. For a while, I just stared at her, unable to respond. I held my phone in hands that visibly shook.

"Your striking was slow and predictable with no defense to speak of. I'd rate your Muay Thai at a second-level warrior grade or worse. I should've beaten you easily."

I couldn't argue with that, even if I had the voice to. She had been kicking my ass before I was able to wrap her up and drop my weight on her.

And the comments probably wouldn't have stung as much if they were mockery. But her expression and mannerisms were that of a detached critic making a cold assessment of my skills.

Just thinking of the fight aggravated the pain in my shoulder. I'd popped a Percocet at the house that hadn't kicked in yet.

This had just went from bad to all the way fucked-up. I could tell by the way they were trailing me on Woodward that they had some form of training; then the way she'd fought at the condo proved they were highly trained. I would've been good if these were run-of-the-mill killers or even Navy Seals. These mutha-fuckas were much worse. Because they were the same thing I was. I finally stopped my hands shaking long enough to fire off a quick question: *How many others on your team?* I wanted to know about her partner waiting outside Amelia's building, who had shown the tactical and defensive driving skills to prove that they were also the real deal. I knew I was facing at least two Shango-class warriors. I was just hoping like hell that it wasn't three or more.

She just stared at me. "We are not a team. We are a tribe." Her facial expression made the words seem emphatic.

If the church had dispatched two of his most elite killers, when one would do in most situations, they were extremely motivated to silence Amelia.

Then I started to worry exactly how much did they know about me. Did the old man know where I was? Had they been surveilling me, or was the fact I was involved just an unfortunate coincidence?

She read the inquiry off my phone and just shook her head. "You don't have the slightest idea of what you are involved in. Just walk away, Lutalo."

I guess she thought she would get some sympathy by invoking my given name. I pulled my pistol, placed the barrel under her chin. I let her see the eyes of a killer losing patience.

The look she returned was that of a killer's calm. As if Life and Death were inconsequential and she would be comfortable in ei-ther form. "If I am killed here, more will come. You are the one who is alone. You have no tribe."

I let her know I didn't need one. I'm a one-man wrecking crew.

She laughed at that.

Amelia's political stance grated my nerves, too, but for them to assassinate her felt like a bit much. I asked the brown-eyed girl if they planned to kill every Black person who went against the fold and adopted a right-wing ideology.

"We will protect our people from those among us who would sell their souls."

To me, that came off like a company line, something instilled early and repeated often.

I wanted to know who the second one was and where could I find them. She gave me a look that indicated there would be no more information forthcoming.

We seemed to have reached that inevitable but mutually understood conclusion. I stepped back two feet and leveled the pistol at her head. I lowered my gaze a bit. Part of me didn't want to see what the bullet was about to do to her face.

She pierced me with those brown eyes. "Being among the scarecrows has taken you far from the path of Dhwty. I am a child of Shango. You would send me back to the ancestors like a dog. Have you lost all honor? We have crossed spears."

We didn't actually cross spears. The point she was making is that we had fought.

It had been instilled in us early in our training to have respect for your opponent, especially if that opponent presented a worthy challenge. A warrior who did not die on their feet was shunned in the Afterlife.

I had been gone from the church too long for this weak-ass play on my religious sympathies. She had earned just enough of my respect to humor her final requests, but I gestured with the pistol to assure her that I fully intended to blow her brains out the back of her skull.

I scavenged the floor until I found a small painted stick about eight inches long, that could've been part of a window jamb. I used my own knife to cut her ropes, let her get to her feet while keeping sufficient distance between us.

She thanked me with a nod as she stood, rubbing the rope

burns on her wrists. I tossed her the small stick. It was the best I could do for her.

A warrior who died on their feet made them favored among the ancestors, but to die on your feet with your weapon in hand earns you a smile from the Thunder God Himself. The small stick was a poor excuse for a spear. I hoped Shango would not hold that against her.

I used my phone to ask her name. I wanted to know who to offer prayers for once I sent her to the Other Side.

"Zakiya. It means—"

I waved her off. She might have been another one who thought deaf meant dumb. In Swahili, her name means *intelligent*. In the Arabic languages, it means *innocent*, *pure*, or *flawless*.

Just like mine, Lutalo, literally means *warrior* or *fighter*.

"Mzee Chifu speaks of you often."

Nice try, but trick no good. The UOTA had clearly expanded their training to include psychological tactics. There was a time when my father's approval meant everything to me. But I'd grown too much since then for that to be effective bait.

"Your mother, as well."

Now that one nearly put the hook in my mouth. I frowned at her, offered a snort to say she was full of shit.

"I was just sparring with Dada Mkubwe before departing for this mission. It is going to break her heart to hear how your skills have declined."

Bullshit. I would've spat the word if I could. There was no way my mother was back in the church.

"You think I'm lying?" She said this through a chuckle that made it difficult to read.

I most certainly did. This was just more psychological warfare. The daddy card didn't work, so she went for the mommy. I didn't think my story was a well-kept secret inside the UOTA. If she had been dispatched here with the expectation of facing me, I'm pretty sure she'd been briefed on the situation with my mother.

I met her eyes when I raised the gun this time. I even offered her a small salute before I sent her to the ancestors.

"A grilled cheese sandwich cut diagonally, a bowl of warm tomato soup, and a handful of Lorna Doone shortbread cookies." It was exactly what my mother used to make me for lunch every day when I came home from kindergarten. It was one of the few memories I had from our life before the church.

I stared at her, trying to gauge her for sincerity. Her smirk was enigmatic as the Mona Lisa's.

"Would you like to know your strawman name? The one on your birth certificate?"

Chapter Twenty-nine

I looked over her closely, searching for deception. My disability always forced me to understand better than most that ninety percent of communication is nonverbal. During my time in prison, I had spent a few years studying body language. People told on themselves with tiny unconscious gestures called micro-reactions: nostril flares, finger taps, wandering eyes. These reactions were too small and quick to be noticed by the untrained observer. And they were too deeply embedded in our psyche to be avoided without specialized training.

I had no doubt that she was working me, but her body language was giving up nothing. In my day, the UOTA could coach up a ten-year-old to beat the polygraph six out of eight times. I'm sure they had probably expanded the training to include other preventative interrogation techniques.

"I'm probably the only person who knows that Dada Mkubwe still hides a pack of Lorna Doones in her drawer. She even sends me out to the store to buy them for her."

I aimed the pistol at her head, but Zakiya's return stare revealed no fear that I would use it. She knew that I was already on the line and sufficiently reeled in.

"The more I stare, the more I see you actually favor her more than your father. She would love to see you."

Bullshit. If she wanted to see me, she could've done so. And she damn sure could've done that instead of going back to the UOTA. She peeped the negative expression on my face. "If you returned, the tribe would embrace you with open arms. Even Mzee Chifu would rejoice. Return of the prodigal son."

That one froze me. Up until that point, going back to the church was something I had only peripherally considered that first year.

"Do you really prefer this life? Lost in the wilderness, and at the mercy of the puppeteers and scarecrows?"

Scarecrows. That was one from my past that I hadn't heard used in this context since leaving. Scarecrows were how the elders labeled outsiders. It was a double entendre.

My father explained to me that anybody born into the system who has a birth certificate and social security card automatically becomes associated with a corporate entity in the same name known as a straw man, and the government makes no distinction between you and this legal entity—you are your straw man. This is your name in all caps as it appears on most important documents. My old dude claimed it was how the government controls us, keeps track of us, even reduced us to chattel property when they monetized our births by using us as collateral for its national debts. Those who woke up had to go through a long and arduous process to divorce themselves from their straw man. Most lived their entire lives as an agent of this corporate entity, never knowing it existed. The people still living as their straw man were considered scarecrows. It was an easy reach.

The second reason outsiders were called scarecrows was because a scarecrow was only an imitation of a real person. It was miscellaneous bulk stuffed in human clothes, designed to fool unintelligent animals. It had no brain, it had no heart, it had no guts. This was the UOTA's critique of pretty much anybody who wasn't them.

She had me deep in my memories, thinking on possibilities I never considered before. But then I realized, a little too late, that it was all crap. I fell for the setup.

Chapter Thirty

All that talk about my parents was just a stall tactic, a distraction. I saw the shadow creeping into my peripheral. Another black-clad figure was coming at me, moving low and fast. I was trying to figure how to deal with the threat at my back when Zakiya lunged and threw herself into me.

She grabbed my gun hand just as I was bringing up the Glock, put both hands on the weapon, and purposely cocked the pistol back for me. I didn't know what the fuck she was doing until Zakiya jammed the side of her palm down into the ejection port. This kept the slide from engaging and wouldn't let me fire the pistol.

It was an adaption of a move I'd used myself when I was running security for a group of strippers who work for my baby momma. Only I'd stuffed my thumb into the trigger guard to act as a backstop. I had been taught that move in the UOTA as a youth, but clearly the instructors had developed a safer, more effective technique since my departure. The sliding mechanism and ejection window pinched her hand hard enough to draw blood.

She took my arm and tried to send me into a hip-toss, which was her first miscalculation. I'd fucked up by letting her get too close, and me, of all people, should've known better; however, this simple karate move—one of the first taught in the UOTA— that used an opponent's size and weight against them, wasn't about to happen against me.

With everything else taught, the church didn't particularly put an emphasis on strength training. I had already been blessed with inordinate size, but it was the twelve years I spent in prison that had allowed me to bulk up to 270 pounds with less than three percent body fat.

While she struggled to leverage me for a slam, I clean-and-jerked her 130 pounds. I muscled her body over my head. I threw her about six feet, where she bounced off the gym wall, then landed sharply on the warped and rotted hardwood.

I swung my pistol in the direction of her partner, but they were close enough to take a hold of my wrist. Twisted in a way that caused me an involuntary hand spasm. Then smacked the weapon from my broken grip and kicked it away.

The partner was definitely a male. Four inches taller, with a lean muscular frame under a snug exercise shirt. He wore black cargo pants tucked into heavy boots that looked like they might be steel-toed. They must've recruited some decent barbers since I left, because he had a short, tapered afro with a crispy line-up. Above the black face mask that covered his mouth and nose, his eyes cut like knives.

We fought hand-to-hand. I attacked with a three-piece, but the first punch only grazed their temple. The other two caught air. This muthafucka slipped my punches like Mayweather in his prime. The few that actually came close to making contact were deflected by their hands and forearms.

I attacked two more times before I realized that my opponent was only playing defense. While he neutralized my punches with, I'm almost embarrassed to say, minimal effort, he returned none of his own. I was missing badly. He moved with almost a dancer's grace. I started to get the impression that I was being toyed with.

I squared up and made the *C'mon* motion with my fists. He

went into his own fight stance, and I assumed he was going to take this shit seriously.

I attacked again, and again he easily dodged my punches, only he did counter. He brought his fist up for an uppercut and stopped it an inch away from my chin. I slapped that hand away and tried a shot to the throat that was blocked. But I realized a split second too late that I left myself open for a punch to the solar plexus. I looked down and saw his fist already there, an inch away from my sternum. His other fist was at my jaw, for what would've been a knockout blow.

I'm a nigga who was far from slow, but this dude was unbelievably fast. And I could tell by his shoulders and arms, those blows would've made an impact.

I let my frustration get the best of me and just charged at him. I knew if I could get my hands on this slippery muthafucka, then I'd fuck him up.

Even though I was about five inches taller, and easily fifty pounds heavier than my opponent, I somehow got flipped. Before I knew it, I saw my feet go over my head and was looking up at the world from my back.

My right hand fell a few feet from the gun, but he put his foot down on my arm before I could lift it. His own pistol was aimed at my head, one he had plenty of opportunity to use. I couldn't discern the make or model from my angle.

Zakiya had shook off being thrown into the wall and joined the other. They loomed over me like skyscrapers. His muzzle was aimed down at me. Zakiya pushed his hand aside before he could pull the trigger. She told him, "He has information that we need."

They pulled me from the floor and sat me in the very same chair I'd just interrogated Zakiya in. Our roles suddenly reversed. She asked, "Where is the newscaster? Anything other than the truth gets a bullet put through your eye."

My right hand formed a flat O shape by pressing my thumb to my fingertips. I touched my cheek, right next to the corner of my mouth, and again, closer to my ear.

I liked having both of my eyes, so I hadn't lied. If neither of these muthafuckas bothered to learn ASL, that wasn't my problem. Zakiya said, "These are not your people. This is not your place. You are a dog on a leash for the black devils." I felt some type of way at being called a dog. I didn't give two fucks about anybody's agenda or their politics. I was just in one man's debt, and didn't plan to be for long.

"You have no real idea of what's going on here," Zakiya said. "There are forces at work in the world who are trying to usurp all the power for themselves. All political, educational systems, and media outlets are just shepherds used to keep the sheep in line."

Wow. She definitely was a true believer. It had been such a long time since I'd heard all this shit. It was like listening to my ol' dude right here in the flesh.

"I mean what I said. You were once Shango, and the elder chief's son. Give us the girl, and we can all go home together."

As fucked up as it might sound, in that moment my pride was so hurt that I would've sold out Amelia and her son just for another shot at dude. I was shaking with rage and humiliation. That I was fiending for Round Two could be seen in my eyes when I mugged him.

Zakiya offered me a pitiable headshake. "You are like the first iPhone. A marvel in 2007, innovative, genius, and we'd never seen anything like you. But we've had seventeen years to improve on your original design. With each generation getting better and better: more gigs, faster data speed, better cameras."

The bitch was basically saying I'm obsolete. And after the way dude just tossed me around, I couldn't argue with her.

Things really have changed in the church. I'm surprised she even knew what an iPhone was. During my time, we had no computers, no TV, extremely limited contact with the outside world. We raised our own cattle and grew our own vegetables. It was like we were Amish, if you traded the Bibles and barns for bullets and bombs.

Zakiya looked at the second shooter and spoke. I couldn't tell what was said from my angle looking at her. From his gestures, the second shooter seemed to be responding, but his face was covered by a mask.

But I didn't need to see faces or read lips to know what was being discussed. They were debating whether to kill me or not. Animated hand gestures suggested that the second shooter was very much in favor of.

The second one raised his pistol. I was then close enough to see it was a FNX .45. I resisted the urge to put my hands up to cover my face. Most people did this whenever a gun was pointed at their head, and I always found it to be cowardly and futile. Like your hand was really going to block a bullet.

I wouldn't have begged for my life even if I had a voice. I just hate that it had to end like this. I hadn't been at my best for a minute, but still, to lose like this was painful. I would earn no smile from the Thunder God.

Chapter Thirty-one

So on top of getting my ass kicked by a girl, and again by a dude who didn't take me as enough of a threat to fight for real, I'd fucked around and let myself get captured, too. My ego was taking quite a beating. I was one of the most feared muthafuckas in the city—my name carried weight and inspired respect. Even in the church, I was always top of my class. I was the elder chief's son, being groomed for leadership, so I was expected to excel at everything. And I pretty much did.

But that was a long time ago. Now I was the traitor who'd turned his back on his tribe. A cautionary tale about what happened to those who left Shango.

"For so long, we have been told that this war is black against white. But it is those with our own faces who are the true enemy.

"Bring us Amelia before the sacrifice. This is the only way you can save the boy. And yourself."

Without my phone, I couldn't ask this bitch what the fuck she was talking about, but my quizzical expression should've conveyed it. What sacrifice? She was sounding more and more crazy. But again, that's what life had been like in the church. An entire community swept up in one man's paranoia and delusion.

It was the reason I could never go back. And the very reason I couldn't believe my mother ever would.

I could tell by his gestures that her partner was speaking again. I began to suspect that the mask he wore was about keeping his words as shrouded as his face.

He brought the pistol back to my head, but Zakiya pushed his hand down again. She said something to him about me being useful. Her head was angled away from me so I couldn't make it all out.

Zakiya's argument centered around me being a pawn to bring them Amelia. That and whatever points they would earn with my parents by returning me to the fold, as if that was going to happen.

"When Mzee Chifu and Dada Mkubwe look at you, they will only see the man who killed their son."

He clearly disagreed, and from his body language, he did so vehemently.

"They will not understand because he is no longer Shango. There is no honor in this. You might've earned a smile from Him if you had defeated the one who was promised to be our next Chifu. But that Lutalo is not here. He has been too long away from his training and his studies. He is lazy and an undisciplined fighter, and despite his size, has no real skill. You have crossed spears with him, so you know he is not worthy. There is no warrior here. Just another lost nigga."

And I proved her right, because next I got on some real nigga shit. I was still seated, and her partner had inched toward Zakiya to rebut. He took his focus off of me. Another one who pay for getting too close.

I brought my foot up quickly, and he reacted too slow to block. It doesn't matter your level of training or how nice you were with your hands. Getting kicked in the nuts erased all advantages, and I caught his clean with the heel of my shoe.

He grabbed his crotch and folded around his pain. He slowly

sank to his knees, then toppled over on his side. He continued to curl himself on the floor until he was a fetal ball of agony.

Zakiya's mouth was still hanging open when I sprang to my feet. The east wall of the gymnasium had been built with large casement-style windows, only all the glass had been broken out long ago to be replaced by plywood. I went at the closest one in a full sprint and dove at it headfirst. I hoped I'd hit it hard enough to clear out the boards and not crack my skull open.

Chapter Thirty-two

I drove home, my pride more wounded than anything done to my body. The cut on my forehead leaked a thin stream of blood into my eye. I wiped that with the back of my hand as I yanked the wheel for each turn. I was a road rage incident waiting to happen.

I got through the window with nothing more than a small cut and a few splinters to show for it. I got up, scrambled around to the other side of the building, where I'd parked my truck.

While my record was flawless, I was under no delusions that I couldn't be beat. No matter how good you think you are, there's always somebody who's better. And I could've accepted that, had he just drug my ass all around the gym. But the fact that he didn't even bother, pulled his punches just to show me how easily I could've been hit. That was more humiliating than anything he could've done with his fists or feet.

In the Universal Orthodox Temple of Alkebulan, the children start their fight training as soon as they are able to walk—at first with boxing gloves, padded sticks, and rubber knives. Only up until ten are the kids separated into training groups based upon age. After that, it was purely your skill that determined your placement, and ultimately what would be your function in the church as well as where you ranked in its caste system. The weaker and less-skilled youths continued to receive low-level fight training, but were pushed by elders more towards farming or intellectual pursuits.

The gifted children were filtered into the more elite combat units, and of these, Shango warrior-class was the highest. But in these elite training groups, there was no distinction based on sex or age. So that meant an eleven-year-old girl might be sparring with a nineteen-year-old boy, who was also being taught to never hold back. And as long as the girl could handle herself, she remained Shango.

In the church, it was only forbidden to fight somebody who was beneath your status. It sullied you as a warrior even if this person was bigger and older than you. Back in my day, lower-tiered individuals often tried to make a name for themselves by calling out an elite. But the higher ranked could embarrass them by simply refusing the challenge. There was no greater shame for anyone in the UOTA than to be considered not a worthy opponent.

Here I was, once the most skilled fighter in the most elite group, trained in rifles and small arms, multiple hand-to-hand and close-combat fighting techniques, knives and other edged weapons, survival skills like bow hunting and tracking prey, wet and dry demolition. But Zakiya had argued for my life based on that there was no honor in taking it. And I had needed to save myself by taking what they teach soccer moms in some YMCA self-defense class: kick him in the nuts and run.

I had been out the church for seventeen years and was long removed from its indoctrination, or so I thought.

I came home and found my house permeated with a tense vibe that I wasn't used to, or was I feeling. My mood only added to it.

The moment I made it through my security barriers, I raided my stash of Percs. And not for the pain.

The question of what happened was already waiting on

Amelia's face. Through a series of texts, I told her, making sure to leave out the most embarrassing parts.

"How did she manage to get away from you?"

The face I made let her know that details would not be forthcoming.

I went downstairs, needed to think and to punch on shit. I'd dropped about $20,000 to turn my basement into my personal gym—saw it as an investment. In my line of work, staying in shape was mandatory.

I spent about twenty minutes taking my frustration out on the heavy bag, unloading hooks, elbows, and knees, pretending it was my opponent. I was stuck in my mind, replaying the fight over and over again, only this time countering effectively and making the necessary adjustments. I was so deep in that battle with my imaginary opponent that I didn't even realize that Antwon had crept down the stairs and had been watching me for I don't know how long.

I nearly forgot he was there and really didn't feel like engaging with him. I hoped he would pick up on my negative energy and find his way back upstairs. Couldn't get that lucky. He picked up two forty-pound dumbbells from the rack. Started trying to muscle up the weight with a strained face, rocking back and forth.

Kids usually didn't like me any more than I liked them, but Antwon was a rare exception. I just wasn't trying to fuck with him right then. I narrowed my focus to the heavy bag and what was directly in front of me. And if he tried for my attention, I could always play on my handicap.

But after a few minutes of this, I started to feel like a lame for ignoring little dude. Plus he didn't know what the fuck he was doing with those dumbbells, and that shit was starting to irk me. He was about to fuck around and throw his back out.

I went over to him, took away those forty-pounders, and replaced them with some twenty-fives. I got him to keep his back straight, used his wrist and forearm to guide him through the motion of a proper bicep curl.

He asked, "Could you teach me how to fight?"

I didn't have a problem showing the boy a few things just to get the bullies off his ass, but didn't plan on being in his life long enough to be a sensei.

First I showed him how to throw a punch. I stood him before me, made him square up. Using my hands as targets, I urged him to show me how he threw a punch before I corrected him. I explained that the power came from the legs and hips. I adjusted his feet and demonstrated how to twist his torso.

Antwon practiced on my palms; then I had him spend a few minutes working with the heavy bag. He cracked a smile. "Maybe I should ask ol' girl to teach me. In the kitchen, it looked like she was getting in yo' ass a little bit."

I made a face to let him know how close I was to getting into his. He couldn't know, but this was the wrong time to hit me with that one.

I was surprised, though, that after everything that happened with the car chase and the shootout, this little nigga still had jokes.

I showed him a wrist lock he could use that would make an opponent, regardless of size, beg for mercy. If he applied a little pressure, the pain would be intolerable. And as I was teaching him something so dangerous, I had the thought that maybe I should ask his mother's permission first.

He dismissed it. "Don't worry about Amelia. She's good. I told you, she already tried to sign me up for karate before." I had already forgotten about that, but still thought I should have a talk with her adult-to-adult. This shit would have him breaking bones and not just boards.

I noticed that it wasn't the first time he referred to her as *Amelia* and not as *Mom* or *Mother*. I used my phone to ask what's up with that. I'm from the old school where fifteen-year-old boys didn't call their mother by their government name. Even though Antwon was respectful enough to never do it to her face.

He gave me a view of his face so I could read his lips, but his eyes avoided mine. "For most of my life, it's been me and my dad. I knew Amelia from TV, was told she was my mother, but she didn't come around like that.

"Then about three years ago, she start popping up, wanting to spend time with me. My pops left it up to me, and I was curious about her, so I started hanging out with her, just for a few hours, every other weekend. We'd go to the museum, the science center, the opera. She was interested in my coding, and always wanted to know what I was reading or working on. Amelia even took me to this place where they gave me this test, I guess like to gage my IQ or something. That was when she sued for full custody."

Wrinkles creased my forehead. Something came to mind that I filed away for later.

Chapter Thirty-three

Antwon continued: "I was cool with every-other-weekend thing. My dad works in sanitation, but Amelia was able to hire a whole team of lawyers and psychologists to testify that I would be better off with her. Said some shit about my gifts needing to be nurtured. I testified that I wanted to stay with my father, but it was like the judge was on their side, wasn't trying to hear shit me or my dad's lawyer was saying. Now, I only get to see him for a few hours every other weekend."

That was pretty much the what I picked up from the exchange between Amelia and Terrence at his job. Antwon didn't know that I already blew down on his old dude when I thought these were just ordinary street punks who could be hired for a couple of dollars. Or even niggas like me who could be hired for a lot.

The problem was that these were not ordinary muthafuckas. This was the UOTA. These were not mercenaries. Antwon's father couldn't hire them, even if he owned every garbage truck in the city. Amelia was being targeted by a group of militarized, pan-African, Black nationalist radicals.

The very same group started by my father, and that I had been a member of. And nobody was going to convince me that was just coincidence.

He looked at me in earnest. "I don't want my mom to get hurt."

I nodded and tapped my chest. I made a silent promise to him that I was going to make sure that didn't happen.

Kierra was right on time, came down the stairs carrying two bottled waters so cold that they were slushed. Antwon looked at her like she was made out of chocolate cake when she offered him his bottle, even twisted the cap for him. Kierra did a little flirting with the youngster that I thought was harmless. I didn't catch everything she said, but if Antwon had been a white boy, he would've been blushing.

Not only was my girl five-foot-ten, with the long, lean frame of a runway model, she was one of those free spirits who couldn't stand to be in clothes—the type who came in from running errands and started snatching her shit off right at the door. She walked around the house, if not butt-ass naked, just about.

So the fact that she was standing in front of him in nothing but a throwback Rasheed Wallace jersey had fat boy looking like he was ready to explode. Those caramel legs ran forever before terminating in pretty painted toes peeking from pink fuzzy slippers. Her rock-hard nipples damn near dotted the I and punctuated the word: PISTONS.

She gave him a smile, then climbed the basement stairs with a lot of extra swing in her hips. I didn't know what Antwon was on when he took both my hands into his.

His expression was earnest. "I think if we both prayed hard enough, God might let us switch bodies just for one night." He stole one last peek at Kierra as she disappeared around the landing. "Or just seven minutes. That's all I need for real."

I snatched my hands back and slapped him upside the head. This little nigga was a fool.

I made Antwon strike the heavy bag until his chubby ass was glazed in sweat, then sent him upstairs for a shower. Even though

I hadn't welcomed the distraction, working with him did temporarily take my mind off Zakiya and the shit at the gym. I spent another half an hour shadowboxing and practicing my footwork before I finally followed him.

On my way upstairs, I stopped on the landing to double-check my side entrance. Both of the exterior doors had been replaced with heavy-duty commercial metal doors. They were one-and-one-half inches thick, cast from solid iron. Each one had cost me $14,000 without the installation, but the salesman had assured me that a bomb might blow the rest of the house to bits, but those doors would still be standing. So, in addition to the electric handle and two mortise cylinder locks that came standard, I had augmented this with four industrial-strength dead bolts, a floor bolt, and a locked bar.

Through the kitchen, I went into the living room and saw Amelia sitting in my one piece of furniture. I never entertained, and wasn't trying to turn my shit into a showplace. So I hadn't wasted any money on a sofa set, coffee and end tables, cheap paintings, or 80-inch televisions. My home wasn't designed for comfort or company.

The only thing to sit on in my living room was an old recliner I bought at a secondhand shop. Amelia was curled up on it with bare feet tucked under her lap. She looked up from her phone when she noticed me.

"How long are we going to be here?" she asked. "I need to go home to grab some things for me and Antwon."

I just breezed past her without acknowledging. We would eventually do that, as soon as I decided it was safe. Just like we would eventually have that conversation.

I stepped into my bedroom and right into Kierra's attitude. She sprang up from the bed the moment I came in. "Hell naw, what that bitch doin' here?" Knowing Kierra, she had purposely said this loud enough for Amelia to hear. "That's the bitch from TV who always—" So much for hoping that Kierra didn't recognize her.

I stopped her with waving hands before she could repeat what we both already knew. I used my phone to give her a summarized version of my job description. Until I found a safer place for Amelia and Antwon to be, they would be staying there. I broke that down for Kierra in a way that killed all debate. It was what it was. She could either deal with it, or not.

She flopped down hard on the bed, pushed out her pouty lips even more.

The bedroom right across the master was used for my home office. It was another Spartan space that didn't have much in the way of furniture. All I needed was a desk and a single chair. My simple desktop couldn't fuck with the computer Antwon had at home. This collected all the footage from the two dozen cameras I had mounted around the house.

I spent a few minutes checking the perimeter of my spot on the monitor.

About a year back, a parole violation had landed me with forty-five days in a detention center, and I came out to a gift from my baby momma: $800,000 in stolen cash. Like I said, thanks to Tuesday and the home ownership programs sponsored by her company, I purchased the house for pennies on the dollar. But me knowing that I would always make enemies in my line of work, a huge portion of that duffel bag my BM had dropped on me got spent on security. I basically turned my house into an urban fortress.

Aside from what I'd done to the doors, all the windows were made from a thick plastic that was shatterproof and fitted with wire-mesh security bars mounted from the inside.

I know I ruined the aesthetic the designers were going for when I spent nearly eighty grand to have actual chain-link fences built inside a personal residence. Two floor-to-ceiling fences along with a swinging gate at the front entrance. Two more gates on the landing at the side entrance that stood at the opening to the kitchen and at the top of the basement steps. So on the off chance somebody was able to breach those iron doors, they would only find themselves trapped in a fenced pen. These were fitted with cameras and secured with heavy chains and padlocks. I had another smaller gate separating the dining room from the hall that led to the rooms at the rear. I typically kept all these barriers unlocked during the day, when no threat was present. This was why Antwon had been able to come up and down the stairs freely.

But even more expensive than that was the other 120 grand I spent having all the exterior facing walls reinforced with thick bulletproof fiberglass. That same shit that separated you and clerk in every bank and liquor store in the hood, I had to find enough, cash out for, then have mounted on the inside of my exterior walls. Niggas in the city was getting access to Chinese and Israeli-made assault rifles that could cut through bricks like butter—the same type of shit that nearly killed little Nika at Mrs. P's house. That incident had made me vow to never let that happen to myself or anyone under my roof.

Back down in the basement, I checked my weapons cache. In a metal storage locker, I had twenty-three assault rifles with munitions for all, six rapid-fire tactical shotguns, and fourteen pistols. More guns were stashed throughout the house in case of emergency.

I had a backup generator connected to the circuit breaker just in case I somehow lost power. In my storage pantries were enough dry and can goods and bottled water to withstand an eighteen-month siege. And thanks to Kierra's Sam's Club membership, it was enough toilet paper in this bitch to wipe my ass until 2044.

My father was a paranoid conspiracy nut with a doomsday complex, and I had inherited the defective gene. I was ready for the complete collapse of the government and all social systems—civil unrest, riots, looting. I felt I was even ready for the alien invasion and the muthafuckin' zombie apocalypse.

But even with all the renovations and preparations I'd done, I didn't think for a minute that my house would keep Amelia safe from two Shango warriors. They had spent their entire lives being trained for shit like this. Zakiya and the other would eventually find out where I lived. They would eventually find a way to get inside.

Chapter Thirty-four

I took a shit and a shower. Needed to wash the smell of funk and the smell of defeat off of me. I let the jet spray right on the back on my neck while I rolled my sore shoulder. Being hip-tossed by Zakiya's partner had reignited my old injury. I dried myself, then popped two more Percocet from the bottle I kept in my medicine cabinet.

I looked at myself in the mirror and wasn't happy with my reflection. I was still a handsome nigga, still had a sick beard game, with low brush waves spinning hard enough to make a bitch seasick. I had managed to keep my 270 solid, although, thanks to fast food, I could no longer boast to having less than four percent body fat, like I could when I first came home from prison.

Yet, I was still disappointed in the man I saw looking back at me. What had made me so dangerous wasn't just the fighting skills I learned in the church, but my focus and discipline. Zakiya and this other fighter reminded me of what I once was, and what I had lost. I was smoking too much, drinking too much, and swallowing too many pills. Zakiya had said that I was no longer Shango. Said that I was just another nigga. That was more of a blow than she could've known.

I went to my bedroom, lotioned up, and threw on some black sweats and a matching hoodie. I wasn't no bum-ass nigga, had a few designer brands hanging in my closet. I just learned that you can't be fly all the time in this line of work. Having to get blood out of Gucci and Louis Vuitton every other day—them dry-cleaning bills be a muthafucka.

I came out the back, through my dining room to the kitchen, and walked straight into some *Real Housewives*-type of shit. Kierra and Amelia were in the middle of a full-blown argument. I could tell just by the energy and body language of the participants that it had been going on for at least ten minutes. I was just oblivious due to my permanent pair of noise-cancelling headphones.

I was trying to creep and dip out the side door when they noticed me. Amelia ran up on me, followed by Kierra, clearly wanting me to mediate. I knew this having two women in the house shit was going to be a headache.

They came to me, both talking at the same time, giving me two pairs of lips to focus on. I couldn't make out anything they were saying. I capped my hands to quiet them, made the time-out T with my hands. I pointed to Kierra, indicating that she would go first.

"Could you please tell this bougie-ass bitch that she don't run shit in this muthafucka!" This came from Kierra, with a rolling neck and a bunch of hand waving. "She ain't been here one day and already trying to talk to me like I'm the help or some shit. Silence, get this bitch before I prove her right. I show her I am one of those ignorant-ass eastside bitches she be talkin' bout on her show, when I'm dragging her all through this bitch, snatching tracks out her hair. 'Cause I don't give no fuck, and ain't nobody bout to—" I had to cut Kierra's ass off with an aggressive hand gesture.

I looked to Amelia with visible agitation. I made a twirling motion with my finger to indicate that I wanted the short version.

She seemed a bit more composed. "First off, I don't know who this person is to you, or why she needs to be here, but—" I frowned to let Amelia know that it wasn't none of her goddamn business. Kierra was right that only I run shit in this muthafucka. And I'll have in my shit whoever the fuck I want.

Amelia clearly read that in my expression and backtracked a bit. "Look, all I did was politely ask your friend if she wouldn't mind putting on some clothes. She walking around naked in front of my fifteen-year-old son. She has Antwon around here with his eyes big, and his dick harder enough to cut diamonds."

Kierra wasn't naked, but not far from it. I never did company, and she had gotten used to being in a T-shirt with nothing on underneath.

Antwon would never forgive me if I told her to cover all the way up. I texted Kierra to at least make sure she had on panties before she came out the room. Let's give the little nigga the NC-17 version before we took him to triple-X.

"You need to be thanking me. At least now you know there's something he love as much as food." Kierra dropped that bomb strutting out of the kitchen.

To me, the matter was settled. I turned and was ready to go when Amelia grabbed my arm. "How long do we have to stay here? We don't have clothes, I don't have my cards, and Antwon has school."

I didn't have time for no pampered princess shit. Through my phone, I told her I didn't want her there any more than she wanted to be, but I had no other options. She was stuck there until I figured this out. And I didn't know how long that was going to be, so she should get comfortable.

"It's not as if I'm complaining about the accommodations or anything. I just wanted a timeline on how long it's going to—" She stopped and shook her head. "You know what, fuck you! I've been bending over backwards trying to be nice to you, and I'm done."

Where was this coming from?

"You don't think I see the way you look at me," Amelia cried. "Silence, you don't speak, but you damn sure don't hide how you feel."

It wasn't the first time I'd heard that one.

"You think I'm a sellout because I dare to tell our people what they need to hear. To get off their asses and stop waiting for handouts, because those always come with strings that ensnare you in the long run. That reparations aren't gonna happen because the white man who walks around today feels about as disconnected from the ones who were responsible for slavery and Jim Crow, as today's gangbanger feels from the original Ghana tribe his ancestors were stolen from. I love my people enough to tell them the truth, that Black nationalism doesn't work and never will. That the only way to change the system is through the system. And yet, I'm labeled as a traitor.

"But you, who has made a living off hurting and killing people. And while you might have been trained with the intent of being a super soldier in the Great Race War, we both know the primary color of all the people you've murdered. Meanwhile, you are accepted, and me, maligned."

Amelia saw that I was about to get defensive.

"I only use this to illustrate my point. I'm not judging you. Which is funny considering, since we've met, you've done nothing but silently judge me."

I stood there for a moment, having to eat that because she was right. My perception of Amelia had been based on the two hours of content I'd watched on the internet and not the two days I'd been in her actual presence. During that time, I'd seen none of her television personality. She carried no soapbox and preached none of her conservative ideology, other than when she had defended herself at the clothing store.

I typed: *My bad.* I was a man who rarely apologized for shit. This was the most eloquent one I was capable of.

"So now all of a sudden you wanna kiss and make up." She said this with a hand on hip, flirtation in her eyes.

I was trying to keep things professional, but I had a thing for dark-skinned girls. And thanks to my bid, still felt I had twelve years' worth of fucking to catch up on.

I gave Amelia a look that warned her to be careful.

Chapter Thirty-five

It was ten o'clock, and I had to make a run. I hated to leave my guests at the fort unattended, but it couldn't be avoided. I told Antwon to make sure Amelia and Kierra didn't kill each other.

I had to pull up on somebody I hadn't seen in a year, and who probably never wanted to see me again. The never wanting to see me again part applied to damn near everybody I knew.

From my arsenal, I chose my Walther P99, a short but powerful .40-caliber pistol that could easily be concealed under a hoodie. I left the house on foot, hoping darkness aided in concealing me. For the first few blocks, I kept the pistol in my hand. I made sure to check my six every few feet to make sure I wasn't being followed.

The Ram was done, too damaged to be driven inconspicuously. My last mission had forced me to carjack somebody every time I needed a ride. After an old man made me shoot him for a raggedy-ass deuce and a quarter, I decided I didn't want to go through that again.

I hit the auction and bought a few vehicles that I put in Kierra's name. Low-key shit that wouldn't draw attention from the jack-boys, or the police if I needed to do dirt. This allowed me to have different shit to jump in and out of to keep people off my trail. Plus, they were cheap enough to where, if I managed to make one of them hot, I could just firebomb that bitch and not miss it, then let Kierra report it stolen. I had five of these disposable cars that I stashed all over the city.

The nearest was four blocks from my house. A twelve-year-old Chevy Malibu that I kept in the parking lot of a closed-down Burger King. Navy blue over gray, no rust, with minor dents. To make sure nobody fucked with it, I stuck a FOR SALE sign in the window, along with an asking price that was way too goddamn high. The few buyers stupid enough to still be interested would be calling a fake number anyway. I hid the key under the car, behind the front bumper. I jumped in, and she started on the first try.

I slid to the Grandmont area on Detroit's west side. This was a small tucked-away neighborhood for people living slightly above the mean, grossing about sixty to ninety grand more than their middle-class peers. Each block was shaded by mature trees and centered with an island adorned in decorative landscaping. Homes that would fetch a quarter mil in a fair market sat far back from the curb, Colonials and ranch-style in majority; long driveways held mid-range luxury SUVs while the backyards had privacy fences and aboveground swimming pools.

His house was five off the corner on a street called Ashton. A long, contemporary ranch with huge picture windows and double doors. A late-model Lincoln Navigator was parked backwards in front of an attached garage. My friend had did well for himself, because of, and in the wake of all the drama I stirred up last year. It was time to call in that return favor.

I parked on a side street, tucked the P99 into my waistband that I hoped not to need. I slipped out the Malibu.

I walked the block like somebody who was supposed to be there. This was the type of area with block clubs and neighbor watch groups, so a big black-ass nigga like me trying to look sneaky would be noticed.

I picked up a handful of small rocks from the sidewalk. I casually strolled past his house, knowing full well that the doorbell camera recorded me. I whipped a few pebbles at the back of his Navigator, saw the blinking of the head and taillights that told me I'd set the alarm off. I continued on past.

I was about two houses down when I saw the lights stop flashing. He must've assumed something incidental triggered it and hit the remote from the house.

After half a block, I turned around, did a walk-by going back in the other direction. I flicked a few more rocks at the back of his white Navigator, this time hard enough to crack the right taillight.

More flashing light, and most likely the sound of a horn, accompanied it. About thirty seconds later, the front door opened up, and I hurried to conceal myself behind a nearby tree.

He charged out the house in a T-shirt and pajama bottoms, pistol in his right hand. He walked a circle around his SUV, inspecting the shiny Lincoln. He stopped at the rear when he noticed the damaged taillight.

I got on his ass before he could raise that pistol. I slipped out my hiding place, took control of his gun arm. I twisted that in a way that made him break his hold of the weapon. Then I slammed his head against the back of the vehicle, pinned him there like I was the cop and he was the perp. I knew this had to be familiar to him.

Bates's face was pressed against the glass of tailgate. He was babbling some shit I couldn't make out.

I spun him to face me while cupping a hand over his mouth. He didn't have his glasses on, so I gave his nearsighted ass a few seconds to bring me into focus. I watched his eyes dart around from fear and confusion, then widen with recognition, after that they narrowed with anger.

He finally calmed enough for me to let him go.

"You? What the hell are you—" I cut him off by clamping my hand over his mouth again. I nodded towards the front doors, indicating that we should do this inside.

His rigorous headshake announced he was in strong opposition to that. He used his key remote to raise up the garage door. I followed him inside after I scooped up the Glock .19 he dropped.

His garage was a well-organized space that reflected a well-organized mind. All his gardening tools were neatly arranged and hanging on a peg board. The heavy-duty Craftsman tool chest was for someone who did automotive work as a serious hobby or a side hustle. A workbench with a circular saw suggested his interests also went towards woodwork.

But I was most impressed by the new Gold Wing motorcycle. This was the Rolls-Royce of luxury touring bikes, luggage compartment, backrest for the passenger, 1800 cc's. Black-cherry paint and black leather, custom chrome snowflake rims. I would've never guessed that his corny ass was a rider.

Bates lowered the door on us. "Goddammit, Silence. What the hell are you doing here? How do you even know where I live?"

I just looked at him like, *C'mon man.* He knew who I was and what I do. In fact, he knew enough about me to make it my business I damn sure knew enough about him. Just in case I ever needed to reach out and touch his ass.

He mouthed, "It's my service weapon, registered to my name. I can't show up to work without that." He apparently peeped how smooth I tried to tuck his Glock into my waistband and cover it with my shirt. I returned his pistol back to him.

Me and the lieutenant here had a very interesting history. At first, he had wanted nothing more than to see me back in a cage. He was working undercover as an IAB mole, investigating a crew of dirty cops. These same dirty cops were blackmailing me into finding 3.8 million in stolen drug money. When the shit hit the fan, we were forced to become unlikely allies. I had saved his life, and he had saved mine.

"Are you fucking insane? After all this time, you just pop up at my house at eleven o'clock at night. You and I should never ever be seen together. In fact, I should never be seeing you."

I wasn't feeling this nigga talking to me like I was some stalking ass side piece. I was his dirty little secret, but not in that way.

I was the one who took out all those dirty cops in the case that made his career. So while he had received a promotion—which obviously came with a significant pay bump—and was getting commendations and metals pinned to his chest, his little buddies inside the department could never know that somebody like me had did the heavy lifting. A street nigga with no badge, an ex-con, and a convicted murderer at that.

I felt like he owed me, and it was time to call in that favor. Without his glasses, Bates had needed to squint long and hard to read what I typed on my phone.

"You need information. Do I look like Google to you?"

I explained that he looked like somebody whose entire life I could blow up, somebody who was in my pocket whether they knew it or not.

Bates tried to put on his most fearsome face. It was a weak attempt.

"Yeah, if the truth ever comes out, I would lose my badge. Maybe even be brought up on a few obstruction charges.

"But you, on the other hand, will be on death row waiting to get a needle in your arm. Dirty or not, you snapped the neck of a lieutenant on the DPD, who just happened to be an unarmed female." I just shrugged. It wasn't the first time.

I politely reminded him that it was he and that same partner who started this blackmail shit, but he was free to call my bluff if he wanted to. I had already been to prison, and wasn't going back under any circumstances. I knew how to go underground, been taught how to live off the grid, could go in the woods, hunt, fish, and build my own shelter if I needed to—I was practically a ghost right now. But if I ever got boxed in, I was prepared to bang it out and take as many of them with me as I could.

I assured Bates that he wasn't the same type of individual. He had a comfortable life, nice home, vehicle, and a career on the upswing. While the consequence might be more serious for me, he was the one who had more to lose.

We became locked in a staring match, playing a game of Chicken with our freedom. Seeing who would swerve first as our futures sped towards each other for a head-on collision.

It didn't take long for him to surrender. "Just this once, and we are done. You never come here again, and I never see you again for any reason."

I nodded that the terms were acceptable.

I had needed both my hands for this next part. Typing on my phone in long run-on sentences and misspelled words.

Gamble had been his ex-partner, and before I snapped her neck in the beverage aisle at a gas station, the slimy bitch had done some digging into my past. I asked Bates if she ever managed to discuss any of that with him. Did he know anything about the UOTA?

Bates rubbed the back of his neck. "She only said that your father raised you in some type of cult that turned kids into killers. That you never really had a chance. It actually made me feel sorry for you."

Not the whole story, but not entirely untrue, either.

The old man might be paranoid, but not all his fears were unjustified. I know there was some branch on law enforcement that was keeping tabs on the church. I had no doubt that it was way above Bates's pay grade, but I needed him to find out whatever he could. Who was keeping track of their movements and what were they suspected of being involved in.

Bates looked at me like I just asked for a kidney and a lung. "From my understanding, this compound is in Washington state. If there is somebody keeping them under surveillance, which I'm sure there is, it'll be one of the alphabet boys: CIA, FBI, DEA. I'm just a city cop. What makes you think that I can get anywhere near this?"

I typed: *I never expected it to be easy.*

Just then a light came on in the kitchen, and someone appeared in the doorway that connected the garage to the house.

Black woman, late thirties, and top-tier fine. She had an athletic build with no enhancements that was only dressed by a T-shirt. Her hand tugged down the hem in the front to cover up panties or exposed pussy.

I quickly turned my head and threw up my hood before she got a good look at my face, but saw enough of hers to be impressed. Bates had clearly undergone a rebranding of himself. The four-eyed nerd I used to refer to as "fake-ass Norbit" was out here riding motorcycles and fucking bad bitches, upper body even looked like he'd done a pushup or two.

He said to her, "Monica, go back in the house. I'm in a meeting with a CI that I'm running."

Without comment, she quickly ducked back into the house and killed the kitchen light. No sooner than she was gone, I snatched Bates by the collar, damn near took him off his feet.

I'd watched enough cops shows to know that CI stood for confidential informant. I wasn't with being called a snitch, not even as a cover story. I normally don't fuck with the police at all, and our purposes had only aligned because we had mutual enemies. But make no mistake: my help only came in the form of dropping bodies. I never passed along information, and Bates knew better than to ask.

He whined, "I had to tell her something."

That was the problem. He could've told her anything. That I was a homeless relative coming to bum a few dollars. That I was a crackhead he caught trying to steal his lawnmower. Either of these would have been preferable. Even inferring to someone that I might be a rat was a serious violation of my personal ethics.

I'm one of those people who believe that disrespect should come at a cost. Now in the past, I've charged broken bones, even as much as a life.

Even though he was a cop, me and Bates had been through

some shit together that bonded us, so I let him get this one for a discount.

When I told Bates what the cost would be for his transgression, he looked at me like I was joking.

The look I returned told him I was as serious as prostate cancer. And that if he didn't pay, the outcome would be just as deadly.

Chapter Thirty-six

I left Bates with the understanding that I expected delivery soon. Of the information I requested and on the payment for calling me a snitch.

I left my move-shooter parked at the corner, but as I headed back towards the Malibu, I was struck by a feeling that raised the hair on my forearms.

Sometimes I had these flashes of intense paranoia, something I'm sure I got from the old dude. I suddenly and inexplicably became aware that I was being watched. And that I was walking into some sort of danger.

Because I can't hear the approaching footsteps of an enemy creeping me from the rear, I've learned to survive by being keenly observant. Like how the wind had shifted from the northwest to the east and carried the scent of burnt wood from a house fire about a mile away, and the fainter smell of a rainstorm that would be on us in another forty minutes. The subtle shift of fabric in the corner of the living room's picture window that told me either Bates or the Monica girl was watching me from behind the curtains, to make sure I walked away from the house.

But my primary focus was a car on the next block that wasn't there before I went into Bates's garage. I'd made a mental note of every vehicle parked up and down this street on my way in. The Toyota was dark-colored and mid-sized, something that didn't stand out—the same reason I'd chosen the Malibu. They had parked in the middle of the second block, knowing the corner would be too obvious, and had purposely avoided the shine of the streetlight. The driver had also chosen a spot that gave them a direct sight line of my car.

In the distance, I was just able to make out the silhouettes of two figures in the car. I assumed Zakiya and the other was watching from behind the darkened glass.

They were halfway up the next block while I was only a few houses away from my move-shooter. My first thought was to run to the Malibu, figuring I'd reach it before they got to me.

While all of my stash cars were just cheap auction-bought vehicles, I had invested a few extra dollars under the hood. They might look like nothing but ran like champs. I couldn't have some shit stalling out on me in the middle of a police chase.

I took off at a sprint, expecting the doors to spring open on the Toyota, or for it to race down the block. But the driver made no move to intercept me. The closer I got to my vehicle, the more I started to think that I'd let my paranoia get the best of me again. The two in the car might just be a pair of drinking buddies sharing a pint out of the view of their nagging wives, or lovers sharing a last moment before he drops her off.

I was so focused on the dark Toyota down the street that I noticed too late the white sedan coming from my rear. It was speeding along the same side street where I had parked, and on me around the same time I pulled the P99 off my waist.

I raced for the Malibu, but the white Lexus swerved around me to block. I turned and raised my .40-caliber at the driver, only to see that Zakiya already had her own pistol aimed at me through the passenger window.

She switched on the interior dome light so I could see her face, read her lips. "Get in. Now."

I wasn't with letting myself be taken captive again. Even though she had the drop on me, I was ready to take my chances. But I also saw a killer's calm in Zakiya. I knew she was capable and ready to pull the trigger on that H&K PV40.

Time can do weird things in moments like this. Our standoff might've only been ten seconds but felt so much longer.

Zakiya finally lowered her gun. I kept mine trained on her, but backed away toward my Malibu.

"If you get in that car, you're dead." I froze, my hand inches away from the door handle. This came off as a warning and not a threat.

She smacked the steering wheel. "Get in the fucking car!"

When I hesitated, Zakiya launched herself out the passenger door and tried to take me down. I slung her to the ground, fucked around and slipped in the wet grass, and landed on top of her.

My car exploded.

Chapter Thirty-seven

"A device was connected to your vehicle while you were inside."

Zakiya said this to me while I was lying in the grass, shattered glass and Chevy shrapnel raining down on us. It really didn't take a GED to figure that out.

We scrambled to our feet as I examined the wreckage. It was a small explosion, about the equivalent of seven sticks of dynamite or one hand grenade. The blast had blown out all the windows and totally destroyed the interior. The driver's door hung off its hinge.

I had some experience with explosives, so I knew it was expertly done. The trigger was a remote detonator. The bomb was most likely planted under the seat, designed to kill only the occupant of the car, while doing little collateral damage to anything nearby.

This is why the white Lexus only suffered shattered passenger-side windows, even though it was parked less than five feet away. It crumbled to the street in tiny glass pellets when I slammed the passenger door.

Zakiya slid under the steering wheel and sped off like somebody being pursued, even though I saw no one when I turned back in my seat. At the service drive for the Southfield Freeway, she took a right so hard that it tossed me in my seat. She swerved around a slow-moving conversion van, then at the next cross street, sped through the red light. I knew that as a Shango warrior, she'd had the same training in evasive and defensive driving that was mandatory. Zakiya wasn't out of control but still had me reaching for the seat belt. She took the entry ramp for the South-field Freeway.

I studied the interior of the Lexus. It was clean, but under the scent of new leather, I detected old woman smells. I didn't need to ask how she'd gotten it—the same way they'd gotten the van and the Taurus, the same way I'd acquired many vehicles in the past. It was just the way we were taught to do things inside the church. We were survivalists trained to live off the land. Zakiya didn't see these people she'd robbed at gunpoint as innocent citizens; they were just a resource, and she was just foraging.

I pulled my phone, let her know that all this trying to save me shit was for nothing. I wasn't going back to the church, so she could kiss my ass.

She turned to me. "Or you could just say thank you."

It was only then that I noticed the bruises. There was swelling above her right eye that was slightly discolored. Her bottom lip was split and bleeding. More blood smeared her cheek, wiped away from where it leaked from her right nostril.

I knew there was only one person who could do that to Zakiya. I wasn't even sure if I could.

She saw me studying her face. "Don't look at me like that. I did way better than you." I imagined she must've, because he had at least considered her enough of a threat to fight back. But the question I typed onto my screen was why were they fighting in the first place.

"Muuaji has gone rogue. I only just learned that he took this mission for his own reasons. Some personal vendetta that he has against you."

Against me? The only person in the church I had beef with was my old dude, which was why I left. Plus I'd been gone seventeen years, so I didn't know who this Muuaji nigga was or why he had a problem with me.

My Swahili was a little rusty, but I did know that *muuaji* meant *killer*. And if the elders had seen fit to give him that name, then he had most certainly earned it.

Zakiya corrected me. "His full name is Muuaji Mkuu."

This just got better. They actually named his ass Supreme Killer.

"You did something to him back when you were in the temple, and being kicked in the ancestral stones made him even less of a fan. I tried to remind him that Amelia and her son are the mission, but he won't hear reason."

Zakiya glared at me. "I'd nearly had him convinced to spare you. Once he'd fought you and saw that you were no longer Shango, he could've let it go.

"But then that cheap shot. You dishonored him as a warrior and yourself as a man." She noticed the frown I was wearing, then shrugged. "His words, not mine."

The night was cool, and Zakiya had the Lexus up to eighty. That wind coming through the broken passenger window assaulted the hell out of me, and started to carry tiny specks from the rain I smelled earlier. I pulled up my hood, tightened it with the drawstrings.

Zakiya said, "You are now Muuaji's target, and I'm about the only person who can protect you. But my price is not cheap."

I looked at her like she was crazy. Since when did a nigga like me need protecting. I'm the one people ran to for protection. Or in most cases, needed protection from.

"In the last ten years, Muuaji has become one of the two top warriors in the tribe. He is the best marksman, the best at demolition, has the best survival skills, and is unmatched when it comes to hand-to-hand combat.

"But lucky for you, I am the other top warrior in Shango. But as a mercenary man who sells his own talents, you know these things come at a price."

I decided to entertain the bullshit. I asked her to tell me the cost of her services. I usually charged between ten and fifteen thousand a week. I was curious as to the dollar amount Zakiya placed on hers.

She explained: "You have been among these people in this corrupt society for so long that you think everyone is motivated by power and greed. Dhwty and Shango provides me with everything I need. Bullets and bombs are not expensive. Neither are books.

"I have two conditions that will not cost in money, but are still not cheap. First, you will take me to Amelia and the boy. You will turn them over to me and let me complete my mission.

"Next, once I have dealt with Muuaji for you, you will come with me back to Alkebulan. And you will do this willingly."

Chapter Thirty-eight

This girl was clearly smoking the best dope if she thought I would turn over Amelia to her, then go back to the UOTA. And the idea that I needed her to protect me from Muuaji was insulting on more levels than I could count.

I was in the middle of typing Zakiya a descriptive message telling her exactly how much of my ass she could kiss when she suddenly spun the Lexus into a 180-degree turn right in the center of freeway traffic. The abrupt motion caused me to fumble my phone and lose it out the broken passenger window.

At first, I thought Zakiya had lost control, because we were doing ninety and a slight mist had started from the approaching storm. But then from the way she swerved, I could tell that one of our tires had blown. The rear right rim chewed up the rubber and spat it out in chunks. We skidded over the shoulder, sparks flying, bounced off the concrete divider.

We slid to a stop, blocking the passing lane. Cars swerved to avoid running into us. A late-model Nissan narrowly missed our stalled Lexus, but the driver over-corrected the wheel, spun directly into the path of a school bus, and got T-boned.

Traffic around us started to slow to a halt. The two accidents created congestion as the freeway was suddenly reduced to one open lane.

Zakiya snatched the Hecklar from her waist and rolled out the driver's door firing. I copied her action even before I noticed the black silhouette in the burgundy Ford Raptor that was right behind us.

Muuaji ducked low in the cab as bullets shattered the glass and pinged the cab's metal. He threw the pickup in reverse and backed into another driver as me and Zakiya sprinted across two lanes of freeway traffic. I saw enough people in their cars holding up phones to know that we'd make the eleven o'clock news.

Muuaji returned fire through his passenger window from a weapon I couldn't quite see, but lucky for us, a car-hauler in the next lane blocked his sight line. He destroyed the bottom row of new Hyundai crossovers with something that sprayed fully automatic.

On the other side, me and Zakiya scrambled up the grassy embankment to the service drive. She leaped the four-foot fence like a gazelle. I cleared it with less grace.

Top side, I was thinking about how far we were from one of my stash cars, and how we could get to it. I looked up and saw Zakiya already solving that problem for us.

She was down at the corner, snatching open the driver's door of a rusted old Cadillac stopped at the red light. Young dog, about twenty-three, jumped out ready to defend his Fleetwood. A natural reaction but still a mistake. He must've saw the skinny girl with the Bantu knots and thought she was just another hoodrat Keisha, trying to play carjacker. He put a hand on Zakiya and got the surprise of his life.

She twisted his wrist, and I could tell by the expression of pain that blossomed on his face, she had just broken it. He took a shot to the throat from her open palm, and this was followed by three quick punches to his kidneys and solar plexus—one of my own favorite combinations. While he was coughing, gagging, unable to breathe or swallow, Zakiya took his head and bounced it off the top of the open car door. He went down, writhing in the street.

In watching her, it did highlight to me how far my skills had deteriorated. Zakiya fought like there was music playing in her head—her movements had the grace and fluidity of beautiful choreography. A violent ballet. Call me weird, but the shit almost made my dick hard.

But what immediately killed the vibe was what I peeped through the Cadillac's rear window. The boy was only about five years old. He was in the back seat, wide-eyed, staring horrified as Zakiya beat his father.

She snatched open his door, and I hurried to jump in the way. I pulled little man out the car while he twisted and whined. I sat him down on the sidewalk.

Seeing his tears hurt my heart. The rain had picked up a bit, so I reached back into the car for a tiny Lions skullcap and placed it on his head. While Zakiya jumped in the driver's seat, I went into my pockets. I forced a wad of folded bills into the boy's tiny hand, as if 900 dollars was adequate compensation for the way we'd just traumatized him.

All I had else to offer was a look of apology as I jumped into the passenger side of his father's Caddy. We peeled off, left the boy standing on the curb and his father lying in the street.

After we bent a few corners, Zakiya turned to me. "You really thought I was going to hurt that child."

Shango warriors were trained to never show mercy or sentimentality when it came to outsiders. Even though we were supposed to be soldiers for a Black nationalistic cause, it had been drilled into us that we should never hesitate to use lethal force on anybody not in Alkebulan. It didn't matter if they looked like us, didn't matter if we were ultimately fighting for their freedom. They were like the people still plugged into the Matrix—potentially inadvertent agents of the system.

I didn't know if she would've hurt the boy, just knew that I couldn't put it past her. Shango warriors were also drilled that the mission came first. The first person I'd killed had actually been a boy a few years younger than me, one that compromised a mission. This was back when I was a true believer, thoroughly brainwashed.

If the boy had tried to fight back or just not responded to her quick enough, I couldn't say for sure that Zakiya wouldn't have killed him. I didn't have my phone to communicate all of this to her and didn't need to. It was shit she already knew anyway.

Zakiya turned left on Schoolcraft, seemed to just be taking corners randomly. "Muuaji can track a falcon on a cloudy day. He's going to keep finding you. Have you given my offer any more consideration?

"Or if you want, I could just pull over right now. I'll let you out, and you can take your chances on your own."

I didn't like the energy she said that with, and I damn sure didn't like the idea that I needed somebody to protect me. I'd always been able to handle my own business. She might think I'm old and obsolete, but I'm still that muthafuckin' nigga.

I was ready to give Zakiya my one-finger response, but then I remembered some of the lessons I'd learned from the books I'd read while in prison. Because they were on the banned list, I had to stumble across photocopied pages of *The Prince* by Niccolo Machiavelli and Robert Greene's *The 48 Laws of Power*. I decided to employ some of the game I absorbed from these masters.

Zakiya had information that I needed, as well as a skillset that could be useful. Her weakness was that she had been in the church living a sheltered existence. She exuded that same bright-eyed gullibility I had when I first came to the hood. Before I learned that lies, betrayal, and unkept promises were not the exception, but the rule. Sun Tzu had said that all war was based on deception.

So I agreed to her terms with a slow shake of the head, knowing full well that I wasn't turning over Amelia, and damn sure wasn't going back to the church. First, we had to negotiate the terms of our agreement.

Zakiya wanted me to turn over Amelia right away. That wasn't going to happen. I rummaged through my pockets for my second phone, the one that only buzzed on occasion and always had to be answered. I told her that she could only have Amelia after Muuaji was dead. I also included two provisions: 1) That no harm could come to Antwon. 2) That I only needed her help getting Muuaji to the proper place at the right time, but when the moment came, I had to fight and kill him myself.

Zakiya glared skeptically at the unsent message on my screen. Then she turned back to me. "This is unacceptable. Because when Muuaji kills you—and I promise you he will if you try to fight him alone—I will not be able to complete my mission."

I thought about that for a minute, then motioned for the phone back. I typed out a promise that even before the fight began, I would text her Amelia's location so that she could still have her target whether I was alive or dead.

I saw wrinkles crease her forehead as her eyes bounced from me to the post-midnight traffic on West Warren Avenue. She didn't agree as much as she surrendered. Her acquiescence came in the form of a frustrated sigh.

After a few moments of quiet driving, she turned back to me. "I only agree to this because Dada Mkubwe is a mother to me, which makes you my brother by default. I jeopardize my mission and my personal honor, not for you, but to see the shine in mother's eyes when her son is returned."

Zakiya mouthed this next part slowly to make sure I understood. "But if at any point, I sense treachery in you, Dada Mkubwe and Mzee Chifu be damned. I will bring your severed head back to your parents minus your lying tongue."

The lies didn't come from my tongue, but the statement to me and the tribe would be unmistakably clear.

And even though I was on bullshit, I could tell by the look in Zakiya's eyes that she was deadly serious.

Chapter Thirty-nine

For a while, I just had Zakiya driving randomly just to make sure Muuaji wasn't on our trail. Even though we had switched up cars, I was still being cautious. My advantage was that neither one of them knew the city that well, other than probably studying a few maps before the mission. I used finger pointing to guide her along an unnecessarily circuitous route through downtown Detroit and the riverfront. While she drove, I kept my head on a swivel, staring paranoid at any pair of headlights that stayed behind us too long.

Once I was sure we weren't being followed, I directed her to an area right off West Jefferson down by the waterfront. Because he had been sentenced to twenty-eight years in federal prison for corruption, it was easy to discount what Kwame Kilpatrick had done as mayor of Detroit. All the city parks that had sat neglected for decades, overgrown with weeds and used for the dumping of bulk trash, had been cleaned up and renovated. Pretty much had been upgraded with pavilions and picnic tables, swing sets and jungle gyms for the kids; some even had outdoor workout equipment. What had gotten Kwame in trouble was that he had given all those building contracts to his friends, and had received a hefty kickback.

We pulled into Hart Plaza park. We were less than a mile from the Ambassador Bridge, close enough for me to see the head and taillights of all the semitrucks crossing the river over to Windsor. Without me having to tell her, Zakiya backed into a spot that well-away from a streetlamp but still gave us a view of anybody trying to enter and exit. She killed the motor and lights to drop us into a darkness nearly pitch. At the same time, we pulled our pistols from our waists and placed them on our laps.

I pulled my phone, wanting to know why was the UOTA interested in a local talk-show host. It had to be more to it than just her conservative views and hate speech. If that were the case, every television anchor at Fox News would be on their hitlist.

"This doesn't have anything to do with politics—this is about good and evil. Witches and warlocks. Oaths taken in dark hoods and human sacrifices." Zakiya dropped that casually like it explained everything, like it made all the sense in the world and didn't sound bat-shit crazy.

It just reminded me of all the bullshit we were spoon-fed back in the church. Plenty of lethal skills were taught, but what wasn't taught was independent thinking. My mother had called it a cult back before she left, back before I even knew what the word meant. My father was the type of man who believed in the Illuminati, Bigfoot, and alien coverups. The ideology came from top down, just like the orders. Neither were to be questioned.

Zakiya had been tasked to do this job from the tribal elders. That whole thing about witches and warlocks was probably all they had told her and was the sum total of what she knew.

Zakiya said, "Dada Mkubwe said that she had suffered a crisis of faith. She was unable to see Chifu's vision and the ultimate purpose of Alkebulan. She had needed that sabbatical, to go out into the world to have her eyes opened. What she saw brought her back to us even more focused and steadfast in her purpose.

"I understand that you left to find your mother. But Lutalo, why did you never come back?"

That question sent deep into my memories, to a pivotal event in my life. One that ultimately helped to shape me into the person I was. One that showed up occasionally to haunt me on nights when I was alone and sober.

I was the son of Mzee Chifu, destined to be the next elder chief. I wasn't just expected to excel at everything, but to overachieve. Nobody had come into the game with more pressure since LeBron James, and just like Bron-Bron, I lived up to the hype. I had been my father's pride and joy.

Until I was seven years old, and I lost my hearing to a rare but treatable disease. After that, the old man looked at me like I was defective, something that pointed back to his own inadequacy. Among the leaders, expectations for me were lowered to someone who'd do tasks like feeding the livestock and shoveling shit.

What they didn't expect was that my disability would fuel me. I trained harder than anybody else, studied longer, sparred with the toughest instructors, and got up every time I was knocked down. Eventually I became Shango, and then rose to the top of that class.

And the old man still looked at me like I was a reject.

By the time I was seventeen, I was so thirsty for his approval that I would've done anything. And I did.

So many hours of wilderness training was mandatory for every child in the UOTA, regardless of tribal class. The elders would wake up a group of us in the middle of the night, strip us naked, and put sacks over our heads. A van would take us deep into the woods of Washington state or up into the Cascade Mountains, where we were kicked out. A group of teenagers and preteens with no supplies of any kind left to fend for themselves for up to six weeks. No clothes, no tools, no food, no adult to whine to for help. It was a grueling experience, and this, more so than the fight training, was what psychologically broke many trainees who thought they were ready to level up to Shango warrior status.

And it started to break a boy in my group who was two years younger than me. I'll never forget his face as his soulless upturned eyes gazed up at me.

My mother had left the church a little after that, and it seemed to be the perfect time for me to dip, as well. I came to Detroit, the city of my birth, to find her, but instead I found a surrogate family. A new tribe.

I never went back because my mother didn't take me with her, and my father never came after me. So in the end, neither one of them ever gave a fuck about me. Which is why I don't give a fuck if I ever see them again.

Even with my phone, I would've lacked the patience and the inclination to explain all of this to Zakiya. To answer her question of why I never returned, I simply scribbled on a napkin in my sloppy block print: *Family is who you chose.*

Zakiya gave me the same look I hit her with earlier. Like I had just said something that was bat-shit crazy.

But when I thought about Mrs. P, Quianna, Trayvion, and even Doc's slimeball ass, it made all the sense in the world to me.

Chapter Forty

Each of us retreated into our own thoughts for a while. I entertained memories of Mrs. P, the woman who took me into her home, taught me American Sign Language, and had basically civilized this savage—as much she could. I had no guess as to what Zakiya thought about, only that it had her absently staring through the windshield at the black geometry created by the pavilion and children's play maze.

Movement in my peripheral drew my attention to the street and the car that was cruising along the access road. My mind immediately went to Muuaji, then thought we might have been better off if it were him when I saw the white sedan, blue stickers and decals, beacons.

Before I could alert Zakiya, she already had the squad car under the gaze of her narrowed brown eyes. She palmed her pistol, and I did the same, hoping like hell they just continued on pass.

I cursed myself for not having Zakiya take me to one of my stash cars. Figured we had at least until tomorrow to ditch the Caddy. While it had most likely been reported stolen, I honestly didn't think the police would prioritize an old-ass rusted '81

Fleetwood Brougham with a mismatched front end. It was technically a carjacking, but the vehicle wasn't taken at gunpoint. I also kind of imagined dude would be too embarrassed to admit that he'd gotten his ass kicked by a girl—the same girl had kicked my ass, and I was still sick about it.

The accident and the shootout on I-96 had definitely come over the police scanner. Had probably made the news right along with our faces, recorded via cellphone. Even with my hood on, I would be easy to recognize. So would the girl in the all-black catsuit, dressed like a fucking ninja.

I saw the silhouettes of two officers inside as the squad car slowed to a stop right at the entrance. It was clear that they were studying us. The park closed at nine p.m., and posted signs warned that parking didn't resume until seven in the morning. They sat there for a while as if debating whether if they should investigate our illegally parked car or make that donut run.

I scanned around, seeing that the logistics didn't play in our favor. The parking lot only had one way in and one way out. To our back was the grass leading down to the riverfront. If they blocked us in, we were gonna have to bang it out with the cops. Or else try to swim for Canada.

Zakiya and I sat next to each other, both with hands on our Glocks. I was trying so hard to will that police car into driving past us that I could've fucked around and got a nosebleed. I could feel the energy coming off Zakiya and knew she was doing the same thing. Shit seemed to be breaking bad against me all day. I sent a mental prayer up to the ancestors asking just for this one-time lookout.

That long-distance call didn't go unanswered, or either they were just like, "Fuck you youngster, figure it out."

On came the red and blue flashing beacons. The squad car pulled into the lot, directly towards us.

Chapter Forty-one

As soon as that police car started to pull into the parking lot, I began to weigh options. I could just roll out the door with my Ruger busting. Not even give them a chance. I could air them out, hopefully, before they got off that call for backup. The park was semi-secluded with practically no onlookers this time of night. So nobody to watch as Zakiya helped me push their car to the river's edge. Throw it in Neutral and send those pigs to a watery grave.

Jumping out and running on foot was another option, but not much of one. On this part of the riverfront, there were no places to go and few to hide. This was not a residential area, mostly in-dustrial, factories that were typically closed during the night. Even Usain Bolt would find himself surrounded in twenty min-utes, handcuffed face down on the ground while them boys got in some baton practice.

The patrol car approached the Cadillac slowly, as if somehow sensing the danger inside. I was just letting them come closer, ready to exercise Option A.

I hardly noticed Zakiya next to me hurrying to untwist her knots. Once her hair was down, she slid over in the passenger seat and straddled me face-to-face. She snatched down my hood and just like that, stuck her tongue in my mouth. Didn't see it coming, and damn sure could've stopped it, but fuck it, why would I? Zakiya kissed me slow and deep, used her fingers to play in my beard.

I quickly put together the type of play she was running. I'm not the sharpest knife, but Deaf doesn't mean Dumb.

So I got into the role, tongue-wrestled with her, and grabbed a fistful of natural hair. Started caressing her body, rubbed her thighs. Grabbed an ass that was firm but soft, no BBL, a product of African genetics and exercise. When I did that, Zakiya bit down on my lip to tell me I was taking this too far.

The driver slotted his car on the left of ours, window-to-window, only facing the opposite direction. They shined the spotlight in on our make-out session; Zakiya and I both jumped like we were startled and only then just noticed them. We did the whole thing of trying to look embarrassed. But what the officers couldn't see, was that we both had our hands on them burners, aimed sideways, ready to blow straight through the driver's-side door if this shit go left.

The uniformed who was driving looked Hispanic and way too young. I'm hoping for his own sake that he doesn't do anything other than tell us to leave. Because if he get out the car for any reason, I was letting 'em have it. We not doing pat-downs, vehicle searches, and ain't got a scrap of ID between us. I didn't see much of his partner other than she was a white female, but if either one of them cracked their door, it was gonna end bad for both.

The cop pointed towards the sign that stated that the park was closed after nine. Zakiya climbed off me as we made apologetic hand gestures. She slid under the wheel, and the young officer backed away without saying another a word. To be on the safe side, Zakiya pulled off right behind them.

Then she punched me in the arm hard as fuck, and I assumed it was for the groping. *Aye, I was just trying to make the shit look real*—I scribbled that on a napkin and tried to hand it to her. Zakiya balled the paper up without reading it and threw it at my face.

Her warm body had felt good on top of me. I wondered what the fuck was going on in the church these days, because I had left a virgin; Zakiya had kissed me like she knew what she was doing. She was fine with her hair up in the Bantu knots, but letting her locks fall down past her shoulders feminized her appearance. And it was refreshing to see a Black woman with an all-natural vibe: no makeup, weave, or fake lashes. I stared at her hungrily, my beast wide awake. I wanted to finish acting out that scene.

Zakiya turned the corner, took us back towards Michigan Avenue, then looked at me like *what now*. I could probably get us access to a crash spot, but that wouldn't be until the morning. Zakiya nor me carried ID, and my guilty conscience caused me to give little man all the cash I had on me. So a motel room was out of the question.

Of course I had money at the house but didn't quite trust Zakiya enough to take her back there. I still wasn't totally convinced that she wasn't actually working with Muuaji, trying to rock me to sleep.

Luckily, I always had a place I could go to pick up some quick cash. I drove over to the spot on Cascade that I had a minority stake in. Dirty Red still owed me the second half of my payment from the bricks I sold him. I honestly didn't expect him to have all of the money so soon, but I needed whatever he could give me.

When I pulled in front of the big-gated Venetian, Zakiya scanned around cautiously at all of the activity. An endless procession of cars cruised this particular block as if it were designated as a parade route. Dusty muthafuckas who habitually scratched themselves shuffled on the sidewalks looking like zombified extras from a horror movie. The influx of traffic was expertly handled by three young dudes dressed in red; they were positioned one on each corner and one in the field directly across the street from the house, and their quick hand-to-hand interactions with the people never lasted more than a few seconds.

I glanced over at Zakiya, wondering if she actually understood what she was seeing. It was a total culture shock for me when I left the church and came to the hood. We had been told our entire life we were descendant from kings and queens, and while we had been warned about the fallen state of our people, nothing could prepare us for experiencing it firsthand. Zakiya scanned the block with some combination of sadness and disgust in her eyes, enough to tell me that she did know what a trap house was, even if she didn't know it by that term.

Seeing her face stabbed me with a slight pain of embarrassment. I had been raised and trained my entire life to fight for my people, but in the end, I turned into somebody who killed them and contributed to selling them drugs. This never really bothered me before. Being around someone from the church was a reminder of the person I used to be: the good and the bad. I couldn't stop replaying when Zakiya told Muuaji that I was just another lost nigga.

But then I told myself *Fuck her too!* because it wasn't like she was innocent. She was a killer dispatched on orders to kill another Black woman, so she had no right to judge me. I had been trained to adapt to any environment in order to survive: I had assessed its threats, built a shelter, found the best prey to hunt in order to feed myself. I would have done the same thing whether it was forest, mountains, rural countryside, or Detroit's urban jungle.

I don't know how long I sat there having a mental argument with Zakiya, acting as my own prosecution and defense by leveling and rebutting accusations that she never spoke. I finally turned to her and found her waiting on me. I could tell that she wanted to know where I was during that brief space-out, but I dismissed her with a wave of my hand.

I gave her the one-minute finger, but Zakiya threw open her car door before I could open mine.

Three youngsters were on the porch, sharing a blunt and sipping from red plastic cups. Their eyes tracked Zakiya as she followed me through the gate and up the front steps. She was still in her all-black jumpsuit, giving off sexy ninja vibes. I saw six eyes take in her form with appreciation, but not one mouth opened to make some out-of-pocket comment or catcall. It could've been that she was with me, and they were showing me that respect. Or it might've been Zakiya's overall demeanor projecting that she was not the one—that and the Hecklar holstered on her hip.

We walked inside to what was a typical scene. More young niggas huddled around the huge 85-inch TV while *Call of Duty* played on the screen. One of them was in the dining room at the pool table practicing his bank shot.

Dirty Red came from one of the rear rooms, noticed me, and rolled his eyes. I know he didn't expect me to be back so soon. That little feminine display of his annoyance was due to the fact that whenever he saw me, he typically had to come out of pocket. This time was no different.

He sat on a ripped leather couch and started breaking down another Backwoods leaf, even though three blunts were already in rotation. He knew he had to look at me when he spoke.

"Aye, man. You gotta give me time to work. It's a few niggas lined up to push them bricks off on, but I ain't made no plays yet. Why is you hounding me?"

"Silence needs whatever cash you have on hand. Plus he also requires all the weapons you can spare—pistols are acceptable, but assault rifles are preferable." When Zakiya explained this, Red gave her a look that was a combination of *Who the fuck are you?* and *Bitch, you must be crazy.*

Coming in, I knew this was going to be a difficult conversation. So I appointed Zakiya to be my voice. I had prepped her for the negotiation on the way there, hoping to speed along the typical back-and-forth I had to go through with Dirty Red using messages and facial expressions.

She continued, "He is hoping to borrow somewhere in the area of ten thousand dollars. He says this amount can be deducted from the funds that you already owe him."

Red looked to me, not even acknowledging Zakiya. "I just put sixty racks in yo' pocket two days ago. How you fucked up already?"

That was a question she couldn't answer, and one I didn't feel the need to.

Zakiya said, "We would like the money and weapons now. As we have important business, and I personally don't want to be in this element with you people any longer than necessary."

I didn't put those exact words in her mouth to say, but I shared the sentiment. A sense of urgency was needed.

Dirty Red finished construction of his blunt. He fired it up, took the first three hits. "Look sis, no disrespect, but I don't do business with people I don't know. And truth be told, he shouldn't have even brought you here. So I'm still trying to figure out why I'm speaking to you about an understanding me and this man already had in place."

I swear I could always feel drama coming, deep in my bones, the way some muthafuckas with arthritis could feel the approach of a storm. So when Dirty Red's girlfriend entered from one of the rear rooms, I knew she was going to be the match that sparked the bullshit.

She arrived at his side just in time to receive his blunt. She was repping hard, with a head full of red weave; her fake tits were braless, with nipples pushing though the fabric of a red-and-white baby tee; the over-inflated paid-for ass fell out the bottom of her red denim cutoffs. Even though she wore Air Max 95s of the same color, I learned later on that she actually went by Red Bottoms, a not-so-clever pun connecting her set and her body to the expensive shoe. I watched her put the weed to her glossed red lips, all the while throwing Zakiya a funky look through false eyelashes that projected nearly two inches from her face.

I flagged for Red's attention. I gestured between me and Zakiya, trying to indicate that she was speaking on my behalf. It wasn't like I brought the police up in here.

Plus, I was keeping watch on the rest of his boys out of my peripheral and could tell by the way they were watching the exchange while shifting in their seats that the energy was getting hostile. I slowly waved my hands to the floor, communicating for everyone to calm down.

I thought it would be Red's hoodrat, but it was actually Zakiya who started the bullshit when she went totally off-script.

"You could just give us what we want, and make this more convenient for both parties. But I'm perfectly fine if I have to kill you and take it."

Chapter Forty-two

I looked at Zakiya like *What the fuck is you doing?* She had threatened to kill Dirty Red in his own spot surrounded by his own boys, and said it as calmly as if she were telling him the time.

It was second nature for me the moment I walked into any room to do a preliminary scan just in case I had to shoot my way out of it. So I had already peeped that out of the four dudes sitting in the living room, two of them had pistols tucked. Two more out of the three guys on the porch. There was at least one more in the house that I hadn't seen, and he most likely could get to something long and fully automatic before I could get to him.

Growing up deaf had taught me to master the use of my peripheral vision, so I used the corners of my eyes to keep watch on the front door, the hall leading to the rear, and everybody sitting in the living room. I had a very profitable arrangement going on here that I wasn't trying to fuck up, but if I saw anybody raise up or reach for a gun, I was ready to start spilling noodles like a clumsy waiter.

"Look man, ain't no need for this to go left field." Dirty Red kept his response measured, because he already knew who I was and how I got down.

However, Dirty Red's girlfriend was a new acquisition; she hadn't been around during the time I was beefing with these niggas to see my work firsthand. And whether out of ignorance or pride, he hadn't told her my pedigree. This alone would've cued her not to fuck with me or anybody I was with.

"Hold up, bitch, you don't threaten nobody in this muthafucka. You got us fucked-up. Don't nobody care about that thang on yo' hip. You ain't the only one who strapped." This came from Red Bottoms, with a lot of neck-rolling and animated hand-waving.

It was the reasonable response, because Zakiya had been out of line. It just wasn't the smart one, because this little chick had no idea of who she was playing with. I gave Red a look that told him to check his girl before this shit go bad.

Zakiya looked over the girl as if she had only just noticed her then. She wore the quizzical amusement of a child at the circus seeing his first clown.

"Is there something wrong with your eyes?" Zakiya was talking about the fake cum-catcher lashes that had come in vogue over the past few years. In the church, the girls didn't do makeup, lace fronts, or fake anything.

"Bitch, keep talkin' and it's gone be something wrong with yo' eye!" Everybody got a laugh out of that, and even I thought it was funny.

"I imagine the modifications to your anatomy are for male sexual pleasure. Do you find that they heighten the experience of intimacy? Were the procedures painful to endure, and do they impact your common activities like fighting or exercise? What about hygiene, is it difficult to clean yourself after bathroom use?"

A few of the fellas laughed, but it didn't seem to me that Zakiya was trying to be comical. One of them mouthed, "Damn R.B., I been wantin' to know that myself. Can you really wipe that big muthafucka or do all yo' thongs got a brown string?"

Her face went flush from embarrassment, especially when she noticed her man biting down on his lips. Tears shined his eyes. As much as he tried, Dirty Red couldn't stop the trapped laughter from causing his big belly to shake. That's when her embarrassment exploded into rage.

Of course, Red Bottoms misdirected her anger towards Zakiya, and I knew this was gonna end bad for her when she snatched that pool cue off the table. I just didn't know how bad.

She held the business end of the pool stick and tried to club Zakiya with the wider, fatter handle. Red Bottoms swung twice, but Zakiya effortlessly avoided those with that lightning speed and ballerina grace. All the fellas stood up and even those on the porch filed inside, cheering for what they thought was going to be a typical catfight where some hair got pulled and maybe a titty bounced free.

Ol' girl took another big swing, and Zakiya bent backwards like she had rubber bands for bones. Red Bottoms missed her target but did smack the hell out of the television. Spiderwebs spread through half of the 85-inch screen.

And that was the last swing she got off, because on the very next attempt, Zakiya caught the pool stick in her right hand. She brought her left elbow down to break it in two. Then she jammed the broken end right through Red Bottoms's throat.

Seeing somebody get shanked like that gave me flashbacks of being in the joint. Zakiya had pushed it in hard enough for it to come out the other side, and I watched ol' girl feebly grasp at the half of pool stick skewering her neck. Fluid matching her name and outfit poured down the front of her shirt. She stumbled three feet back into the dining room, her eyes wide from disbelief. She bumped the pool table, then collapsed like a puppet whose strings had been cut, sank to her knees, toppled over onto her side.

All the fellas were still wearing identical masks of disbelief, and I had to take advantage of that moment. I pulled the .40 off my waist and gave out headshots to two of the gangbangers that I already knew to be strapped. Zakiya followed my lead without hesitation, just upped her mag and started blowing shit. Four of them were dead before they snapped back to their senses.

But at this point, everybody was in panic mode: scrambling, ducking, trying to hide behind furniture. Most of these young niggas out here carry guns, but few had been in an actual firefight, and fewer still had been trained in their proper use. They would've had their hands full with me alone, but really didn't have shit coming against two muthafuckas who had been taught marksmanship since six years old, but most importantly, how to remain cool under fire. Only one of the Joy Road Boys had the thought to go for their own weapon, but Zakiya made his head explode before he could free it from the waistband of his jeans.

The gunshot must've been heard outside, because I peeped out the front window to see the walk-up fiends running off the block as the driving customers sped for the corners to purchase their heroin elsewhere. So much for solidarity, because two of the dealers busted up, too. The loyal one who came running towards the house got his dumb ass shot right through the window, slumped him coming up the porch steps.

It hardly took ten seconds for us to turn the living room into a scene from a horror movie. Eight bodies were slumped on the floor all around us in various positions. Blood and brain matter sprayed the walls. The acrid smell of gunpowder filled the confined space. The cracked television was still frozen on a game of *Call of Duty*. We had played something much more graphic in real life.

Dirty Red had tried to run for the rear, either to the freedom of the back door or for a gun stashed somewhere near it. Zakiya found him belly-down in the hallway, feebly inching along on his elbows. A much-darker shade of crimson had spread across the jacket of his red Adidas jumpsuit from the bullet he caught in the back. Zakiya stood over his body, watched him struggle for a few feet, then looked to me for permission.

Even if I had wanted to spare him, it made no sense to. We could never come back from this. I granted it with the subtlest nod, and she sent another slug down through the top of his cranium.

I took Dirty Red's chain off of his neck, the huge Figueroa-style links hanging the huge diamond-encrusted Old English D. The chain was solid, and those stones had clarity. My rough estimate was in the area of $80,000, but I didn't take it for the money. The chain had belonged to someone who was like a brother to me. The value was purely sentimental.

We went through the rest of the house to clear it. I found a girl cowering in the bathroom upstairs, hiding in the tub. Through her trembling lips, I was able to make out most of her pleas. She begged for her life, and for some reason I flashed back on the girl I had tried to help but had ultimately left at the house being gang-banged. I didn't know why my mind took me there.

But we played a game that could be very messy, filled with collateral damage. The number one rule was: no witnesses. I had made that mistake in the past, and months later watched a woman that I spared, that I loved, get up on the stand to testify against me. I swore it would never happen again.

So I stopped all the girl's blubbering and the tears by pumping two into her skull. Then I closed the shower curtain on her, as if that were some type of small consideration.

I didn't need to search the whole house, because I already knew where Dirty Red's stash spot was. In the basement, there was a utility closet with a false wall at the back stacked with shelves. A small windowless room was behind that hidden door. There was unsold heroin in the refrigerator and cash bundles on the table.

I swept all the cash into an empty grocery bag. Thought I might have a plug for the drugs.

Chapter Forty-three

We pulled away from the scene of the massacre. Didn't burn rubber and didn't speed. That was the type of shit that drew attention.

No sooner than we were a few streets away from Cascade, I grabbed Zakiya by the collar and shook her.

She was smart enough to understand my frustration. "Was I supposed to let her harm me?"

No, she wasn't. But she didn't have to kill her, either. Zakiya could've disarmed that girl easily, or just fucked her up while she was armed. I wanted to ask her where was all that Shango shit about only fighting a worthy opponent.

I was starting to think this chick just likes to kill, but couldn't judge her, because I was the same. Once I left the church, I didn't go to a factory to make twenty-six dollars an hour. Being a goon paid well, but I really didn't do this for the money. In the end, I did this because I loved it. I briefly considered if it were nature or nurture. Did the church do this to us, or were we just inherently fucked-up?

I didn't go there looking to do these youngsters dirty like this. I'd had a very lucrative relationship with Dirty Red that I didn't

SILENT JUDGMENT • 173

want to end. But when Zakiya killed his girl, I just started laying niggas down, because I knew it was over. There was no coming back from that.

I didn't count up what was in the money bag, just pulled out five bands. Now we could afford a motel, but it was too damn hot to be in these streets. We had to find someplace safe to crash for the night. The problem was that my house was the safest place I knew.

Bringing Zakiya to the same place where I was keeping her target was the equivalent of bringing a fox to the henhouse. But at the moment, I had no other play, didn't stash houses around the city the same I did cars—at least not yet, anyway. So with hand gestures and finger pointing, I directed her back to my hood.

Not far from where I lived, there was an abandoned industrial area with the gutted shells of steel factories that had been closed for over thirty years. I torched the Cadillac on a rarely used service street that stopped in a dead end. This was where stolen cars came to die—the scorched frames of three other victims were already there.

My house was less than a mile away, and we reached it on foot. But not before we stopped at a hardware store only minutes before it closed. Zakiya didn't seem the least bit curious as to why I needed duct tape at nearly two o'clock in the morning.

It only became apparent to her when we reached my front gate. She looked at me like I was kidding. My expression indicated that I was now the one deadly serious.

Chapter Forty-four

I demanded that H&K PV40, then made her hold out both hands. I tore off a length of industrial-strength Gorilla Glue duct tape and bound her wrists together in front.

She mouthed, "I did just save your life." And the look I returned indicated how little that mattered in the moment.

I led Zakiya into my house through the rarely used front entrance. And that was all she got to see of my house, because she made it no farther than the pen that was built behind that door. She looked at me with a smirk when I locked the gate from the other side.

"Very hospitable."

This was what I had planned from the jump. Bringing her here was one thing, but I damn sure wasn't about to let her roam.

Kierra came out the rear, drawn simply because she knew I never entered through the front. She joined me at the gate, looking quizzically at our guest. "You just coming home with a new bitch every other day now."

Antwon joined her, followed by Amelia. She put a protective arm around her son. She looked from Zakiya back to me with disbelief.

She ordered Antwon back up the stairs to the room I was loaning to them. He backpedaled slowly, staring at Zakiya the way zoo patrons stared at the tiger cage. She mocked him with a friendly wave.

She turned to me. "He is a wide one. How do you think he would fare in wilderness training?"

Most of us in the church had to endure it at around that same age. Personally, I liked Antwon but knew he wasn't built to survive six weeks in the woods without clothing, shelter, or food. It would've broken him—I seen it happen firsthand.

As soon as her son disappeared up the steps, Amelia hissed at me: "Why would you bring her here? Why haven't you *dealt* with her yet?"

"What do you want with me?" She screamed at Zakiya, and I had to grab her before she got too close to the fence. "What have I ever done to you?"

Zakiya was calm. "It's not so much about what you've done. It's what you will do."

Kierra frowned at me, pursed those huge sensual lips. "Wait a minute. This is the person who's supposed to be after her? You came home with the ops?"

Zakiya had already proven to be useful. And having her here, where I could keep an eye on her, was better than having her out there where I couldn't—I was playing the game of keeping my enemies close. Plus, there was still a lot about this that didn't make sense, and she potentially had information that I needed.

I could've explained all of this to Amelia and Kierra, but I didn't go through the trouble.

Zakiya scanned her cage, searching for weaknesses. "This does seem foolish even to me, Lutalo."

Amelia spoke with animated hand gestures. "I'm paying you to protect me, and you come here with the very woman trying to kill me?" Well, when she put it like that, it did seem fucked-up. "Get rid of her now. Take her out back. I don't care where and how, just do it."

I returned an expression that told her to chill the fuck out. Just because I worked for her didn't mean I took orders from her.

I was still holding the Hecklar I took from Zakiya in my right hand, when Amelia snatched my Walther from its holster. She held it with two shaky hands and aimed it at the cage.

"I could just save myself the trouble of paying you right now."

"Oh shit, this bitch trippin." Kierra said, then hid behind me like I could stop bullets or something.

I guess Amelia was expecting me to jump in and stop her. I just shrugged, my expression nonchalant. I didn't think she had that in her. Part of me was curious to see.

"You don't think I'll do it?" Nope. And I just stood there, practically daring her.

Through it all, Zakiya stood behind the fence wearing the same amount of calm, but she voiced less skepticism. "I don't have any doubt that she'll do it when the time comes. She's a daughter of darkness. Seeking entry into the legion of demons."

In that instant, I saw Amelia's hands stop shaking. I stepped forward and snatched my pistol from her.

She looked at me, fuming. "Who are you being paid to protect? Where is your loyalty?"

Kierra came from behind me to stand at Amelia's side, briefly in solidarity with her. "Yeah, Sy, you know I ain't the one to speak on your business, and you damn sure know I don't care for this bougie bitch. But to link up with the ops while you already locked in with her, is just crazy to me."

I couldn't believe this shit. Just a few hours ago, Kierra was ready to kill her; now she's going to preach to me about taking sides.

Zakiya asked, "You're really going to keep me locked in a cage? And here it is, I thought we had bonded when we at the park and I was sitting on your lap."

Kierra glared at me. "Hell naw! What is this bitch talkin' 'bout, sitting on your lap at the park?" She went all eastside hoodrat with the waving hands. "I'm sitting here playing babysitter for you while you out here living your best life."

Amelia folded her arms. "Why was she sitting on your lap at the park?"

Kierra spun on her. "Bitch, why you so curious? He ain't yo' nigga."

I glared at Zakiya, who stood there wearing a playful smirk. She tossed that grenade, and it had the exact impact that she intended.

"I didn't even say anything about the kiss. Whoops!"

Kierra shook her head, caused the ponytails to swing around. "No she didn't just say y'all kissed."

I started to use my phone to explain that we had only did that to throw off the cops, then I paused and got mad at the fact that I even had to explain myself. I was a man used to living alone, not having to answer to anybody. All of a sudden, I had three women in my house. All of them questioning me.

I looked at all of them like, *Shut the fuck up!* Turned and walked off.

Told myself I knew what I was doing. Then tried like hell to believe it.

Chapter Forty-five

When I finally found a pen and paper, I left strict instructions. 1. Nobody was to give Zakiya anything. 2. Nobody was to talk to Zakiya. 3. Nobody was to get too close to her cage. Then I scratched out number three and just banned everybody from the living room.

Before I crashed for the night, I checked the cage and found Zakiya seated with her legs crossed at the ankles, squeezing her thighs together so tightly that her face strained with the effort. Another instance where body language told the story. I would eventually have to figure something out for her. I couldn't just toss in a bucket and tell her to go for what she know. I was a savage but not that type. My face warned her not to be on no bullshit before I unlocked the pen and escorted her to the bathroom.

At the door, she presented her hands, looked at me expectantly. I went into the kitchen and returned with some large scissors. I flashed another warning, then cut the duct tape from her wrists. Five minutes later, when Zakiya came out the bathroom, I had real zip ties waiting for her. Police-issue. I rarely took prisoners, but sometimes my line of work did require me to kidnap a muthafucka.

"We made an agreement, and I am honor-bound to keep it. I swear on the ancestors that I will not kill anyone in your home. Where I am from, a person's word has weight."

Well, where I'm from, a person's word only weighs as much as the air they used to speak it. Muthafuckas will have tears in their eyes, swearing on the souls of their kids and dead parents, knowing they lying they ass off.

That was the reason those zip ties went on her wrists, and she went back in her cage. Zakiya seated herself with her back against the front door. The cage wasn't long enough for her to stretch on the floor. I pushed a bottled water through the chain links of the pen as a small consolation.

It was damn near three in the morning, and I had been in constant motion for most of the day. I was headed back to my room to steal a few hours of sleep when I passed Amelia in the hallway.

She was charging down the stairs, dragging Antwon by the arm. The boy threw me a look that asked for help. Amelia brushed past me like I didn't exist, made a beeline through my kitchen. I met them at the pen at the side door, fumbling with the chain that secured that gate that separated the kitchen from the stairwell. Bitch knew she wasn't going anywhere without the key to the padlock. I just let her play with it for a while, until she turned back to me and the *fuck is you doin'?* look on my face.

"As long as she's here, I will not be. This is clearly a breach of our contract, and you can expect to hear from my lawyers." Amelia said this with hands on hips, and I could've died laughing.

First off, we didn't sign any contract, because I don't sign shit. Second, any process server walking up on me with a summons was gonna get served a Level 7 ass-whipping with all the fixins.

"Open this gate. I'm taking my son, and I'm leaving now."

I explained as best I could in hastily typed texts with misspelled and omitted words the agreement I worked out with Zakiya. Of course, I conveniently left out the fact that it was temporary and that I was sure Zakiya still intended to kill her.

I alerted her that the second assassin was still loose, and just as determined to stop her heart. I also avoided the reasons why Za-kiya had agreed to help me with him, but wasn't above stating that her help was our best option.

For now, my spot was still the safest place she could be, but I wasn't anybody's jailer. I undid the chains on that pen for her, then stood poised to unfasten the many locks on my side door, meeting her eyes. Amelia was smart enough to see that I was offering her a choice. Any indication that she really wanted to go, I would've bust that door open and wished her good luck.

But luck was all I was offering. She had paid me for the week and wasn't getting a refund. I don't do those.

So we stood there for a full minute having a staring contest as she weighed her pride against her survival. Ninety percent of communication is nonverbal. Because of this, I'd studied several books on body language. I saw in her eyes the exact second when the decision was made, but Amelia felt it necessary to stare me down for a while longer.

She finally turned Antwon's shoulder and pushed him back towards the hall. He had made certain to keep a solemn face while his mother was watching, but behind her back gave me a goofy smirk and two raised thumbs. I felt the vibrations from his heavy ass jogging up the stairs.

Amelia waited for me to close and lock the gate. "Silence, I need to know that I can count on you to protect Antwon. There is nothing more important to me than my son's future."

I nodded to signify that I understood.

Amelia became weirdly intense. "I mean it. You might feel some sort of kinship with her because she's from the same place you're from. But I need you to promise me, that if it comes down to it, and Antwon's life is in danger, you won't hesitate."

I tapped my heart to say *I promise*, and it was one that I meant. Shango or not, I was prepared to kill Zakiya, just as prepared as I knew she was to kill me.

Amelia grabbed me, buried her face in my chest, and started to cry. I rolled my eyes, thought she was being overly dramatic. I snatched a fistful of paper towel off the roll by the kitchen sink. Offered it to her.

I was in my own mind, filing something Amelia said away for later, when she stretched up on her tiptoes to kiss me. It was slow and sensual. She tried to slip her tongue into my mouth when I stepped back from her.

I frowned to let her know she was on bullshit. I was doing everything on my end to keep this professional, didn't need to complicate things any more than they already were.

Plus, I had sense enough to know that Amelia was mostly doing this to get back at Kierra for all the dick-teasing on Antwon.

But my nonverbal scolding probably would've landed better if my beast hadn't come alive. I bricked up the moment she kissed me and figured she felt it. I was making the neck-slit motion with my hands to let her know she had to kill that type of shit, but Amelia's eyes were focused on the print going down the leg of my loose sweats.

Amelia walked off with the swagger of someone who felt their mission was accomplished.

From the corner of my eye, I saw Zakiya laughing, clapping her bound hands. Her eyes were open again, and she had witnessed the whole exchange.

"Lutalo, I never would've guessed you had such a way with the ladies."

Chapter Forty-six

I rolled out of bed around ten thirty the next morning, which was a full two hours later than I intended to. I didn't take my ass to sleep until around three thirty, got woke up by Kierra's mouth after four. Zakiya's little acting job still had me feeling some type of way, so I spent a quick twenty minutes pounding Kierra before I drifted back off. Now she curled up on her side of the bed, sleeping peacefully with a thumb in her mouth. I started to wake her ass up just to be petty.

I was still groggy and half asleep when I walked into the kitchen. So I really couldn't trust my eyes when I saw Zakiya casually leaning against the counter, sipping coffee from my favorite mug. I checked the pen, as if expecting to find a double locked at the front door wearing zip ties. Of course it was empty, with the chain and lock still secured.

I quickly snatched one of the knives from the butcher's box on the counter to my left.

Zakiya was quicker. By the time I turned back to her, I was staring down the barrel of a pistol, already raised and waiting.

"Unless you're about to use that to make breakfast, I suggest you put it down."

I was sure I'd locked that gate. Zakiya read the quizzical expression in my eyes.

"Before I finished puberty, I knew how to make a fertilizer bomb strong enough to bring down the Capitol building. You think they didn't teach me how to pick a lock?"

That's when I realized that she didn't just have any pistol pointed at me, but her pistol. The same H&K PV40 that I took from her at the front gate. I had placed it on the nightstand next to my Walther before I dozed off. Maybe it was fatigue or the fact that she was drinking my morning coffee that caused me to take too long to realize that she had actually been in my room, had stood over me and Kierra.

"For a man who makes many enemies, you sleep too soundly. I could've slit your throat, then went upstairs to kill Amelia and her son. The only reason you woke up this morning is because I made a promise. Let your life be the currency that purchases your trust."

She motioned with the gun as she spoke. "Or you could try to come at me with that knife. See how that goes."

I was thinking over my options and not liking them when Zakiya quickly tucked the Hecklar behind her back. I sensed before I saw Antwon slide into my peripheral from the rear. He took an oblivious first step into the kitchen, then froze and stared warily at Zakiya.

She put on what was probably her most disarming friendly smile. "Hey big man, I was just trying to talk this guy into cracking a few eggs for some French toast. Don't that sound good? I know you're hungry, too."

Antwon just stared at her, unblinking. "Is that a fat joke?"

"It's more of an educated guess. I wasn't trying to be comical."

"Well, I'm not trying to be comical either when I say you look like Erykah Badu's less-fuckable homeless sister: Erykah Ba-do-you-got-some-spare-change."

I could tell by the look on Zakiya's face that went totally over her head.

Other than that initial reaction to her, Antwon didn't appear disturbed by the thought of Zakiya being free. He took his phone to the table and stared into it while he waited for breakfast. The prospect of French toast seemed to outweigh any concerns over his safety.

Behind his back, I threw Zakiya an irritated glare and nodded my head towards the pen. Zakiya returned a look that challenged me to come make her go back. She knew I didn't want to do that with Antwon right here waiting to be collateral damage.

Zakiya had planted the seed, and I actually started to crave French toast. I went to the refrigerator, pulled the eggs and milk. I'm a big goon-ass nigga who don't really play around in the kitchen like that. But like most men, I can put together a decent breakfast. So I started to cook.

Zakiya discreetly checked the .40 on her waist, then offered to assist me. She looked confused when I handed her a roll of ground turkey sausage and I had to remember that she was used to being in the church, where all their meat was fresh, either raised or hunted. So I demonstrated how to open the wrapper and cut the first few slices for her. She was able to pick up after that.

But while she was busy prepping, I snatched the Hecklar from her waist. Made a face to let her know I didn't give a fuck what she promised, she wasn't walking around this bitch with a gun. She made a face like she wasn't concerned, like she knew I'd slip up again and she'd get it back eventually.

I made enough breakfast for five, even though only three of us currently ate. I left plates for Kierra and Amelia in the oven and just enjoyed this brief moment of peace. I didn't expect either of them to adjust to Zakiya's new level of freedom as easily as Antwon had. I was preparing myself for a whole bunch of drama when those two woke up.

"So I'm just supposed to sit here and pretend like this isn't the woman who's trying to kill my mother?"

"It's not too late for your mother to change her path. If she denounces the devil and turns away from iniquity, I would spare her." Zakiya said this casually while shoveling herself with forkfuls of French toast. "But the snares of the beast are sharp, not easily broken."

There she go talking that crazy shit again. I just shook my head and continued to eat.

Antwon looked at Zakiya as if genuinely concerned. "You know they have medications for that stuff, right? There's people you can talk to. We can get you help."

Zakiya turned to me. "I am impressed by the considerable thought you put into your home's defenses, but you have to know none of it will matter if Muuaji ever finds this place."

I ignored her, focused back on my plate. She wasn't telling me anything I hadn't already figured out.

When I had made all the modifications to my home, I was thinking of threats in the form of regular thugs, or potentially a police standoff. I had unbreakable windows, impregnable doors, and perimeter walls that could probably stop an anti-tank round. But I never thought that I would be facing off with another Shango warrior.

The average street nigga knew how to play with guns, but very few knew anything about demolition. That comment Zakiya made about being able to take down the Capitol building wasn't just cap. In the church, they gave us classes on how to make a wide range of incendiary devices, many out of common household products like sugar, concentrated oxygen, and ammonia.

The point she was making was that, unlike most enemies, Muuaji didn't have to break inside the house to get to us.

He could just blow this muthafucka up.

Chapter Forty-seven

After breakfast, I took Antwon downstairs to hit the heavy bag. Zakiya pretty much invited herself.

The whole time I was training Antwon and helping him to develop basic fighting fundamentals, I noticed Zakiya from the corner of my eye, repeatedly shaking her head with pursed lips. I wasn't facing her the entire time, but could tell from Antwon's reactions that she had made a few comments that were less than encouraging.

Half an hour later, I had him jumping rope to improve his cardio when Zakiya finally got tired of just discreetly hating from the sideline. She felt the need to give an unsolicited critique of my coaching techniques.

"You think skipping rope and punching something that doesn't hit back will prepare him for a real fight? Shango frowns on this.

"You know what it takes to make a warrior because you have been made one, even though this world outside of Alkebulan has undone our work. Train him the way you were trained."

I was only teaching him enough to deal with the bullies at school. Zakiya seemed to think that I was trying to prepare him for covert operations and assassinating foreign dignitaries.

She called to Antwon after going into her fight stance. "Come, spar with me. I'll teach you how to make Eve—how to snatch a man's rib right out from the side of his body."

Antwon looked excited, was actually about to square up with her, until I stepped between them. I placed a hand on his chest and pushed him back. My face should've warned him of the gravity of the mistake he was about to make.

He didn't understand that when Zakiya and I were both adolescents, we had adults with military training punching and kicking the shit out of us without mercy or restraint. Black eyes, broken bones, and chipped teeth were a common sight, even in kids as young as six. Antwon's horny ass probably thought he and Zakiya were going to do some light playfighting where they wrestled on the floor all tangled up and he got to squeeze a titty or something. Zakiya wasn't going to hold back. She was gonna fuck Antwon up, because that was the way she had been taught, and she still didn't see anything wrong with it.

I sent Antwon upstairs before his dick got him into any more trouble. Turned and glared at Zakiya like, *What the fuck?*

After a quick stretch, she started in on the heavy bag. Her punches and kicks had the precision of a machine; the power had the bag swinging wildly.

"The boy is heavy and slow, just like most of the children I've seen out here, because their elders are failing them. They have been too soft with him his entire life. And now you continue the trend with this foolishness you label as training."

She continued to work the bag while I turned the subject to Muuaji. Even supreme killers had to rest. I knew the UOTA hadn't put them up at the Four Seasons, but there were too many abandoned houses in Detroit to choose from. I asked Zakiya about the place where he was crashing at.

"We keep moving, rest on the road. Muuaji will sleep just long enough to recharge and never in the same place twice."

It made sense for him to sleep in his car, just as we had done.

He had no identification, no connections, and at the slightest sign of trouble, he could just drive off, taking his bedroom with him.

She said, "We have to lure him out, use yourself as bait. If he doesn't find you, he will tear your life apart to force you to come out of hiding.

"Our best play is to get him to an open area, with no obstructed views. Find me a good rifle and put me up in a sniper's nest. We end this with one bullet."

I reiterated to Zakiya that I had to fight him. She didn't seem surprised, but the expression on her face indicated how stupid she thought that was.

"A pack of hunters can track and kill a nine-hundred-pound grizzly bear with the proper bait and trap. But you don't jump in the cage and try to wrestle with him."

And that was exactly why I had to do it. Because in my mind, I was the muthafuckin' bear. I was supposed to be the animal that men feared.

"You have been away from Shango for too long. You've been affected by this slave culture: Individualism, Materialism, Hedonism. Poisoning yourself with this unhealthy food. Your kundalini is low from wasting your seed in these toxic women. You are not going to beat Muuaji in a hand-to-hand contest."

I explained to her that I'm a savant when it came to fucking people up. I ain't never lost a fight twice to the same person. I learn my opponent and adapt.

She laughed, "You didn't lose to him the first time because he didn't actually fight you."

She stopped striking the bag, turned to me in earnest. "You gauge yourself based on the pitiful opponents you've faced in this world, scarecrows who've never been taught the correct use of arms or even how to throw a proper punch. You had the benefit of being raised in Alkebulan, so you will always have advantage over common men. But don't get puffed up in your own conceit. You are a four-foot giant in the land of dwarves.

"But we've also seen how you fare when you have faced skilled warriors. You had to resort to a cheap shot against Muuaji. And you wouldn't have beat me if you didn't grab a frying pan."

That screwed my face up. I let her know how close she was to getting choked.

"Very convincing." She mocked me with false applause. "The size, the muscle, the big beard and tight scowl. I bet the scarecrows all quake with fear when you make that face."

This bitch was running her mouth a little too much, and I was done with it. I loosened the muscles in my shoulder and neck. Put my fists up. I'm always with the shit.

Zakiya stepped back, went into her fight stance. "Just remember. I don't have testicles."

Chapter Forty-eight

We began to circle each other. She feinted a couple times with the left. I didn't feed into it by giving up any defensive, didn't bob or weave either way. Just waited for her to throw a real punch.

She threw a real right, and I moved to counter. I realized almost too late that she had baited me. I came in at the perfect angle to catch a knee strike. Luckily, I blocked that and stumbled backwards and out of the way a moment before her rising patella would've clipped my chin and probably knocked me out. Like me, she could switch seamlessly from traditional boxing to Muay Thai.

She gave me a little smirk, knowing how close she was to almost having me.

I fell back, hands up, and began to circle her again. I would have to think more defensively. I was used to being able to overwhelm my opponents with my offense.

Next I snapped a couple jabs just to test her, but she gave up nothing, didn't fade to the left or the right. Not even on my second one, which came to within a quarter inch of her face. Zakiya didn't blink. She just continued to move laterally with this weird shuffling of her feet.

We continued to circle each other, waiting for the other one to make their move. Perhaps we were each showing the other too much respect.

Then I saw the walls slowly start to close in at the edges of my vision and realized what she'd been doing. That strange, sideways shuffling with her feet was actually cutting off the room to me. She had been permitting me to go so far left before sending me back to the right, then not as far back to the left, and not as far back to the right. It was the same effect of a swinging pendulum with the distance getting shorter with each swing. It was so subtle that I didn't even realize she had been slowly herding me into the corner until my back was nearly to it.

Desperation forced me to attack. I pressed forward, doubling up my jabs. Zakiya dodged everything like this was a scene from a movie she'd already watched thirty times. She skillfully used her forearms to deflect what she couldn't avoid.

She stepped back after she swatted away my latest punch. "There's no point to this if you're not going to fight for real."

The sad part was that I actually was fighting for real. Granted, not real enough to try to kill her, but I wasn't exactly pulling my punches to the degree that she thought I was.

So with that I came in, faked like I was about to chop her in the throat, and when she reacted, I gave her a shot to the kidney. That explosion of pain widened her eyes, and the blow lifted her off her feet.

But she recovered quickly, stepped under the second punch of my combination, and sent three into my body. She finished with an uppercut that stunned me and sent me back into the corner.

We exchanged blows a few more times with me on the losing end, but what had always been my strength was that, if given enough time to study my opponent, I could figure them out. Most fighters had a sequence in which they liked to throw their punches. Something taught early that worked for us so often that we had a tendency to lean on it, without even knowing. Under

Cus D'Amato, Iron Mike Tyson had favored the left hook to the liver, followed by a quick uppercut with the same hand. I had always tried to avoid this, because having a favorite move made you predictable, and a very attentive fighter could notice and exploit a move that you used too often.

Zakiya was lightning fast, lithe, and could hit hard as any man. She was an extremely gifted mixed martial artist, but I slowly started to realize that she favored a specific side of her body. This manifested in a tendency to lead with her left. Whether it was a straight jab, or a low kick, her combinations always started with a left-side appendage.

Being that I had her cheat code, I decided to end this quickly. I still felt bad about that blow to the kidney. I promised myself not to hurt her too bad, but she was going to damn sure know that she'd been in a fight. So I stood facing up with her, watching and waiting for that telltale sign to make my move.

And it came when she stepped back to put all her weight on her right leg. This was a necessary pivot point for someone about to use the left side of their body. Either to throw a big punch, or possibly the low leg kick, which she had shown to favor. I didn't care which, and didn't wait to find out.

I lunged in, ready to absorb that weak-ass leg kick, to get my hands on her, but then I watched that girl damn near defy physics.

While her left leg was still up for that low leg kick, she sprang off her right foot. Launched herself in the air for a Superman punch that caught me right in the forehead. Then with that ballerina form, she went to the prettiest roundhouse I'd ever seen. Put the heel of her foot right on my jaw and dropped me like a stone.

I was suddenly on my back, looking up at her with the room spinning.

"All war is based on deception." She mouthed this, quoting one of my favorite lines from Sun Tzu. "Do you really think I'm so predictable that I would start all my combinations with a left jab or leg kick. I am Shango. Zakiya Ra-El. The beautiful light. The sword that sings." Her mouth kept moving, talking a bunch of shit that I wasn't trying to make out.

I couldn't deny that: She tricked the hell out of me, and I fell for it.

But she was also tricking herself, because I knew for a fact that her instructors taught her to never celebrate a win until the fight is over.

I swept her ankles with my arm and dropped her onto her back. Once she was on the ground, I switched over to my jujitsu. I scrambled to mount her, but Zakiya raised her knees to keep me in half guard. But this was only deception by me, because I really wanted her wrist. I rolled across her chest laterally and pulled her right arm between my knees.

I felt Zakiya frantically tapping my thigh before I could fully extend her forearm. She knew as well as I did that an arm-bar was an inescapable hold that would only result in her shit being broken.

I released her, rolled away, and for a moment we lay side by side, breathing heavy. I rubbed my chin. That still hurt like a muthafucka.

Zakiya turned to look at me. "Muuaji would've killed you inside of ten seconds."

I gave her a *Bitch please* look. I just beat her, again. I didn't doubt he was good, but she was playing me like I wasn't shit.

"Muuaji is much stronger than me and just as fast. If he had kicked you like that, it would've taken the head off of your shoulders.

"A sniper nest is still our best plan. Take him down from distance."

She didn't get it. I couldn't let this stand. Win or lose, I had to fight this nigga again.

Zakiya seemed to read that in my face. "Don't let your wounded pride destroy you."

I used my phone to explain to her that I planned on doing this no matter what. I knew that bullet in my back had affected my shoulder and diminished my speed. But I was going to train hard, rehab the shit out of that bitch with the time I had.

Zakiya looked at me and shook her head. "The reason you are not ready has nothing to do with your body."

Chapter Forty-nine

The shit that damn near happened to Antwon let me know that I had to keep Zakiya on some type of leash. She was like one of those pit bulls that had been bred only for fighting. She still hadn't been acclimated to family life. She had to be kept in a kennel until it was time to come off the scratch line.

For the time being, I kept her down in the basement. I knew that Zakiya could just as easily pick the locks on the gates that separated the stairs and the landing. She found the cellar preferable to the pen at the front door. There was a bathroom down there, plenty of room to move around, and to work out if she wanted.

Upstairs in the bathroom, my head was still ringing from that kick she gave me. I reached for my Percocet but just palmed the bottle without opening it. This had become a crutch, and I was getting to the point where I couldn't keep lying to myself. I thought about pouring the pills in the toilet but didn't quite have the strength. I thought I'd earned a small victory when I put the bottle back in the medicine cabinet.

It only took the time needed for me to finish pissing for that brief flash of willpower to crumble. I popped one after I washed my hands. Then patted myself on the back because I only popped one.

I walked into the kitchen to find Kierra in nothing but a T-shirt and panties, bent over the kitchen counter staring at her phone, pretending not to notice that she was giving young Antwon an eyeful. He stood across the room playing with his tablet, trying to act like he wasn't watching her like Netflix.

I wasn't in the mood for no bullshit between her and Amelia this morning, so I used hand motions to tell her to go put on some pants before the bougie bitch got up. With rolling eyes and sputtering lips, Kierra strutted out the kitchen. Antwon's eyes following her the entire way. I smacked her on the ass just because I knew he'd get a kick out of it, and because she likes that type of shit, too.

Amelia stepped in the kitchen right on cue, looking like someone who hadn't slept longer than an hour. Brown eyes heavy and swollen with fatigue.

I saw them momentarily brighten when they flashed on the empty cage. I quickly snatched her hope when I jerked a finger to the floor.

Amelia rolled her eyes at me, went over to the coffee maker, snatched the pot. She made sure to snatch the cabinets open in a way to broadcast her mood. I didn't know what the attitude was from and didn't care enough to try to figure it out. I couldn't wait to get this shit over with. It was too much damn estrogen in my house.

Zakiya talked all this shit about being a world-class sniper, but then didn't even think to bring a rifle. So it was basically on me to find her one. I was a pistol and shotgun guy, had plenty of assault rifles but nothing for long-range. I preferred to do my work up-close and messy.

I was headed out with plans to take Zakiya with me, but first I asked Amelia for the key to her condo. I was offering to swing by her apartment to grab a few things for her and Antwon. I knew it wasn't safe to bring her along but agreed to call her when I got there to learn what she wanted.

She tossed me the key but not before I got hit with another eye roll. She had been acting funky towards me the entire morning. I used my hands to ask, *What's up with you?* but she turned her back on me and strutted out the kitchen.

I turned and saw Zakiya standing behind the gate that separated the basement from the kitchen. She had been watching our exchange with a smile. "I think she upset because her sleep got disturbed late last night. Let's just say that your girlfriend sent a message to everybody in the house. Loud and clear."

I just glared at her frustrated. It was already hard enough for me to understand people, so I really hated when they talked in riddles. I eventually caught on, though; then it all made sense.

That little pound session Kierra and I had in the middle of night, after she woke me. She had apparently screamed loud enough for the whole house, and probably the neighbors to hear. I was working with a monster, so there's no doubt that I could do damage. But Kierra had gone overboard with a hell of a acting job just to fuck with Amelia. I could see her being that petty.

I left on foot with Zakiya at my side. My second car was stashed about half a mile north, so I counted on a ten-minute hike.

I had my Walther P99 on my hip and had returned the PV40 to Zakiya. These pistols could handle everyday action, but our mission was to find something that could knock a nigga down from 900 yards. I deferred to her expertise on this matter. She claimed to have had a lot of trigger time on the McMillan TAC-50 but would accept a FN Herstal Ballista .338 Lapua in a pinch. I had about ten bands stuffed in my pants because I knew that quality sniper rifles weren't cheap.

There was only one person I knew who would possibly have a line on that type of hardware. He was no longer in the arms business but more than likely could point me in the right direction.

The problem was that this was just another in the lost list of card-carrying members of the We Hate Silence club.

It was about fifteen minutes before noon on an overcast day that was unseasonably warm. A drab gray blanket had been pulled over the city. Dark thunderheads gathered in the eastern horizon, but the weatherman had assured this was an empty threat.

I never left my house without making sure my head was on a swivel. I walked in a way that allowed my eyes to sweep over everything while staring too long at nothing.

I knew my block too well. I hadn't engaged with any of my neighbors on a personal level but knew what everyone drove. From the old white lady three doors down who owned the burgundy Honda, to the young Arabic family on the corner who all shared a silver Subaru with a dented rear end. I had made it my business to memorize every car, van, or SUV that lived on my block, and even those who lived on the next block and came down my street with any frequency.

So when I saw the early-model Chevy Tahoe parked on the corner just idling with someone inside, I didn't bother to waste any time.

I raised my pistol and started punching slug right through the windshield before that driver's door could open.

Chapter Fifty

Zakiya didn't hesitate to follow my lead. By the time I spit the third round from my Walther, she had the Hecklar raised and firing right along with me.

The driver of the Tahoe peeled off in reverse, went about six houses before he backed into the rear of a pickup parked on the opposite side of the street. The man behind the wheel was some six-foot-three nigga who I'd never met. He stumbled out of the door with an FNX 9-millimeter in his left hand. He swayed on his feet, then went down before without getting off a single shot from the weapon.

But he wasn't alone, and the two on the passenger side returned fire. The body of an AR-15 came out the front window just as I slotted myself behind a tree. I guess these were the real hitters, and the driver had only carried something for protection.

Those semi-automatic rounds peppered the trunk of a fifty-year-old maple. Zakiya had concealed herself behind the one planted by the curb next door.

She looked at me to ask: *What the hell?*

This had nothing to do with Muuaji. It was related to some shit I already had going on.

The two shooters climbed out both passenger-side doors, continuing to fire. They circled around the back of the SUV and shot at us from cover. We were pinned down and outgunned. Pistols versus semi-autos. I had a whole arsenal of high-powered shit locked in my basement not seventy yards away.

These were Prime's boys. I recognized the one who jumped out the rear passenger door from the gas station a few nights ago. I guess he finally felt strong enough to make a move on me.

I peeked my head out from behind the tree but couldn't get off a shot. I clutched my pistol, waiting for my opportunity. I had to snatch my foot back when an errant slug skipped off the sidewalk. I couldn't stay here like this. Eventually they would chop through this tree and me right along with it.

Zakiya was about fifteen feet away in the exact same predicament. But as I looked at her, she appeared to be smiling, even blew me an air kiss. She was enjoying this shit a little too much.

I blindly fired a couple of shots around the tree just to keep them honest. If they just strapped their nuts on and ran up, we'd be in trouble.

Then came the moment I was waiting for, that pause they needed to reload. I motioned for Zakiya to cover me as I made my move.

Sprang out from behind that tree running low and fast. My pistol was up and firing as I scrambled across the street. Over the roof of the Tahoe, I saw one head snap backwards and bloody mist spray from his skull.

I was halfway across the street before I saw the second car. Maybe Zakiya had tried to call out to warn me. Anybody else would've heard it coming.

I didn't know what kind of car had hit me, only that it was dark blue and fast. Then from the position of someone tumbling, I saw my feet go over my head, the hood and roof. The sky for a brief moment and then the ground as it came racing towards me.

I landed on my stomach, and the impact shook me to my

bones. Later on, Zakiya would swear on the ancestors that I went twelve feet into the air. Luckily, I didn't come down awkward enough to break something. And I had the presence of mind to hold onto my gun.

From ground level, I looked up to see that I got ran down by a Chrysler 300. My head was about seven feet away from the rear bumper and plate. The white lights came on that signaled the car was thrown into reverse. This slimy muthafucka was about to run me over.

The tires peeled rubber before the 300 launched at me in reverse. There was an internal mutiny going on because, in that moment, I was telling myself to get up and run, but my body didn't respond to any of the commands.

I barely had the time to roll over onto my back and tuck my limbs. I flattened myself against the asphalt as much as I could. I smelled gas and felt the heat from the engine when the car raced over me with hardly four inches of clearance to spare. Some unidentifiable 26-inch mag wheels was a hair away from running over my left arm. I was grateful that the owner didn't put on a low-profile custom kit.

When it had passed, I sat and sent three bullets at the front of the Chrysler. The windshield was coated in a deep illegal tint, so I couldn't tell if I hit anyone inside. Then I aimed for that front right tire and popped it.

Zakiya stepped into the street, firing until her Hecklar went dry. The blue 300 continued to speed down my block in reverse, wobbling bad as the deflated tire came off the rim. The driver backed into a turn at the corner, smoked the tires again, then took off down the side street.

Zakiya holstered her weapon because she needed both hands to pull me to my feet. I didn't realize how much that shit had hurt until I tried to walk. I stumbled the first few steps, limped some after that, and slowly tried to regain my stride.

I didn't even see Zakiya take down the second shooter, just noticed his body slumped on the curb with blood and pus leaking from his left eye. She really was a helluva markswoman to catch him like that in the middle of a firefight.

My neighborhood was filled with middle-class homeowners who took pride in their lawns and formed block club associations. In short, the type of place where people called the cops and they actually showed. I figured we only had about sixty seconds left before squad cars bent the corner.

I was too damn sore to try to run, so I went over to the gold Tahoe. The keys were still in the ignition. From the dead, I snatched both AR-15s and tossed them on the rear seat. I climbed behind the wheel, hoping that it didn't suffer any frame damage when it backed into the old pickup truck.

I pulled off in the same direction as the Chrysler 300, but hit the opposite turn at the corner. I was four blocks away on that side street when I saw blue-and-whites with flashing beacons race down mine in the rearview.

I was hunched over the wheel in pain, gritting my teeth and squinting to see through the shattered windshield I'd filled with P99 holes. I felt her eyes on me, then turned to find Zakiya grinning at me like a kid.

"This is the type of stuff you get to do every day? I see you didn't want to come back to the temple."

I understood her excitement. Many inside the church will and have spent their entire lives training for shit like this but never got to use any of it in real-world situations. We were on standby for some apocalyptic scenario when the government collapsed, anarchy spread, and the proud boys made their final push to get rid of all the minorities.

So I could relate to the shine in Zakiya's eyes, and how she bounced in her seat from the surge of adrenaline. I was addicted to this shit, too. I had chosen it time and time again over stability, love, and family.

But as I clutched my bruised ribs, I gave her a little shake of the head. Life in these streets ain't always the roller coaster she thinks it is.

Chapter Fifty-one

We only took that bullet-riddled Tahoe the half of mile we needed before switching out.

My second car was stashed about in the parking lot of a small apartment complex that offered assisted living for seniors. I had watched the place long enough to learn that it had assigned parking but was never quite at capacity. My twelve-year-old Buick LaCrosse had been sitting there for three months, slotted in the spot right next to the smelly dumpster, the one I figured everyone else avoided.

I reflected on something Zakiya had said in the basement that forced me to call an audible. We were still going to get the sniper rifle we needed to set up our trap. But something slightly more pressing had to be done first.

I drove to West Outer Drive, to a long brick single-story office building inspired classic Colonial design. White doors, plantation shutters, and exterior lights in imitation of the old oil lamps was supposed to create the illusion that they were long established and dependable. The stake out front hung a shingle for Waterson Realty.

I cut the motor, gave Zakiya the one-minute finger, then switched it to ten. I didn't expect this to go smoothly.

I pushed through the doors and stepped into a well-lit reception area with blue carpet and brown leather wingchairs, mahogany furniture. I stood in the entrance for a moment, scanning the layout, searching for cameras and anyone working security. I hoped I wouldn't have to tear shit up, but that was always a possibility when it came to me.

The white guy at the front desk had looked me up and down with skepticism, but put on a plastic smile when he asked me if I had an appointment. We both knew I didn't. I was in a dark hoodie, wrinkled sweatpants, and muddy boots. Looking like a nigga who'd just got hit by a car, not one ready to cash out on a three-million-dollar listing.

I stormed off towards a door at the rear where I figured the offices were, but the receptionist was mouthing some more shit about No Walk-ins, then stood up like he was about to stop me. Wasn't about to happen. Not at five-foot-ten and hardly pushing 170.

I turned and froze him with a death glare. I shook my head, warned him with my eyes not to fuck up his life. He clearly got the message from the way he stood there rooted to the floor. But then I saw him glance at the office's landline. I drew his attention back to me, promised him that calling the police would only get him fucked up worse. Ninety percent of communication is nonverbal. He seemed to get the message.

At the rear of the reception area was a narrow hall with doors on either side. The doors had nameplates in various colors: imitation bronze, silver, and gold. My guess was that said something about your status within the company.

I came to a door hanging a silver nameplate stenciled with: ALEXIS COCKBURN—a last name that I knew got her teased in school and was just a bad look for a woman. I didn't bother to knock, because no tiny display of etiquette was going to help me anyway. I threw open the door like someone announcing their entrance.

Alexis was behind her desk with an older white lady, mid-fifties, seated across from her. Both ladies looked to my interruption wearing confusion and irritation like masks. But when my size and overall demeanor registered with the elder, irritation melted into a primal fear.

Lexy's face went from mild irritation and confusion to recognition, as she sprang to her feet. Then I watched her expression intensify to some combination of fury and fright. She shot daggers at me, but underneath that was a quiet appeal for me not to embarrass her.

I didn't know if the white lady sitting with her was a superior, a colleague, or a client. Really didn't give a fuck, either. Whatever this meeting was about, I'd just adjourned it. I stood to the left of the open door, silently inviting the bitch to beat it.

Lexy quickly jumped in and used words to do what I was seconds away from doing with my muscles. "Forgive me, Farrah, I'm so sorry about this. It's a family emergency. If you could just give me five minutes to deal with this."

The woman excused herself without comment but stared at me warily. She inched her way towards the door slowly, giving me a wide berth. She treated me like I was a pit bull without a leash. Once she was clear of me, she practically sprinted down the hall. I slammed the door, hopefully loud enough to make a statement.

I imagined it was a good-sized office, about twenty by forty feet long—never worked in any type of corporate setting, so I couldn't be sure. Large windows that unfortunately only looked out on the back alley and the rear of a Foot Locker. The same ubiquitous royal blue carpet ran throughout the entire building, but the overuse of dark wood made her office appear masculine. As I would expect, she had adorned the space with African art: tribal masks hung on either side of the large bookshelf behind her desk, ten-inch figurines in the shape of Egyptian gods served as bookends. The real estate license she'd earned and the master's degree she finally completed hung side by side on the wall, obvious points of pride.

I could tell from the way Miss Cockburn glared at me that she had a thousand questions. Showing up at the house for those once-a-month drop-offs was tense enough, and the most she ever wanted to see of me. So pulling up to her job was well beyond those unspoken boundaries we'd set in place a year prior.

She dropped herself into her seat, flopped down hard. She seemed to accept that this was going to happen, right here, right now, regardless of how she felt about it.

"Get the fuck outta here, Silence!" she mouthed. "That was the branch manager. You trying to get me fired?"

There was a stationery pad on the desk with her own personalized letterhead. Luckily, I wouldn't need it.

I pushed my hands forward, palms up, fingers curled, then pulled them back into me. Next, I brought the fingertips together of both my hands, palms facing each other, forming the top side of a triangle. I pulled my hands apart, then brought them down in straight vertical columns.

"Home?" She looked at me quizzically. "You came through here like this because you're in the market for a house?"

I was so rarely able to use it lately that my signing was rusty, but my sloppy hand formations and delayed responses finally conveyed that it was her home that I was referring to. She needed to go there, get her daughter, pack some shit, and be on her way out of town by tonight.

The way she rolled her eyes at me brought back memories. Back when we were two sixty-degree edges of a love triangle. "So I guess all this wild-ass thug shit you out here doing in the streets about to blow back on me and my family."

Chapter Fifty-two

"Boy, I got a job, relationships, obligations. I can't just pack up and leave town at the drop of a hat. Just 'cause you live like some bum with a shopping cart."

That twisted my face up. I understood what she meant in terms of my life being transient: I had no social media accounts, no real paper identity, and wasn't connected to anything that I couldn't walk away from in ten minutes. The bum comparison just stung a little bit because I owned a nice home, could drive whatever I wanted, and was getting money out here.

With my hands, I apologized for potentially putting her in the mix, but also expressed how important it was that she listened to me. Personal attachments were a liability in the game we played, and I knew for a fact that predators often exploited those weaknesses. I'd been taught to do the same. I didn't beg, just spent several minutes urgently imploring that she needed to leave home. I conceded that she didn't have to go far, somewhere outside of Metro Detroit should suffice. And she wouldn't have to stay long, because I planned on having this Muuaji shit wrapped up in a day or two—one way or another. Either I'd be dead, or he would.

Lexy finally surrendered, but only reluctantly. She confessed to having a few vacation days in her bank, even though the timing was poor. She claimed that meeting I interrupted was due to her being in the middle of closing on a property that would earn her a high five-figure commission.

"I just gotta figure out what excuse I'm gone tell my man." She delivered that with calculation. Even though we shared a child, this was the first conversation of any real significance we'd had since I learned she was pregnant. Lexy didn't want me to get it twisted and start thinking that being on agreeable terms meant we were fucking again.

I reiterated that she would only have to lay low for a day or two. But learning about that real estate deal did bring me to the second reason I was there.

I made the sign for house again. Then I curled my fingers into a circle, palms up, and snatched my hands back to me.

"You want me to give you a house? This is the place you come when you're actually looking to spend money. If you want something for free, go apply for Section Eight."

I wasn't looking to buy or lease. I just needed to borrow one of her unsold properties. A place where I could squat for a few days. I was hoping for a spot out in the boonies, rural, secluded, not too close to any nosy neighbors.

She stared at me in disbelief. "You asking me to risk my job for you. We only deal in luxury listings. Silence, shit blows up, people die around you. You think I'm gonna hand you the keys to a seven-figure house that I'm responsible for?"

I informed her that was exactly what I wanted. And exactly what she was going to do, because she owed me that much. In fact, she owed me a lot more, but I'd let her settle the bill for the low.

I simply asked if her new boyfriend ever asked about that tattoo on her big, beautiful ass.

When I first met Alexis Cockburn, she was wearing a neon-blue weave, and her work attire consisted of a fishnet bodystocking. Back then, she went by Lexy Bands, aka The Booty Queen.

All the members of the BANDS Society had the logo tatted somewhere on their body. She had once been co-captain in this all-female group of adult entertainers.

Her new man was a straightlaced dentist, church-going, looked like he didn't have a street bone in his body. I merely hinted that he might feel some type of way at learning that his girl used to shake ass and sell pussy.

I knew about her new fella because I know how to do recon. That's how I knew where she worked, just like I also knew where her mother stay. I read the look on her face and let her know that I wasn't stalking her, just keeping tabs on the mother of my child.

"You thought you was gone come in here and blackmail me on some soap opera shit?" She laughed in my face. "Fuck you nigga, tell 'em! You can show his ass the video if you got it. I stand on every decision I made, and ain't ashamed of none of 'em."

I proved her ass wrong with my very next question.

I wagged the index finger on my right hand. Then with the same hand, I made a quick salute from my right temple to the crook of my bent left arm.

Her eyes widened. My old friend had been raised by a deaf uncle, so she knew American Sign Language better than me.

I asked her where the fuck is my son. I added the curse words for emphasis.

Chapter Fifty-three

I understood that I was a piece of shit for trying to run a black-mail play, but this bitch was in no position to preach. Lexy's energy changed faster than a thrown switch. She got off all that I-don't-give-a-fuck shit, and I saw some of that shame that she swore she didn't have.

People had a tendency to think that deaf means dumb. It was time for her to finally confess what I'd already figured out three months ago. There had been no pictures or videos posted on Facebook, no car seat in the back of her Cadillac XT-6. When I had watched the house, there was no sight of her coming or going with a baby bundle or a diaper bag. My expression was deadly serious, and I let her know it was time to stop playing with me. I had started those monthly drop-offs when I first learned she was pregnant and had faithfully kept them going for the past year. Even after three months ago, when she was supposed to have given birth but never came home with a baby, I was still at her door handing her a bag.

"I don't know his name or where he's at. You know how the rules are. I was just told he was with a good family." Her eyes shied away from mine. "I know I should've told you."

She goddamn right she should've told me. I know we never had much of a relationship, had only fucked twice. And that her whole pregnancy had been somebody else's backfired plan to try to use a baby to trap me. But still, as the father, I had a right to be a part of that decision.

I had come home thirteen months ago on a mission to find my best friend's killer, a conspiracy that pointed back to his own son and little sister. Quianna had bet that by the time I figured out what she had done, she would be protected by my love for her, and by the fact she was carrying my son.

Lexy had been lovers and best friends with Quianna, but she hadn't wanted a child with me, any more than I wanted one with her. But Lexy had ultimately went along with the play because she feared losing Quianna. Then when the whole thing fell apart, and Quianna went into hiding without taking Lexy with her, she gave away my son like a bad Christmas present.

I could see that bringing all this up had touched a nerve. Lexy glared at me from across the desk, fuming. "It was you. If you wouldn't have ever got out. Or just stayed out our lives."

What Lexy didn't understand was that Quianna never loved her. Had only used her as bait and a distraction to keep me from solving her brother's murder. I could've signed that to her, but I didn't see any point in twisting the knife.

I honestly didn't come here with the intent of playing dirty. I had hoped to appeal to Lexy as mutual victims of the same woman's manipulation. Seeing her longing disturbed me, because it so closely mirrored my own. Even with what she'd done to each of us, neither was over Quianna. The little hazel-eyed witch still had both of us helplessly trapped under her spell.

Lexy confessed, "Sometimes when we were in bed together, I would just stare at her. The way you could just get lost in her eyes. It was non-sexual. She was beautiful like a sunset or a painting."

This wasn't cap. Quianna was a bad muthafucka by anyone's standards. A short hazel-eyed mulatto with a face made for *Vogue* and body made for Magic City. She was the type of bad where she could've easily had two million followers on Instagram if she wanted.

But even as her lover, Lexy would never experience Quianna's real gift. That girl had pussy so good that if you threw it in the air, it wouldn't turn into sunshine, it would turn into Heaven. Being in the streets, I rarely get to use words like *spectacular* or *fantastic*, but there were few others to describe that magic box my other baby momma had between her thighs.

I signed, "There was always this part of Quianna that was threatened by you." Lexy looked at me like she couldn't believe that.

I assured her that it was true. I explained to Lexy that the manipulative little bitch had chosen her simply because she knew my fetish for thick dark-skinned girls. Of all the girls in the BANDS Society, Quianna knew that Lexy would be the perfect distraction to keep me from solving Doc's murder. She was my ideal of feminine perfection. Quianna secretly feared that I would never be as attracted to her as I was to Lexy.

Lexy stared at me wearing a different type of disbelief. She was stunned beyond the ability to speak. So for a few seconds, we just sat there as two mutes.

I didn't communicate that with the intention of trying to score any points with her, just thought it was something she needed to know. This hadn't been cap, either. Her own beauty was right there on par with Quianna. The only difference was a matter of personal taste: Quianna was French vanilla, while Lexy was dark chocolate.

Lexy just rolled her eyes at me. "Every time I make up my mind to hate yo' ass, you turn around and do something like this."

I thought things between us were concluded when she got up and went to the door. I assumed it was to let me out. If she wasn't going to help me, then it really wasn't shit else to talk about. I felt like I had been in the same place for too long. Muuaji was still out there looking for me.

I didn't know what time it was when she twisted the lock in

the door, then pulled the curtains tight. Lexy gave me a look that I understood the meaning of. Then she definitely let me know what time it was when she stepped out her red bottoms, unzipped the back of her skirt, and fought the fabric over the wide spread of her hips. She shrugged off her jacket and blouse in one motion. After her bra, the stockings and black satin panties also came off as a set.

Lexy stood before me totally nude, hands on hips as if modeling for me. She looked like a vixen created for a video game by horny nerds. A cover-girl face with a slightly upturned nose that somehow fit her. Small upthrust tits with areolas that resembled Hershey kisses. Tiny waist, but her cartoonlike proportions might repel those who thought the ass wasn't real, even though I could personally vouch that it was.

I wasn't staring at her like she was a painting or a sunset. She was something I wanted to attack like a rabid pit bull. Something that I wanted to give pain and pleasure to in equal degrees.

I didn't realize my hand had drifted down to my dick. I couldn't tell you how long I'd been massaging it through my clothes when her smiling eyes lingered on the bulge in my sweats.

I knew this wasn't the time or place for this, but there had always been something about Lexy that was just irresistible to me. I convinced myself that I realistically could be dead later that day.

I stood up and approached her when she pushed me back. "What you think you doing?"

I gave her a look like *Shit, girl, you know what time it is.* But she slapped my hands away when I tried to touch her.

Her smile was playful. "Oh, did you think you was about to get some pussy?" She hastily collected the shed items off the floor and started to dress.

She found something comical about the disappointment I showed. I could only imagine that *What the fuck?* was written on my face.

"I just wanted to show you that I ain't let the figure fall off. I'm still the queen."

I could tell that through the clothes. Getting naked was just blatant dick-teasing, and should be at least a Class B felony.

I signed a reminder that she needed to lay low for a few days. Muuaji probably didn't know anything about her, but caution couldn't hurt.

"Oh, and before you go, you might want to do something about your little friend."

I looked down. My beast was bulging through the fabric of my loose sweatpants.

Chapter Fifty-four

I made it back to the Buick I left two blocks over, parked at the corner at an angle that gave Zakiya a view of anyone coming or going on the block. She was mugging me before I even jumped behind the wheel. I was only gone twenty minutes, but I had to imagine that it felt a lot longer being out in the open like that.

I could tell Zakiya was about to unload on me, but I held up and jingled a set of keys on a ring. It took a lot of reassurances for Lexy to let me borrow a property, and she only conceded to give me one that she had been trying to unload for six months. She made me promise her I wouldn't blow the house up. Lexy knew me.

Before we went to check the place out, I had to get me another personal phone. I had been using the Big Phone to communicate in person, but the people I cared about couldn't reach me on it. I hit the T-Mobile to get me an iPhone. Not the latest model, but two iterations back. New phone but the same old number. I wasn't with losing my 313 area code.

Next we hit a clothing store, because we had to change up out our shit. My hoodie was peppered with tiny crimson spots, blood spray. And Zakiya needed something more low-key. As much I enjoyed sneaking peeks of her in that black skin-tight catsuit, she couldn't keep walking around looking like a reject from *Blade 3.*

The afternoon temperature was starting to spike as we hit a unisex boutique on Greenfield Road. I left Zakiya to make her own choices, and that was a mistake. She was on the verge of selecting some tiny Ethika shorts and matching sports bra with SpongeBob on them. I used my phone to help explain that the point was trying not to draw attention to ourselves.

She looked at me quizzically. "But this is how the women here dress." I couldn't argue with that.

But still, I directed her towards something that wouldn't have every thirsty nigga in a three-block radius breaking their neck. Form-fitting jeans and decent top.

I took I-94 to the east end of the city, the dividing line between Detroit and Harper Woods. I navigated the surface streets near Moross Road until I came across a large shopping complex that housed eighteen different businesses. The largest and most popular store anchored the south end of complex. I stole the only available handicap spot from a Middle Eastern lady in a Dodge Caravan. She shot daggers at us as I led Zakiya to the front entrance.

I thought that High Score would be a cool name for a marijuana dispensary, but fat boy had wasted that potentially clever pun. After owning a strip club for a while, he had decided that he wanted to own a more family-friendly business. His answer was this 75,000-square-foot multi-entertainment facility that offered everything from bowling, karaoke, billiards, go-carting, and enough arcade games to look like a ten-year-old's vision of Heaven.

We walked in to enough bright colors and flashing lights to give an epileptic a seizure. It wasn't even particularly crowded at one o'clock on a weekday, but Zakiya still seemed stunned by the level of noise.

But I also saw the same wide-eyed fascination that many children must've wore their first time coming here. Church life may not be as sheltered as it was back in my day, but she had never experienced anything close to this. It was fun for me watching her react to some of the nicer things this world had to offer. It revealed a childlike innocence that all the rigorous training and nationalistic propaganda couldn't quite destroy. We walked through a maze of arcade games: fighting games, racing games, first-person shooters, countless others. And Zakiya's grown ass stared like she was dying to play every one.

We made our way to a service door at the rear that led to a hall. The hall housed the manager's office. I tested the knob, then pound on that door with the bottom of my fist like I was the police.

When I felt he was taking too long, I unlocked that bitch with my boot. The door swung in, hitting someone on the other side. I barraged my way inside the small office.

The dude on the other side had the size and look of security. He must've been on his way to answer the door when I kicked it in. He didn't appear to appreciate being hit by it.

He appreciated it less when I fucked his ass up with a quick four-piece. Two short jabs to the ribs, an uppercut followed by an elbow strike, put that nigga on his back and into an afternoon nap.

DelRay was down on one knee, right arm buried deep into an open safe. I drew my pistol to let him know to bring it out slowly. I was tired of fucking up people's workday. He pulled out an empty hand, and I made him seat himself on the sofa.

I peeked into the safe, saw the nine-millimeter Ruger still sleeved in a holster.

He frowned. "The fuck you expect? You kick in a nigga door like that."

But then I took a long, hard look at all the cash bricks stacked up inside. He was eating off all these spoiled-ass kids whose parents dropped down hundreds at a time for tokens and credits. I glanced back to DelRay, let him see the gleam in my eyes.

His fat face twisted into a comical expression. "C'mon, Sy man, we better than that. Big niggas gotta stick together." Then I made the comical face.

I was big. He was fat. At six-five, my 270 was all muscle. This muthafucka was six-foot-nine, close to 400, and built like a Black Michelin man.

If he was anybody else, I would've got him. I saw relief soften his features when I closed the door on his safe. I wasn't going to do him like that.

He looked to his mans on the floor. "Dude, why the fuck you always got to be so extra with shit? You could've stopped at the main desk out front and had them page me."

The fucked-up part was that I never once even considered that. Was I becoming so much of an asshole that violence was just my default setting? I tried to keep it out of my face but felt a little stupid for my entrance.

I didn't make introductions. He and Zakiya exchanged perfunctory head nods on their own. Then she helped herself to a handful of the miniature Reese's Cups that filled a punch bowl on his desk.

I used my new phone to inquire about our mutual friend. The last time I saw her, it had not been a good night for her.

"Bent but not broken. I done been by that girl side for twenty-five years, so I know her pedigree. Watched her go from being a shy stripper at sixteen surviving off Top Ramen, to a jack-girl robbing niggas for Rolexes, to a small club owner barely making it, all the way up to a corporate CEO on mogul status playing with a few hundred mil. Trust when I say, it ain't shit she can't come back from. She gone be okay." I didn't need to hear the words to feel the emotion. It sent chills through me and brought the hairs on my arms to attention.

I was also aware that the rich lady had fronted him the cash to start this little venture, but what I saw in his eyes went far beyond mere appreciation. It ran deeper than Love and was stronger than Loyalty. I knew in that moment if he was given the chance, he would lay down his life for her, and would feel honored for the privilege.

Doc was the only person who had earned a fraction of that from me, until I realized he wasn't one-hundred. Part of me thought he was a gullible fool; the other half secretly envied him. I briefly pondered what was worse: that fact that I didn't have one person who inspired that level of devotion in me, or that I couldn't think of one person who I inspired it in.

Chapter Fifty-five

We finally got down to business. I told DelRay that I needed a big gun, some shit that could bust a muthafucka's melon from three quarters of a mile away.

DelRay glared at me quizzically. "Bro, you already know I don't fuck around in that game no more. My brief little run as an arms dealer ended with some Colombians trying to stick a red-hot iron poker up my ass. I decided to keep that as an exit and left that game to people way tougher than me."

I already knew what the company line was. Them folks spooked him, then he tucked tail and left the game. This new squeaky-clean image he was trying to push for the sake of his benefactor. But my ear was to the streets, so I was also aware that he still had a toe in that dirty little pond. He was still moving guns. He just didn't want to fuck with me.

I pulled my phone out to let him read: *I'm here for bizness. Let's keep the personal shit out the way.* This polite little brush-off he was trying to pull was because he still felt some type of way about what happened between me and his boss. I can't keep apologizing for the same shit. I already told her a thousand times that I didn't know Caine was going to take her daughter.

DelRay stood up, chest-to-chest with me. He was one of the few people I had to look up to. "But you was secretly working for him the whole time you was supposed to be working for us."

He wasn't lying. Tuesday had come to me seeking protection, and I took the job knowing the full time that I already had a deal in place with her husband.

But I had to smirk at him using the word *us*. He never had the bag or the brand to hire a nigga like me. He was just an ex-bouncer getting a ride on the right pair of coattails.

He continued, "In fact, I bet you still working for him right now. Because when a muthafucka like him get his hooks into you, ain't no getting free."

I was about to prove him wrong in the next day or two.

DelRay stepped towards his desk. Plucked one of the Reese's miniatures out the bowl, then gave Zakiya a look like she needed to slow down. "I done sold you merchandise in the past, but that was before I knew you was a mercenary type of nigga, selling yourself to the highest bidder. I don't fuck with nobody who can switch sides that easy.

"I'm gone need a few hundred for the cost of fixing my door." Then he waved his hand dismissively, as if that were the end of the conversation.

I knew if DelRay was back in the gun business, his boss lady probably didn't know about it. She had worked too hard to scrub her gangster past, which included a name change, falsified birth records, and a whole new identity. Even though I knew she was still a gangster, she wouldn't have anybody in her immediate circle connected to anything illegal, especially nothing petty.

So I could've played the whole game of trying to blackmail him, but was getting sick of going through all that trouble. It was time to get back to my old way of doing things.

I still remembered the first time we sized each other up, and peeped back then from his walk that he had a problem with his left knee. Like so many people struggling with obesity, the excess weight wears down on the cartilage at the ends of the bones. So when I kicked him in the back of his left leg, he dropped to that knee.

I leveled my Walther P99 at his head. With my other hand, I used my phone to invite him to play a game of Would You Rather: *Would you rather a) sell me a gun and make a few thousand dollars on the transaction, or b) have me use this gun to redecorate your office?*

Twenty minutes later, we were at one of those storage facilities on the west side of the city. It was the type of place that had a few hundred of those cheap units that could be rented for about thirty dollars a month. I followed DelRay, who drove a triple-black Suburban XL, through a maze of identical tan structures lined with red doors. The streets were wide enough for two lanes of traffic, but narrow gangways separated the buildings on each side just wide enough for a person. We parked outside a unit close to its center, and DelRay let up a rolling door and revealed a redneck's wet dream.

Rifles galore: assault and hunting. Bolt-action, lever-action, semi-auto, and fully auto. Boxes were lined up against every wall, covering them end to end, and stacked on several tables. Many of the rifles were loose, just lying in careless piles. Everything was new and looked military grade. I was three feet from the entrance and could smell the gun oil.

Zakiya stood there with her mouth hanging open, looking like a kid on Christmas morning. I had to tap her arm and motion with my head. She slipped into the rear of the unit, then returned carrying a big, funny-looking rifle damn near longer than her. She boasted that it was the Accuracy International AXMC with a Vortex Razor scope—and said that like it was a bad muthafucka. According to her, it was one of the best modular rifles on the planet; the parts could be switched out in minutes to shoot either .338 or .308 rounds.

DelRay said, "I usually don't get too much business for precision rifles. You know these young niggas want ARs, Dreccos, shit they can just spray wildly and hope for the best. Two in two days is kinda weird."

I pulled my phone to ask DelRay who in the fuck did he sell another rifle to. I let him see in my face I wasn't trying to hear none of that client confidentiality shit.

"I didn't sell him nothing, but one of my little westside niggas I sold some choppers to tried to refer some dude. They say he been running up on anybody in the hood with a pistol, trying to get plugged in. I told them to keep my name out they mouth. That felt like some police shit."

Zakiya pulled her pistol right along with me, because we knew what it was.

DelRay saw this and thought we were on some bullshit with him. He started backpedaling towards the entrance of the storage unit.

I snatched his shirt collar and pulled back away from the open door just as a bullet hole appeared in the wall right where his big-ass head would've been.

Chapter Fifty-six

Zakiya and I were too careful about being followed, had been trained to survey our surroundings while in traffic to make sure the same car or cars were trailing us. Which was why I was certain we hadn't led him here.

Muuaji knew that once he had been betrayed by Zakiya, she would ultimately need guns, a sniper rifle in particular. So instead of trying to track us down, he had tracked down the one person he knew she would need and just waited for her to come to him. He'd probably been watching DelRay for a day now.

I saw wisps of dust high in the wall as two more slugs struck the concrete. Muuaji didn't appear to have the angle to get a shot directly into the unit without exposing himself to us. I placed him somewhere to the left.

We retreated into the rear, away from the open door. Only the space wasn't that deep. A bigger problem being that the storage unit only had one way in and one way out. We were trapped in a box.

But luckily, it was a box filled with guns.

I wasn't looking for anything in particular. I just snatched open the box closest to me, and it was love at first sight.

Even in the middle of firefight, this fat muthafucka was forever trying to sell. "The Sig Sauer MCX-Spear. That bitch right there is the civilian version of the Army's next generation squad weapon, the XM7. Baby girl spit .277 Fury rounds that punch through anything but Level Four body armor at a distance, accurate up to a thousand yards."

I shoved an extra magazine in my pocket and made my way towards the entrance while staying directly out of the doorway. I peeped my head out briefly and let that Sig go about four times. I didn't have eyes on Muuaji, just had to shoot something back to keep him honest. I assumed he had some type of idea of what was in here, so he was going to play us cautious.

Zakiya was at my back, still holding onto her Hecklar with that long AXMC hanging down her back with a carry strap. I gave her a look that told her to get ready.

DelRay read it. "The fuck y'all going out there for when we got everything we need right here?"

In the moment, I couldn't explain to him that while we had the numbers and the firepower, we were the ones pinned down. Having a million guns in here wouldn't mean shit if Muuaji tossed in one grenade.

I folded the stock and switched the weapon to fully automatic. I rolled out the door, firing down the drive lane to my left. Zakiya followed with the PV40. And I'm tripping because the big-time arms dealer didn't think to grab a gun for himself.

I spotted Muuaji about thirty yards away, concealing himself around the corner of the building. He ducked out of sight when I sent a few of those .277 Fury rounds in his direction. They gouged baseball-sized chunks out of the bricks.

DelRay scrambled for the Suburban, but Zakiya pushed him away from the driver's door. At any point, Muuaji could've planted a bomb on his SUV, and it could've detonated while we all tried to flee inside. She motioned for DelRay to run in the opposite direction of the shooter, and he made a face like he couldn't believe this. His big, slow ass lumbered off looking like his every movement was painful.

Zakiya was backing away and calling for me to follow, but I was pressing forward. I had Muuaji pinned down with this powerful Sig. I was trying to end this right then and there.

I emptied my mag, and he returned fire as I went to reload. I had to dive and crawl around the edge of an adjacent storage building. He peppered the ground near my feet with a FN SCAR 165.

I got to my feet, reloaded and ready. I looked back and saw Zakiya ducked behind the Buick. Her hand gestures were warning me not to do it. Waving for me to bring my ass.

But I ran at him low and fast, the Sig again chewing up the building. I was just around the same corner, sided against the wall, gun raised. I was waiting for him to peek his head out so I could erase his whole face.

I waited and waited until impatience got the best of me. I spun that corner firing down the narrow gangway. The rifle he had fired was on the ground, but he was gone.

I only thought he was. I looked up and saw Muuaji using his arms and legs to brace himself between the two buildings. By the time I brought up my rifle to fire, he was coming down on me.

I tried to bring my rifle up, but he batted down and caught me with a two-piece. I tried to bring it up again only to get it swatted back down and chopped in the throat.

At least he was fighting me for real now, and I took some type of victory in that.

He grabbed hold of the rifle and tried to keep me from bringing the muzzle toward him but was losing that fight. He was fast and he had skill, but wasn't about to outmuscle me.

But he angled himself on the side of the barrel and jammed his fingers into the trigger guard. He squeezed the last remaining rounds in the mag.

The Sig was useless, so I let go of it first and punched him in the side of the neck. I hooked him to the kidney and went for his jaw. I would've took his head off, but he slipped that punch.

He countered with his own rib shot that folded me. Then I took an elbow to the mouth. His style was too unorthodox, and he was lightning-fast. He landed a three-punch combo to the body and tried to finish it with a judo chop to my face. I avoided that but not the front kick it had set up. I took that to the sternum and got knocked back a few feet.

He appeared calm. "Do you even remember his name?"

I didn't know what the fuck he was talking about, and was too pissed off to learn. After that shit that happened in the gym, I wanted his ass. I came at him again with a much more ferocious attack.

But even in the narrow gangway, he was elusive. Of the few strikes that made contact, none were as flush as I would like. He either smothered my punches to rob their sting or just flat-out dodged them. I tried some low kicks to slow him down, but he was as surefooted as a mountain goat.

His counters were amazing, and I was unable to fend off most of them. He had the perfect response for my every effort. I was getting my ass kicked, and the margin was wide.

He kicked the already tenderized shin on my right leg, and that brought me to a kneel. I crossed my arms over before my face and blocked the several times he tried to ram his knee into my chin.

But being so low to the ground did play in my favor. I reached down and grabbed his weapon. He stepped on the barrel before I could get it up. Dropped the point of his elbow on the top of my head.

Muuaji asked, "Can you still see his face? Or did you really convince yourself of the lie?"

At that point, any form of technique was gone. I was all rage. I just wanted to get my hands on the nigga and tear him in half, even if I had to take some punishment.

I came in hot, taking every punch, chop, and elbow strike. I just kept pressing forward like a maniac from a scary movie.

Blows that should've put me down barely paused me. I was backing him up, and I saw something close to panic in his eyes.

But this wasn't from me. I glanced back and saw Zakiya at the far end of the gangway. She had the sniper rifle raised and was trying to line up a shot.

The problem was that I blocked her sight line, and I made no effort to get out the way. I wanted this muthafucka so bad that I couldn't let her kill him like that. It had to be me.

Muuaji was still backpedaling towards the corner, and I was this close to getting my hands on him. He turned to run, and when I gave chase, he stopped abruptly and kicked me right in the nuts.

Chapter Fifty-seven

Muuaji bent the corner and was gone. Zakiya never had the chance to get off a shot.

I slumped against the wall and cradled my agony. Tears took the world out of focus. It was just a taste of my own medicine, but it still went down bitter. Zakiya had to help me to the car—I was walking slow, stooped over like an old man.

DelRay's fat ass had tried to climb an eight-foot fence at the rear of the storage yard. Failed at that, then had opted to hide behind a nearby dumpster. When the drama was over, he appeared smelling of old fish grease and cat piss.

Zakiya spent a few minutes inspecting the underbelly of his Suburban, then gave him a nod. She assured him that Muuaji hadn't planted a device on it. But DelRay still made certain to stand back at least twenty feet before hitting that remote start. I couldn't fault him for that.

But I damn sure could when he came at me for his payment. He was the one who brought Muuaji here and damn near got us killed. Zakiya laid that AXMC in the trunk right along with my new Sig Sauer. We grabbed extra ammo for both out the storage unit and counted his ass lucky that I didn't take more than that.

On the way home, I texted Zakiya to stop at any store and get some ice for my balls. She ignored my request and purposely drove over the city's deepest potholes. "We should hurry and get back to your house."

I knew she had an attitude, because she wanted me to run, but I wasn't hearing that shit, even if I had working ears. All we been doing is running and hiding from this muthafucka, and I'm tired of it.

"We had our chance to take him out, but you ruined my shot. We cannot guarantee we will get another."

I just turned away from her lips, didn't bother to read any more.

I was lost in my own thoughts, revisiting my encounter with Muuaji, when my phone started to buzz in my pocket. There was only a short list of people who had my number. I directed Zakiya into a detour from home. She was getting better at using my hand signals to navigate. Two fingers followed by two waves meant two miles down, just as two fingers followed by a single wave meant another two traffic lights.

Bates chose to meet at a coin car wash near the Lodge Freeway. He didn't want me coming back to his house, and I damn sure wasn't going to the station. His black and gray cruiser was slotted in the center carport. Zakiya glared at me skeptical when I had her pull into the one to his left.

I wasn't sure what she was thinking, but I had to let her know this ain't that. I was coming to get information, not leak it.

I left her in the Buick and limped over to the next stall, still cradling my nuts. I made sure my hood was up for fear of somebody seeing me jump into his passenger seat.

He looked at me curiously. "You alright? You're walking like you got a hernia."

I waved him off even as I grimaced trying to adjust myself in my boxers.

"Look, I had to call nearly two dozen law enforcement agencies all over the country. I had to beg, promise to name my first-born son after folks. A friend of mine in the Vegas DEA even got dibs on my organs if something happens to me."

I didn't give a fuck about all his labor pains. I just wanted the baby.

Bates pulled up a screen on his phone that was filled with notes. "There's a DA out in Seattle who's really got a hard-on for your old man. He's been trying to build a case against the UOTA for years. I get the impression he's got a whiteboard with a flow-chart of the whole organization at home in his living room. But he's super pissed, because his bosses won't let him off the leash. I'm not totally sure what it means to be a sovereign citizen, but the last time he took your people to court, he got handed his ass, and a judge lost his bench."

That sounds about right. My father might be nutty as a Payday, but you'll find few people in this world who know more about the deeper secrets of constitutional law. That same knowledge allowed him to legally form his own twenty-acre independent nation right in the middle of Washington state.

"Well, when I finally get a hold of this guy, I pretend I'm working a case on this end that might tie in. I couldn't get him to shut up. He's got them involved in pretty much anything you can think of: gun smuggling, child endangerment, murder, sex trafficking, domestic terrorism."

I knew for a fact they were guilty of all the other shit. Sex trafficking was the one that jumped out at me. Life in the church was weird, but not freaky weird.

"Well, according to him, the UOTA has recently gotten into the business of kidnapping kids. Boys and girls all around the country between eleven and sixteen have been disappearing, and nobody's talking about it."

Bates's eyes got wide, preparing me for the meat in this dish. "This next part is going to sound like something from a sci-fi series, but this guy swears that these aren't just your run-of-the-mill, creepy-guy-in-Ford-panel-van type of abductions. When the kid goes missing, everything about them vanishes, too. Records, personal property, social media accounts—entire archive and digital footprint. It's like they never existed.

"And if you wanna crank the weird factor up another ten notches. The families of these victims aren't even reporting the crimes—always some friend or neighbor. Parents and siblings are just going on with their lives. It's like even the memory of that person is getting erased."

Chapter Fifty-eight

Before we separated at the car wash, Lieutenant Bates commented that him coming through with info made us even. I had to let him know that he didn't get to decide that.

I alerted Zakiya to the change of plans—instead of going back to my house, we going to check out the place Lexy had loaned to me. It was a twenty-minute drive up I-75 North, during which time we were overtaken by a thunderstorm that moved in from the south. The city became a dark place of monochromatic gray. The Buick's high beams silvered the rain that fell on us in diagonal sheets.

There wasn't much communication between me and Zakiya during the ride. I punched the address Lexy gave into my phone, then let the voice from Google Maps navigate for Zakiya. I spent most of the trip behind closed lids, wrapped in a cocoon of my own thoughts and pains. I only interrupted the little robot bitch to point Zakiya towards a KFC.

We finally reached the address, way out on Long Lake Road in Bloomfield Hills. When we pulled up, I saw why Lexy was having a hard time moving the property.

It was a corner house on a tucked-off block surrounded by forest. Three-story, Tudor-inspired, with round turrets that made you think of a miniature castle.

Only the king had long abandoned the throne. It was a fixer-upper. The lawn was over a foot high and choked with weeds, and the bushes were like ungroomed animals. All the windows were covered with plywood. A tarp covered half of the roof. Scaffolding was built on the south wall of the structure, as if somebody had started the renovation process, then quit part way into it. The money probably got funny—looked like it was going to take 100K just to touch up that three-car garage.

But we went inside and were surprised by a clean and livable space. Four bedrooms, three baths. It was furnished, but whoever bought the place was definitely going to need an interior decorator to come in and update the old Empire décor from the 70s. The kitchen was also in desperate need of being modernized, but I tested the sink to find running water. There was no electricity and no gas. I didn't think Zakiya was above taking a cold shower as long as she could flush the toilet.

She said, "This place would make a good fallback position if we need it, but we really should get back to your home. It is not safe to be away for too long." That wasn't about to happen.

Plus, I had already texted Kierra in the car just to check on what was happening at the house. Other than a few complaints about Amelia's attitude, there was really nothing to report. Kierra knew my security almost as well as I did. I told her to keep my shit locked down tight.

For some reason, Zakiya and I avoided the furniture, as if that would minimize our presence. We sat on the floor picnic-style to have our meal. Zakiya removed the PV40 from her hip and lay it next to her. While she wasn't looking, I stealthily pushed the pistol a few feet away from her hand.

I was sore, irritable, and my nuts felt the size of grapefruits, but I still had an appetite. I started in on that KFC. I spent ten minutes trying to convince Zakiya it was safe before I gave up.

Her wary eyes bounced from me to the bucket as I devoured two thighs and a breast.

"Chifu says the food here is poison. Filled with chemicals designed to keep the African in a state of servitude." I waved her off.

I remembered that whole lecture from my childhood. Let the old man tell it, this ubiquitous shadow organization that secretly ran the world had tainted all the food coming to the ghetto with special RNA compounds that specially targets African American genes. We were pumped with steroids to increase our athletic prowess because we made them billions in sports, but we were also given substances that stunted our cognitive faculties, made us more prone to drug addiction and violence. Then, just to keep our households divided, the Black woman was given chemicals to make her overdeveloped and sexually hyperactive, ready to fuck any partner who smiled at them.

And that had made perfect sense to me back when I was still in the church, gullible as to exactly how big the world was. Definitely, back before I actually tasted a double Whopper with cheese.

I watched as Zakiya's resistance slowly eroded in the face of her mounting hunger. She eventually chanced a small, cautious sampling of the mashed potatoes. Within minutes of that, she had plucked a drumstick out the bucket and was tearing into that like something voracious.

Once I was full, I adjusted myself on the floor so I could rest with my back against the sofa, only the movement caused pain to knife through my ribs. Zakiya saw me wince, stared at my bloodied lip. I could tell that certain parts of my face had started to swell.

"Some people can be warned that fire is hot. Some have to actually touch the flames."

The bruises from the experience were well worth the wisdom gained. Muuaji was good—no, he was exceptional, easily the most talented hand-to-hand fighter I'd ever seen. But I had mentally recorded the entire fight and was aware of his speed and technique now. I knew I could beat him. And that's what I was going to do the next time we fought.

I used my phone to relay to Zakiya, but she seemed doubtful. "I apologize, because I honestly thought he would've killed you in seconds. You get some credit for hanging in there with him, but let's not pretend you weren't losing. And if I hadn't shown up, he would've ended you.

"That's why you should've got out of the way and let me take the shot. This already could be over."

Zakiya attacked another biscuit while I typed something else I learned from my encounter. I let her read that off my phone.

"You figured out who Muuaji is and why he wants to kill you."

And boy, did he have a damn good reason.

The next thing I typed was something I'd never shared with anyone. I told her about my first kill.

Chapter Fifty-nine

The last time I had been sent out on wilderness training was brutal. The instructors had purposely chosen a particularly rough part of the Cascade mountain range to test us: rocky terrain, very little vegetation, far from a water supply. There was eight of us, starting from the age of eleven, and I might've been the oldest at sixteen. We'd been taught in class how to build a camp, then forage for the supplies to make simple tools and weapons. The problem was that the area was practically devoid of wildlife. That meant no animals to hunt for food and fur. So after two weeks of surviving off of small game like squirrels and the occasional rabbit, we were all cold and hungry as fuck.

This one kid just wasn't supposed to be in a test this difficult. You just saw from the start that he didn't have it—he might've been twelve or thirteen, small even for his age. Morale was already circling the drain, and his constant whining and complaining was beginning to cause infighting.

Early one morning, I took him with me, presumably to go on a scouting mission. I snapped his neck and threw him into a ravine. When I came back alone, I offered no explanations and was asked no questions.

It was the first time since losing my hearing that my father showed any measure of pride in me. Said I demonstrated true leadership skills, made the necessary sacrifice and achieved the objective. I had been busting my ass for years just for that little pat on the back. But when I finally got it, I only felt resentment because of what I had to go through to get it.

Right after that, my mother had left, and it seemed like a pretty good time for me to follow. But in hindsight, I probably would've left anyway, even if she hadn't.

"Muuaji was somebody connected to the boy. Who knew what you did and had been waiting all this time for his revenge. I was supposed to do this mission alone, but he had insisted on coming."

And that, as much as the pain, was the reason for the strain on my face a few minutes earlier. I was reaching back through clouds of weed smoke fogging my memory to recall that the boy did have an older brother close to my age.

But dude wasn't cut like that, wasn't even a low-tier warrior, let alone Shango class. I remembered him working the farm and helping to serve at mealtimes.

"You better than anyone should know what the proper motivation can do. Desire for your father's approval led you to surpass every other warrior in the tribe. Just as desire for revenge has led a farmer who wasn't even in warrior training to become one of the best in Shango. Second only to me."

Zakiya gave me a playful little smirk that I couldn't return. Now that we knew why Muuaji was there, it was time to find out about her.

When I drew the Walther, Zakiya reached for her waist on instinct. She was shocked to see her Hecklar already laying on my lap. Her eyes became narrow slits as she glared at me from over the barrel.

She had finessed me, and my stupid ass had actually taken her back to my house. Everything she had been doing had only been about her ultimately getting closer to her target. And this whole time, I had been thinking that was Amelia.

"So you're back to not trusting me again?"

I never trusted her. I was keeping my enemies close, and I hadn't killed her because she was useful.

I held the question up on my screen: *What do you want with Antwon?* Then I put the barrel of P99 right between her eyes.

It never made sense to me that they would come after Amelia for her political views. She was just a local journalist. It made more sense for them to target somebody larger, nationally syndicated who has a broader audience.

But then again, it made no sense for them to target Antwon, either. I needed to know why was the UOTA taking kids. And why Antwon in particular.

"What difference does it make? I can assume you brought me here to kill me anyway."

She could miss me with all that tough shit. I looked into the eyes of too many people before I took their lives. Zakiya was no coward, but not as ready to die as she thought she was.

I showed her the eyes of a killer losing patience.

"I told you from the start that this is about good versus evil. There is a war going on that you cannot see. And it is for the souls of our children."

I didn't have to type it. Zakiya should've read in my demeanor that I wasn't in the mood to hear nothing about witches, demons, and blood moons. If she didn't give me the truth without all that Stephen King bullshit, I was going to blow her brains out right here, right now. I cocked the pistol. It was the most articulate warning I could give that this was her absolute last chance.

"Back in West Africa, after being converted by the colonizers, many tribal chiefs unwittingly sold their kinsmen into slavery. The devils convinced them that they were agents of God. And that the Africans leaving on the ships were headed for salvation."

I was versed in our history, but that still creased my forehead. Were these kids being sold into slavery?

"I am a soldier, and soldiers only follow orders. But I can only tell you that they only seek the one-percentile—the best and the brightest. They want to corrupt them early."

But according to Bates, the UOTA was the ones out here taking children. I needed her to make that make sense.

"We are protecting them."

I asked her from who.

"From their parents."

I called bullshit. Amelia was kind of hard on Antwon in terms of wanting him to toughen up and lose weight, but I didn't see anything to indicate that she was abusive.

She stared at me defiantly. "I am here to save the boy."

We became locked in a staring match, as I tried to make sense of this.

"Time is running out, Lutalo. The sacrifice is near. Muuaji now knows what we are planning. Do you think that makes him more or less dangerous?"

She wasn't going to keep playing the we-need-each-other card. We both knew how this was going to end. I wasn't going back to the church, and I wasn't letting her kill Amelia.

Then a thought hit me like a thunderbolt. I sat up so quickly that it drew Zakiya's attention. She looked at me confused as I wore a strained face, struggling to get to my feet. I was slowed by the aches and pains.

I motioned for her to hurry. We had to leave, and right now.

I cursed myself for not seeing the shit sooner.

Chapter Sixty

I opted to drive. I came back down I-75 doing a hundred. The rain had stopped, but the pavement was still wet, six-inch-deep puddles in some places. I had hydroplaned a few times, skidded along without really having control of the Buick. An errant bump would've had me plowing the Buick into the concrete divider.

I was driving with one hand, trying to text Lexy with the other. She wouldn't respond. I was hoping like hell she listened to me and got out of Dodge.

The thought that had me so panicked was realizing that Muuaji had come here seeking revenge. If I had taken somebody from him that he loved, as we figured. True revenge would not be killing me. He would go after somebody close.

The problem was that I didn't really have anybody that close to me. I didn't even know where my first baby momma was at. Lexy had given away the child, but she was the closest thing to family.

I cut what was typically a half-hour drive to eighteen minutes. I sped over the surface streets, blowing through red lights and treating stop signs like they were suggestions. I hit the block and was pissed when I saw the white XT6 parked in the driveway. I had told her she needed to leave; now I was going to have to make her.

I parked in front of the house, then beat on her front door like I had a search warrant. Dude from the upstairs flat peeked his head out to be nosy. When he saw Zakiya and me standing on the porch with pistols in hand, he quickly closed it back, rightly deciding to mind his own damn business.

I was this close to kicking that bitch in when the door was snatched open. It was the dude that I already peeped was Lexy's man, the straightlaced dentist. He seemed to have a bit of an attitude and tried to ask me something, but I wasn't paying attention. I just moved his ass out the way as I let myself inside.

I stepped into a modernized version of the house I had lived in as a teen. The old floral-printed sofa had been replaced with a sleek leather couch, carpet by hardwood floors, the floor-model box television by 70-inch flatscreen. And most notably, all the framed photos of my family with African art.

I was halfway through the living room when he tried to grab my arm. A natural response to an intruder, but a mistake. I clocked this lame ass in the mouth with the butt of the Walther. He stumbled back into the sofa cupping his face, then spit out a broken tooth. Maybe he could do oral surgery on himself.

Lexy appeared in the entrance to the dining room, and I gave her a look like what the fuck was she still doing there. She saw her man writhing on the couch, cupping his bloodied mouth, and started to scream at me.

"Dammit, Silence, you can't just come in my house and put your hands on people!"

I ignored that shit. I went past her, into her daughter's room. Scooped little Kiyuana into my arms and carried her towards the entrance. Lexy blocked me at the door, asked what the fuck I was doing.

I told her in so many words that either she was going to get her daughter to someplace safe or I was going to do it.

"Silence, I don't know who the fuck you think you is. This is my child."

I let her see how few fucks I gave. I wasn't trying to see another kid get hurt because of my bullshit.

"I know what I said at the office, but I can't just leave like that."

The girl started to cry and squirm in my arms, wanting her mother. I just stood in the doorway, silently giving Lexy a choice.

I didn't even give her a chance to pack an overnight bag. I just peeled half of the ten grand I had brought to buy Zakiya's rifle.

A minute later, I was escorting them to the car with my pistol out. Zakiya held them back while I checked out the Cadillac to make sure it wasn't wired for explosives. Once I was sure it was clean, I helped Lexy to put her daughter in the back seat. Her boyfriend climbed into the passenger seat, still holding his mouth, trying to mug me.

Before Lexy pulled off, she screamed at me: "I hate you. Everything in my life has been a mess since I met you. Don't bring yo' ass around me and my daughter ever!"

Understood and agreed. She could hate me all she wanted, as long as she did it from someplace safe. I felt as much relief as she felt anger, watching the white Cadillac SUV back out the driveway and turn up the block.

She paused at the stop sign at the corner, next to the old Plymouth that had been parked there since I was a kid.

The Plymouth erupted, windows shattered, and the body seemed to tear itself apart.

Even halfway up the block, we felt the impact. Tiny bits of shrapnel stung me and took me off my feet. Zakiya ducked down and covered her head.

The blast seemed to tear through the Cadillac. Lexy's SUV almost turned onto its side. It went up on two wheels before crashing back down. It rolled through the intersection at the corner before it was halted by a fire hydrant across the street.

A motorcycle sped off along the side street. His face was concealed behind a helmet, but I didn't need to see him to know it was Muuaji.

I took off up the street, already knowing it was too late.

I ran up the block, still limping a bit from my sore testicles. I reached the corner and nearly slipped in the debris that covered the street. The ground was littered with tiny steel ball bearings.

I approached the Cadillac slowly, as the engine smoked and leaked fluids. The body had been perforated with holes.

I peeked through the window, hoping against hope that they had survived.

But again, my prayers were ignored.

Lexy's head was resting against the airbag, her eyes open but unmoving. The unnamed boyfriend was facing the passenger window, but I saw enough blood to know he didn't make it.

Most of my hope had been for Kiyuana. The girl was stretched lengthwise across the rear bench seat. Eyes closed, looking peaceful, but not asleep.

Chapter Sixty-one

I headed back to the house, driving angry, snatching the wheel for every turn. Zakiya had tried to console me, but there wasn't much she could say. More innocent people were dead because of their connection to me. And this time, a little girl had been more than shot.

Muuaji had turned the old Plymouth into a claymore mine. The bomb wasn't that powerful, but its kill radius was controlled by the steel ball bearings it was packed with. The blast was funneled out to the side of the car, toward anything in the street parked next to it.

What was worse was that he could've set that bomb off any time Lexy stopped at that corner. He had purposely waited for me, had wanted me to see it happen. Had made me be responsible by triggering me to respond.

When I reached the house, Amelia was grilling Antwon about something, and Kierra came to me with a complaint that she didn't even get off her lips. It was clear to everybody I was in a foul mood. Rather than having everybody stay clear of me, I chose to stay clear of them.

Except for Amelia. I pulled her into my room so we could talk alone. I had questions that needed answering. It wasn't like I just found this job on Indeed. I wanted to know what was her connection to my boss.

Amelia looked at me quizzically. "I have never heard of Sebastian Caine. Is he somebody I should know?"

I studied her body language; she didn't appear to be lying. She probably didn't know him, because he dealt with people directly. She'd probably never heard of him, since she doesn't live in the criminal world.

But this was a very serious man who'd come in person to have me take this case. The fact couldn't count as trivial or coincidental.

"You're growing quite attached to the girl who wants to kill me."

I shared with Amelia my doubts that this was even about her.

I went into the basement and started taking my frustration out on the heavy bag. I found punching on shit to be more of a productive outlet than crying. Anger more productive than guilt.

Zakiya was already down there. She just watched me for a moment, then came and stood next to me. Watched me for a moment longer, then pushed me aside. She started working the bag with a flurry of punches and kicks.

"You do alright with those outdated moves, but you need to be faster, better footwork. After you left, we incorporated more African fighting styles: Dambe and Capoeira." Most people associate Capoeira dance fighting with Brazil, but it was actually originated by African slaves.

"It is why we do not train with heavy weights in Shango. These newer techniques require you to be more flexible. You have added power, but at the cost of speed and fluidity. This is why Muuaji can predict and counter you so easily. You are too stiff and slow."

She had the shot at the storage facility, and I stopped her from taking it. This was on me because Muuaji would already be dead.

Zakiya could've hit me with *I-told-you-so*s but decided to go the other way and high-road me.

"The new way of training is to turn an opponent's advantages into yours."

Because in sparring with her and during my two encounters with Muuaji, it was the first time that I actually felt that my size was a detriment.

Zakiya began to move her body to an inaudible rhythm. "Dance with me."

What we did wasn't exactly sparring. She showed me the adaptations of Capoeira and Dambe being taught in the UOTA. I stood at her side and tried to mimic her moves. It was only then that I realized how stiff I really was.

I don't know how long we spent down there training when the power suddenly went out.

When the lights died in the basement, my first thought was that it could've just been something overloading the circuit breaker. And I tried to convince myself of this, even though there was nothing down there drawing that much power. The was no light filtered down the stairs from the side door landing and kitchen, letting me know that it was more than just a single room. Power had been lost to the whole house.

I waited for my backup generator to switch on, but it never happened. I had spent $15,000 on one of the most powerful standby generators on the market, and another seven to have it installed. In the event of a blackout, my shit was supposed to switch on in seconds. I waited nearly two minutes, and we were still in the dark.

I felt my way over to the circuit breaker, started hitting switches with no effect.

I darted up the stairs and peeked out the kitchen windows and then the living room's. All my neighbors on both sides of the block had light glowing at their windows.

I went into my office to check the monitors on my computer.

Like any desktop, mine came with an internal battery that permitted it to work untethered to an outside power source.

I clicked on my surveillance cameras to see what the hell was going on. All my screens were static.

I didn't need to see anymore. I grabbed a flashlight, ran back to the basement. My weapons locker was in a small storage room near my water heater. Behind a door that I usually kept locked. I came upstairs with an armful of guns.

I gave Zakiya my Tavor X95 .300, an Israeli-made semi-auto that looked like some shit from a video game. I grabbed my new favorite toy: the Sig Sauer MCX-Spear I got from DelRay. I even handed out small lightweight pistols to Kierra and Amelia.

Muuaji was here. We were under attack.

Chapter Sixty-two

I grabbed Antwon from upstairs and put him to work on getting my cameras back up. From a tactical standpoint, I needed to see what was going on outside. He sat at my computer, and his fat fingers started banging away at the keys. I didn't think my surveillance system was any more complicated than what he had hacked into at his condo, but for whatever reason, he struggled to get my cameras back online.

I huddled all the ladies up in the kitchen and made them understand that we were putting aside any and all beefs, conflicting interests, and petty rivalries for the time being. They're all on the same team, and I'm the captain. That means do what the fuck I tell y'all to do, when I tell y'all to do it. That's the only way we gone come out this shit with everybody alive.

I placed Zakiya in the living room with the task of defending the front and side doors. These were the most likely points of entry, even though both doors were seemingly impregnable. If he did manage to break through, he would wind up in a cage. Which would result in an easy kill shot for her.

I had Kierra in the main floor hallway, defending the back of the house. I had taught Kierra how to use a gun, had taken her out to a secluded area and had her shoot at bottles. She wasn't a great, or even a good shot, but decent enough to hit whatever she was aiming at in close quarters. The windows were bulletproof, but if he managed to break one and tried to climb in, it was Kierra's job to blow his ass right back out through it.

I had to force a Smith & Wesson CSX into Amelia's trembling hands, because she didn't even want to take it. I took her to the second floor and had her defend the only two windows I had on that level. I sincerely doubted that Muuaji would attempt to come in from the roof, which is why my I put my least lethal girl upstairs. It was for Amelia's protection as much as anybody else's.

I had already guessed that his most likely response would be to put a device somewhere on the exterior. I had to be the one to go out there and make sure that didn't happen.

I was headed out when Zakiya and Kierra both met me at the side door. Zakiya said, "You're still not healed. You won't be able to defend against him in this condition." Kierra took this rare opportunity to agree with her.

I gave them both a look that said I was good before I unlocked the side door. I motioned for Kierra to engage the ankle, bolt locks, and the brace beam once I was on the other side. Both women looked like they wanted to cry, as if I were saying a final goodbye or something. I just frowned at them bitches like they were crazy, because I knew I wasn't heading out there to die.

I poked the muzzle of the Sig through a crack in the door before I followed with my head. Once that I saw that it was all clear, I rolled out into the night and made sure that Kierra pushed it closed behind me.

I tiptoed around the perimeter of the house going towards the rear, sweeping the beam of flashlight from left to right. The LED floodlights mounted on my garage typically had my backyard as bright as day. Without them, the area around my house was dark enough to conceal an attacker.

In the backyard, I checked the utility meter. It didn't appear to be damaged or tampered with. Looking up, I saw the electrical line from the pole running to the house. I couldn't understand how my power was out.

I peeked into my garage, just to look around. No one hid inside.

I continued my circuit around the exterior of the house. From the backyard, I checked the north side of the structure. I didn't see any sign of an explosive device.

When I circled back around to the street side, I shined the flashlight through the bushes that shaded my porch. I saw that my front door was hanging open.

I sprinted back into the house. The gate in the cage behind the front door also hung open. Through the living room, I saw someone down in the kitchen. Kierra was lying on the floor in front of the sink. Blood leaked from a gash in her head. Her eyes were closed, and she didn't respond to the gentle shaking of her shoulder. But I grabbed her wrist and felt a strong pulse.

I took the stairs three at a time to get to the room I was lending to Amelia. She was down, too. A quick scan of her body revealed no bullet wounds. She was also unconscious.

I ran back downstairs, did a quick scan of the first floor and the basement.

No Zakiya. No Antwon.

Chapter Sixty-three

That bitch Zakiya had played me. She must've made her move the second I left the house. The good thing was that she didn't have much of a head start. It had taken me less than five minutes to check the garage and skirt the perimeter of the house. They couldn't have gotten that far, definitely not on foot. She had Antwon with her, who wasn't very fast. They couldn't have any more than a few blocks on me.

I ran down to the short end of my block carrying my big-ass Sig. That ass whooping and kick to the balls Muuaji gave me still had me moving gingerly. I reached the corner, whipped my head in both directions. I didn't see the silhouettes of a slender female and wide teen.

I hurried back down to the house, locked everything down, then jumped in the Buick. I would only need to cruise the surrounding neighborhood in a six-block radius. Zakiya didn't know the area as well as I did. There weren't many places to hide.

She didn't have a car, but thanks to me, she had the means to get one. Anybody getting that big Israeli rifle pointed in their face was going to give up their keys, their money, and whatever else she wanted. I had to find her before that happened.

I sped down the street two over from mine when I damn near T-boned a white pickup with the SPIRIT OF DETROIT logo on the driver's door. I swerved around that and kept heading in the direction of 7 Mile Road. I didn't see how they could possibly make it that far, especially with Antwon's big asthmatic ass. I started with a six-block radius, then expanded that to twelve. There was no sight of them. No sight of anyone on the side of the road looking like they'd been carjacked. Just gone. I drove around my neighborhood for damn near an hour before finally I gave up.

I was absolutely sick when I went back to the house. I kept searching awhile longer, even after I was sure they were gone, looking to prolong and hoping to prevent what I knew was coming next.

I made it back home to find my power mysteriously back on. Kierra and Amelia were up and appeared to be lucid. I dreaded having to tell her that Zakiya had taken Antwon. It went about as bad as I expected.

"You let this happen. You let my son get taken. You brought her here, trusted her—even knowing that she was hired to take my life. Was it just because she was a member of that cult you used to be a part of? Was it just because you wanted to fuck her?

"You stood in this very spot and swore to me that you would not let anything happen to my son!" This all came with screaming, tears, and fingers in my face. Kierra stood next to her, not adding anything, but it was clear from her expression she was in full agreement.

I promised Amelia on the souls of the ancestors that I would find Antwon and get him back. She wouldn't look at my phone to even read my promises or apologies.

Amelia pulled her phone, muttered something about calling the police, and I slapped it out her hand. She looked at me with fury and disbelief as if I'd just slapped her.

I understood I was the one who let the enemy in our gates, and I took full responsibility for that, but I tried to communicate that calling the police wasn't the thing to do here. For Antwon's sake and for mine. Whatever Zakiya's intention is with him, she wants Antwon alive. But if Zakiya gets into a situation where she's boxed in by SWAT teams, we can't guarantee what she'll do. It's best to keep this a simple kidnapping and not a hostage situation.

Plus, for the sake of me, calling the police to my house wasn't going to happen. When they came in and saw my house laid out with bulletproof walls and indoor cages at the entrances, all their questions were going to quickly change from Antwon to what the fuck I was on. Not to mention that I collect guns the way sneakerheads collect Jordans, had somewhere close to 120 unregistered firearms, and many of them illegal in this country.

Amelia was only sold on the points I made about Antwon, gave few fucks about protecting me. She picked up her phone, stormed out the kitchen, and I felt the vibrations when she stomped up the stairs. I started to follow but thought it better if I gave her some space.

Plus, I knew I had to get back out in the streets before Zakiya's trail got too cold. The problem being that I didn't even know where to start.

When Amelia came back downstairs, it was with a bag full of the few belongings I'd brought from the condo for her and Antwon. She appeared to be waiting for a ride. I tried to warn her that Muuaji was still out there, even though he seemed more interested in me than her.

Ten minutes later, a dark-colored Bentley pulled up out front. Amelia demanded to be let out, then carried her bags out to her manager's car.

He stepped out to greet me. "This is the worst possible outcome." Personally, I thought the worst possible outcome would've been Amelia getting killed, since I was hired to protect her, but it wasn't the time to be a smartass.

"I knew it was a mistake to hire you."

He almost made another one when he got too close and poked me in the chest with his finger. He had on a little bronze triangle-shaped pinky ring. He was this close to getting that ring shoved up his ass with the finger still attached.

But I gave him a pass, because I did fuck up, and emotions were running high. But also warned him with a look not to expect any more freebies.

As Amelia climbed into the car, I wanted to advise her one last time to be careful. But that and the apology would just be another in the long list of unvoiced things trapped in my head. I watched the Bentley Mulsanne pull off, making a silent promise to myself that I was going to get her son back.

Having no fucking idea of how I was going to do it.

Chapter Sixty-four

I ran back into the house to grab a few more pistols. The Sig was already in the Buick.

I was ready to get in the streets and do what I do best, but Kierra came at me, wanting to talk. I let her know this wasn't the time for any *I-told-you-so*s or critiques of my decisions. I'd fucked up and had to make this right.

She was adamant in that she had something to get off her chest, trying to block me at the door. I was even more adamant that this wasn't the time or place for the shit, so I moved her skinny ass out the way. I made hand motions to say, "Hold my spot down."

Her face tightened with frustration. "It's bad enough that you can't hear. What's real fucked-up is that you don't listen!"

I didn't know it in that moment, but these would be the last words she ever said to me. Words I would spend the rest of my life reflecting on.

I let unresolved personal attachments to my old life cloud my judgment.

I jumped in my car, not really knowing what to do or where to go. I tried Bates, but didn't get any answer, then spent an hour just sitting outside his darkened house. I didn't know who I could call but him, then realized how few allies I actually had. Zakiya had told me that I was alone, a man without a tribe. I was feeling that now. There was only person I knew who had the connections to track them down easily. The problem was that I had no way to get in contact with him. Whenever the Big Phone rang, it was always from an unavailable number. Our understanding was that he would reach me when he needed me. The line of communication did not go both ways.

I drove around aimlessly for a minute, fighting but coming back to one inescapable conclusion. There was only one other card I could play.

I had to pull up on somebody who I didn't want to see as much as they didn't want to see me. I needed their help. But unlike with Bates, I had no leverage to use this time. I would be reduced to begging or threats. Doubted that either would work against this particular individual. I was scripting our exchange in my head and getting more agitated at each negative simulation.

I drove back out to the rich lady's house, hating that each mile took me farther away from Antwon, and that Zakiya might be taking him an equal mile farther in the opposite direction.

I pulled up to the front gate, buzzed the intercom. She was still mourning the loss of her daughter, so I knew she was home. I stared into the camera, waiting for whoever was on the other end to make a decision.

If Tuesday herself was watching, then she should know that her nine-foot spear-pointed fence wasn't going to keep me out anymore than the low-tier goons she was paying for private security. She knew who I was and how I got down.

After a few seconds, the gate parted and permitted me to slide through. I pulled beneath the portico at the main entrance, then slotted my ten-year-old Buick between a new Lamborghini Urus and a Maybach S600.

I was invited into the house by a female staff member and escorted to the left to wait in a salon. Twelve-piece suede sofa set; large French windows looking out on the manicured green of her topiary bushes; chandelier looking like a hanging piece of glass art.

I didn't have to wait long, but the lady of the house clearly wasn't ready to receive guests. She stepped into the room wearing teal silk pajamas, head covered by a Gucci bonnet. She looked a little better than when I'd last seen her. Still broken, but better. Her mostly gray eyes were rimmed with dark bags.

She took a seat on the sofa opposite mine. "I'm assuming you're here because you got information. Make yourself useful or make yourself gone. I have to tend to the funeral arrangements for my daughter."

Actually, I was coming for information. And really had nothing to provide in exchange for it. I was basically here just hoping that she took pity on me. I let her read the inquiry off my phone.

"You gots to be a muthafucka, to bring your ass here asking for a favor." I was well aware of how this made me look, but for Antwon, I was willing to be whatever in her eyes. I was well beyond principles and pride. She didn't give a damn about any of my apologies or platitudes. She seemed a second away from putting me out when I told her that a boy was missing.

Her raised eyebrows produced forehead wrinkles that disappeared into her bonnet. "How old is the boy?"

It took frustratingly long just to provide her with a summarized version of what happened with Amelia, Antwon, and even my mistakes in trusting Zakiya. She seemed particularly interested in the part that Bates had shared with me, asking follow-up questions.

"The boy who's missing—" She spent a few seconds fumbling for the name until I used my phone to reminder her. "Is Antwon gifted? High IQ? Unusually talented at something?"

I told her that he was a little fat silly muthafucka that would keep you laughing. But also that he had been able to write computer code since he was seven.

On the surface, she was the squeaky-clean owner and CEO of Abel Incorporated, but I knew she was still out here with her hands in some things and her ears to the ground. I asked for whatever assistance she could spare.

"I can't give you shit but advice. If you don't find that boy within the next twenty-four hours, you ain't gone never see his ass again. And in the next day or two, every picture, post, or piece of information about this person is going to be scrubbed off the internet.

"At least, that's how it was with my daughter."

That nearly knocked me sideways out my seat. I'd nearly forgotten that during that brief stint I had served as her bodyguard, she did have a second daughter, around twelve. As rich as her mother was, I had just assumed the girl was away at school. I relayed that thought to Tuesday.

"Her name is Dani, and she's away at the same school your friend might be headed to.

"Like any regular kid, she liked ice cream and cookies, but she was also a math prodigy. At seven years old, you could give her any long-ass number with thirteen digits, and she could tell its square and cubed roots right off the top of her head. By eleven, she could solve physics equations that would stump most grad students."

Tuesday scooted to the edge of her sofa and leaned into me like she was about to whisper this next part. Either forgetting or not caring that my handicap made this an empty gesture.

"Be careful what you do next, and be very careful who you tell this to. You just stumbled onto something that's deeper than you would ever believe." Her eyes seemed to turn a different shade of gray. The gravitational pull of them drew me forward until I matched her, perched on the edge of my seat.

My old dude was a conspiracy nut, so I spent most of my young life in the church hearing about the Rothschild family, the Trilateral Commission, and the Freemasons. Even though it was pretty much gospel in the UOTA, deep down I didn't really believe that there was a fraternity of ultra-powerful individuals who secretly ruled the world. Tuesday assured me that there were actually several.

The Kamku was supposed to have been started in the early 1900s by Black intellectuals like W.E.B. Du Bois and Booker T. Washington. A super-secret organization designed to push a pro-African agenda. This was to be the Black man's answer to the Illuminati.

I didn't know how much of it was true or just cap. The fact that many prominent Black leaders were members in secret, from Marcus Garvey to Thurgood Marshall to Muhammad Ali. And that they were instrumental in founding and funding the NAACP, the Nation of Islam, as well as the Black Panther Party. Tuesday claimed that they had infiltrated the highest levels of politics, finance, business, and media. They were more powerful than the government and more connected than the mob. They were every-fucking-where.

She explained, "In its infancy, the Kamku established the HBCUs as a vetting process to funnel the best and brightest people of color into their ranks. But over the past few decades, they stopped waiting for them to reach college level. They started taking an interest in any child who had a really high aptitude for Law, Business, Mathematics or STEM. They want to groom these kids to be the future leaders of the world; the puppets will become the next generation of puppet masters, all pushing the Kamku's agenda.

"The problem is that ruling the world isn't something that can be taught at your local K-through-twelve prep academy."

What Bates had said about all the missing children. Were they gifted kids recruited by the Kamku? But it still didn't make sense to me, because Bates had sworn it was the UOTA taking the kids.

"Making people totally vanish, erasing their entire digital presence and history, hard copies of their birth, medical, and school records. Even getting to their families through bribes or intimidation. Those are God-tier boss moves. Your old man's little group in the woods ain't got that type of juice."

Maybe they contracted out the child-snatching part of the operation to the UOTA. I asked her if she remembered exactly who it was that snatched her daughter. Maybe she's seen a face. And if so, was it Zakiya?

"I know exactly who it was that took my daughter. Her father. The same man you're working for right now."

Chapter Sixty-five

I left Tuesday's house with her assurance that she would do what she could to help. But the assistance would not be free, and definitely not cheap.

I thought I had some inkling of the type of power he had when a man who didn't exist was able to walk into a prison one night, without being seen, and hand me a phone. I would've gone to my grave never believing that her husband was a very key player in some secret society that was actually trying to take over the world. I thought he was just an ordinary gangster, smart and well-connected. Turns out, this nigga was a villain from a James Bond movie.

I jumped in my Buick, hurried back to the city. During our conversation, some of the loose strands had come together in my brain. I needed to go see a man about a truck.

I returned to the Department of Public Works to find a skeleton crew working the midnight shift. The doors were unlocked. The only security was in the form of a single guard stationed near the south entrance. A Black chick, early twenties, crackhead-thin. It would've only been a problem for her if she had tried to intervene. She was too busy on a FaceTime call, arguing with her man, to even notice or care about the big six-foot-five goon who breezed past her with no uniform or credentials.

I walked into the dispatch office with the name already loaded into my phone. Dude behind the desk was either cooperative by nature, or had heard about my first visit. He told me that Terrence Jenkins had already gone for the day, but offered to place a call if it were important.

It was extremely important, so much so that I needed him to concoct a story. To invent some emergence that only a supervisor could solve, and get him to return to the job. I placed my phone faceup on the desk and let him read that.

He started to mutter this whole thing about how he couldn't do that until I pulled the P99 off my hip. Didn't point it at him, just kept it palmed at my side. Seeing it seemed to be enough to stop the dispatcher midsentence, and to reevaluate his dedication to company policy.

He grabbed the office line, and I watched him carefully as he placed that call. He was probably smart enough to peep my handicap by the way I was communicating. But if he was dumb enough to try some slick shit without knowing my skills for lipreading would put me on to the entire play, he would get his brains blew out. And I would have to do the same to little mama out there working security.

The dispatcher thought for a moment, then came up with a story about an overturned sanitation truck that had spilled garbage all down the street from the mayor's mansion. I could tell from his end of the conversation that Terrence was giving him pushback. He claimed that someone higher up on the totem pole had ordered him to make the call. Terrence claimed it would take him twenty minutes to get back to the job.

During the wait, I told the dispatcher one more thing I needed. I knew a place like this had to keep a log sheet or record of which drivers had taken out which vehicles. The request sounded friendly in my mind, but I guess my pistol made it come off a bit more demanding.

Terrence actually made it there in under fifteen. He got there quick, even though he was looking pissed off. The nigga was at least dedicated to his job.

Soon as he stepped through the door to the dispatch office, I sprang out from where I'd hidden behind it. At first he looked like he wanted to start running. And it was that very reaction that provided the confirmation.

"Not this ol' I-gotta—" Coughing choked off the rest of that insult. I punched him in the throat. We wasn't having all that shit this time.

I gave him a front kick to the gut that sent him back out the door. Then I grabbed him by the neck and dragged him to his office. It was time for another conversation.

I loaded the first question in my phone: *How long was him and his son planning this shit? Why would Antwon help himself get kidnapped?*

It never made sense to me how they were able to disappear so quickly when Zakiya escaped with Antwon. But then I recalled the white pickup truck that I damn near ran into as I was cruising around the neighborhood. It was a city vehicle, the same department where his father happened to be a supervisor. It was a fleet of them muthafuckas parked outside. My inability to hear had caused me to lean heavily on my sight, and that keen visual observation was sometimes a gift as much as a curse. That was why, even in that brief encounter I had with the truck, I memorized the six-digit vehicle code on the door. Checking the logbook proved that it had been the work vehicle on loan to him that day.

That alone was too easy to chalk up to coincidence, but it only all started to make sense when I considered the possibility of Antwon working with Zakiya. Zakiya was a helluva fighter, but not unnaturally strong. Antwon was close to 300 pounds, and far from athletic. Even at gunpoint, she shouldn't have been able to disappear so quickly with an uncooperative hostage.

Plus, I was so sure that Muuaji had done something from outside my house, never considering how easily Antwon was able to hack into the cameras at his own building and take control of them. I'd seen what he could do with a phone; with access to my computer, taking out my security would be simple for a master hacker.

Everything made sense when you factored in that Antwon and Zakiya were working together. The only thing that didn't make sense was the why.

I gave him the crib notes of what I was able to piece together, and just waited for him to try to lie to me.

"All I know is that my son called me saying he in trouble and needed a ride. He asked me to drop the truck off for him."

Bullshit. As much as he might love and trust his son, he wasn't going to leave a city vehicle somewhere unattended based on the word of a fifteen-year-old.

I let pain be the barometer by which I expressed my level of doubt. I grabbed his shoulder, squeezed it hard, pushing my thumb into the trapezius muscle.

He buckled. "Oww, oww, goddamn nigga. How is you so strong? Muthafuckas put steroids in your Similac?"

Like I said, the little comedy shit was cute the first time, but I shook Terrence's ass up to let him know that I wasn't in the mood for an encore.

The pain sank him into his knees, and my thumb damn near had to puncture the skin before he folded.

"Even when he was living with me, I knew my son be going to some real dark corners of the internet. He be in touch with people all over the world, smart muthafuckas just like him who can make those damn computers do anything. I never really tripped because he seemed to be able to navigate that world, and it never brought problems to our doorstep."

I was willing to bet those same friends had given Antwon some pointers and help to cut the learning curve on his hacking skills.

"All I know is that eight months ago, my son started getting into this hardcore, lizard-people-walk-among-us type of conspiracy shit. He started sending me all this stuff off the dark web, articles about kids going missing. Even claimed to know a few of them. Naturally, I think he's just trippin' at first, but then he starts to get obsessed with it, paranoid for real, telling me that they're people out to get him. But then as I started reading the stuff he sent, and doing my own research, I slowly start seeing that there might be something to it. I even saw the pattern.

"Some fourteen-year-old kid in Abu Dhabi who created his own crypto-currency; a thirteen-year-old girl in Waco, Texas who plays piano like Mozart and already has a Grandmaster ranking in chess; another girl in South Africa who engineered a complex pipeline that brought clean water for drinking, irrigation, and sewage disposal to her village, and baby girl was only eleven. All missing, all minorities, all of them gifted or certified geniuses."

So it's looking like Antwon somehow got in touch with the UOTA, and they dispatched Zakiya to help him run. Muuaji insisted on coming when he discovered I was involved.

If his plan was to run, I needed to know how, and where he intended to go. Father and son were too close for Antwon not to tell him. And to set up a final meeting to say their goodbyes.

Terrence claimed not to know, but didn't understand that my expertise in body language allowed me to detect untalented liars. I applied more pressure to that shoulder, making him grimace and grit his teeth. He hissed, then howled in pain as my thumbnail broke the skin, and I pulled like I was trying to tear his shoulder meat off the bone.

Tears slipped from his eyes as I saw the stubborn resolve of a father trying to protect his son. I admired the man and envied the bond. But I'm a goon, and I'd come to extract information. I had to break things in order to make him break his promise.

He suffered through the agony of a broken pinky on his left hand, then the ring finger. By the time I grabbed his middle finger, he reached his limit. I was as grateful as him when he finally surrendered.

Chapter Sixty-six

Henry Ford Hospital was less than a mile from Terrence's job, a straight shot down West Grand Boulevard. I dropped him off at the emergency room, felt that was the least I could do for him. I let his stupid ass know that he should've gave up after I broke the first finger. I guess comedians are always taking people for a joke.

Terrence didn't know where Antwon was, but knew where he was going to be. I was texting Amelia like crazy, blowing up her phone.

The response eventually came from her manager. He texted me explaining that Amelia was distraught over Antwon and couldn't be disturbed. He had her safe, under guard at a motel that he refused to give the location to. But he did want me to meet him at the condo to discuss the situation.

It was after one a.m. when I entered the lobby. There was no receptionist at the front desk, and I thought that was strange. Could be I just caught him away from his station while he went to take a piss.

Cameron sent the elevator down for me, but I only rode up to the seventeenth floor. I got out and hit the stairwell at the end of the hall. I jogged up those last few flights with the Walther in hand, the expectation of drama quickening my pulse.

Clearly another muthafucka who thought Deaf meant Dumb. I wasn't stepping off that elevator into what was surely a trap. As soon as those doors opened into Amelia's penthouse, there would be a gunman there waiting to spray my blood and brains all over the walls.

There was a camera in the elevator, so they would know I got off on seventeen but wouldn't see anything of my movements after that. I didn't know how many enemies I was facing, but from a tactical standpoint, I knew there should be a man posted at the stairwell door on nineteen.

Which was why I'd left the stairs at eighteen. I counted seven doors down from the elevator doors on the left side of the hall. Unit 1808. I gave the door a front kick, three inches below the knob, that sent it swinging inward. Zakiya had been taught to pick locks—for me, a size fourteen foot in a heavy steel-toed boot worked just fine.

During the security sweeps I had done on the building, I made it my business to learn the status of any unit that surrounded Amelia's condo. I had considered the possibility of someone planting a bomb, or just shooting through a wall. Because she was on the top floor, I had inquired about the neighbors on either side of her and directly below. This was why I knew 1808 would be furnished but unoccupied. According to Amelia, the unit was owned by a professional photographer who sold his work to magazines like *National Geographic*. He was always globetrotting to exotic locations, and would be away for months at a time.

His layout wasn't the same as Amelia's, being that she had the penthouse. It had a lot less square footage, lower ceilings, and was without a second floor. But I crossed the living room to his balcony. That was directly under Amelia's.

I took a deep breath, because this next part was the shit that scared me more than the guns and knives I was about to face.

I climbed up and stood on his balcony railing, which was basically a one-foot-wide beam of painted wood. I had to place my feet one before the other and slowly stand from a crouched position. Your boy don't really fuck with heights like that. I could squat damn near 700 pounds, so I knew it was only nerves making my knees feel weak. It was a calm night, but I'd swear the slightest breeze threatened to steal my balance. I'd tried to resist, but eventually gave in to temptation, and looked down. Two hundred and fifty feet below me, the parking lot, trees, and surrounding area looked like a miniature set built by a hobbyist. I felt dizzy.

Times like this made me wonder why I even do this shit. I'm a big nigga with a strong back, and Chrysler was always hiring.

And I needed that strong back to pull myself up to Amelia's balcony and over her railing. The climb hadn't taxed me physically, but I still took a knee and needed a few seconds to get myself together.

I peeked through the sliding door. The rooms were lit and I saw Cameron seated on the living room sofa barking into his phone. There were at least two shooters that I could see in the room with him, but no Amelia.

Sometimes surprise was all I needed. I pulled my Walther. The balcony wasn't that deep, so I backed all the way to the railing to give myself a running start.

I threw myself like a brick and exploded through the glass door shoulder-first. I didn't purposely go into a roll trying to be extra, but tripped over a large shard stuck into the bottom of the frame. I played it off cool, though; sprang back to my feet swinging my pistol from left to right.

The first gunman closest to me got two put in his skull before he could unholster his weapon. When he fell, his bloody head landed in Cameron's lap. I watched Cameron scream, then kick the man away from him like he was a rodent or something disgusting.

The second shooter was deeper into the room, and actually

had pretty good reflexes. He didn't freeze up like most people were prone to do during an unexpected display of violence. He quickly freed his pistol, and slotted himself behind an outcropping of wall in the dining area.

I remembered ol' boy, the one I had to fuck up during my audition for the job. We traded shots from across the room, forcing me to duck behind Amelia's overstuffed gray furniture. Whatever he was shooting punched holes in the upholstery while I sent .40-caliber slugs into the drywall near his head.

He was a big fella like me, and probably wore about the same shoe size. But he fucked up by not tucking in one of those size-fourteen loafers. I put one in his foot, and when his head came into view, put one in his eye. That sent him face down to the hardwood.

From the corner of my eye, I saw the elevator doors start to open and stood just to the side of the frame. As soon as dude stepped in, I calmly blew his brains out without ever getting a good look at his face.

I did a quick sweep of the first floor just to make sure there were no other shooters.

Cameron had also dove to the floor during the shootout. He stood and frowned at the blood that stained his pants. "Well, damn, that was a dramatic entrance."

I wanted to know where Amelia was, but he ignored the screen when I held up my phone.

"Well, you've really made a mess of things, haven't you?"

I shrugged. It's kind of what I do.

He slowly opened the jacket to his teal-green suit to show me he had no gun. He pulled a thick envelope from the breast pocket and tossed it on the table. "Severance. You'll find we've been awfully generous under the circumstances."

He could talk all the shit he wanted, but my job wasn't finished. I still picked up the envelope, grateful for any donation.

He must've read in my face that this wasn't done for me. "I

have people looking for Antwon, and the girl you exposed him to. This whole thing will be resolved in hours. And you can go back to your life of robbing drug dealers and beating up street thugs."

I warned him with my eyes that I just didn't beat up street thugs. His orientation didn't protect him from these hands: gay, straight, or bi. I'm an equal-opportunity ass-whipper. It won't be a hate crime, because it's not coming from a place of prejudice.

Cameron made a tent of his thin fingers under his chin. "Silence, what would you be willing to give for a better future, but one that you might not be alive to enjoy?"

I just sighed, because some people had watched too many damn movies, and had been fucked up by them. I guess Cameron thought we were going to act out this whole scene where he and the killer exchanged witty barbs while he dropped cryptic clues about what was really happening. What he didn't understand was that I seldom watched movies, and when I did, it was mostly with the closed-caption off, because I was all about the action.

I grabbed his jacket collar, snatched him off the sofa so fast that his feet left the floor. When Cameron saw that I was dragging him toward the balcony, he tried to use his feet as brakes. What a time for his own fashion sense to work against him. Those dressy shoes slid easily over Amelia's waxed hardwood floors like he had on skates. The nigga should've had on some Jordans.

I kicked out the rest of the glass and started to pull him through. He tried to hang on to the door frame, cutting his hands on the broken pieces still there. I pulled his body through with one good yank.

I scooped him up WWE-style and was poised for a body slam, only the mat was about 270 feet down. It was time to have our movie moment, but it was the scene from *The Five Heartbeats.*

I imagined he was trying to speak, but I couldn't read his lips from that angle. I could imagine there was a lot of screaming for me not to drop him.

I dangled his ass for about twenty seconds, then pulled him

back over the railing. He fell on his ass, scrambled back towards the door breathing heavy, eyes wide. It was time to see if he wanted to have a real conversation now or did he want to engage in some more witty banter.

I started to type in my question into my phone when I felt the other one buzzing against my thigh. That was the Big Phone. The one I couldn't ignore.

Cameron must've heard the buzzing, too. He dropped his head back against the wall as if exhausted. Relief softened his features.

He mouthed: "I promise you're gonna want to answer that."

Chapter Sixty-seven

The words that came across the screen read: *Stand down. You're done with Amelia Chess and her son. Cameron Sudfield is a brother and friend. No harm is to come to him.* As usual, this was from an unavailable number, and I received no reply when I texted follow-up questions.

Cameron climbed to his feet and began to dust himself off. "That's right boy, Heel. Sit. Good Boy." He smoothed out his jacket and straightened the tie. "You think you live in a world where Strength is defined by how hard you can punch, and Power is all about the caliber of your gun."

He was back on his movie shit again. He already got the save. Don't fuck it up by trying to monologue me to death.

"In my prime, I probably couldn't do fifty pushups, and the only black belt I'll ever own is made by Saint Laurent. But I have power like you'll never know. The type of power that allows me to make a phone call and have Quianna and your one-year-old son murdered in their home."

He saw the stunned look on my face and smirked. "You think you're just in one man's debt. You're not. We all hold your leash."

He held up his right hand, twisted the little triangle-shaped ring on his right hand like that was supposed to mean something. I didn't know what the fuck he was talking about, and I didn't appreciate the way he was talking to me.

"You think we just met, but I already knew who you were when you walked in. And I knew you would get the job, but we had to give Amelia the illusion of choice. That's what we do best, give people the *illusion* of choice."

I thought back on my conversation with Caine. This was the friend he was doing the favor for.

"Silence, you are in the unique position of actually having a real choice here. Even after all the messes you've made, we will forgive you. All you have to do is make sure you go on the newspaper from now on.

"Or, you can continue all this pissing on the carpet and make us have to rub your nose in it."

Cameron was really going there with the dog-on-a-leash shit. Even with Sebastian Caine, who had a reputation for being one of the most notorious gangsters in the Midwest, there still was always a certain level of respect.

I know what I needed to do, just to walk away from the situation and let whatever happens to Antwon. He wasn't my son. At the end of the day, I'd only been hired to protect his mother. But then again, I'm a man who doesn't speak, but feels extremely compelled to keep his promises.

"You just make sure you keep that phone handy. We'll let you know when it's time to go fetch again."

I held up the phone for him to see, then flung it out the door, and it disappeared over the balcony into the night.

Cameron looked at me like I'd just fucked up.

I let him know what power really was, one man deciding that his pride isn't for sale, even at the cost of the things he loves. One man deciding that he's not going to bow down, take orders, or let anyone put a boot on his neck.

One man remembering that he is a warrior and not just a man.

I pulled my personal phone and then gave Cameron a choice.

He could: a) tell me where Amelia was and ride the elevator back down to the first floor, or b) not tell me and get there by a much faster route.

That message, along with the look in my eye, seemed enough to take Cameron off all the smug shit. He told me that Amelia was being kept in a suite at the Atheneum Hotel. There was only one guard with her, to make sure she didn't interfere with the sacrifice.

Cameron said, "His father would let him become a thousand-pound glutton who spent all day playing games. Amelia might ride him towards a life where he's making two hundred K a year as a computer analyst. I'm offering him a path that gives him more wealth and power than most adults could dream of, and at the same time be a transformative force for all people of color."

The way I see the problem is that nobody's asking Antwon what he wants. It's his life; it should be his decision.

Plus, I wasn't buying that he was doing this purely for cause. This muthafucka was an agent/manager, and they didn't do anything without collecting some type of percentage. I'm pretty sure that bringing somebody like Antwon into the ranks came with a hefty finder's fee. Either in the form of money or just status within the organization.

He continued, "We are at war, and it is a war for the future. Gifted children like Antwon are the nuclear weapon. And you'd better believe we aren't the only ones trying to stockpile the biggest arsenal we can."

I let Cameron see how few fucks, then grabbed him by his collars. Pushed him back towards the sliding door.

His eyes were wide, and his lips were moving almost too fast to read. "I told you where Amelia was. You said you wouldn't do this if I told. Said I could take the elevator."

What Cameron didn't realize was that I only gave him the *illusion* of choice. I picked his bony ass up and threw him about ten feet clear of the balcony railing.

I watched him sink towards the earth and felt a satisfaction that made all the bullets and bombs worth it. You just don't get to do this type of stuff at Chrysler.

Chapter Sixty-eight

I anticipated repercussions for disobeying an order that came from the Big Phone, but it had been long past the time to cut those strings.

There had been a lot of gunshots, and one man did a swan dive off the nineteenth floor. This was the riverfront; I figured I had about four minutes before police cruisers had the entire building surrounded.

I found Amelia's keys in her room. In the garage, I transferred my things to her car and took the Benz. I chose the AMG S63 because it was a lot faster than my Buick. And the fact that I just liked driving this muthafucka.

My first destination was Brush Avenue; the Atheneum was one of the most luxurious hotels metro Detroit had to offer. At least they weren't being cheap about where they were keeping her. I slipped the valet a fifty along with a note telling him to keep it close—I didn't plan on this taking more than a few minutes.

Cameron hadn't lied; there was only one guard posted, and he was an easy piece of work. I simply knocked on the door and stood to the side, outside the view of the lens. When he stepped out, I dropped his ass. I didn't expect they would give their most talented men babysitting duty.

I entered the bedroom; Amelia ran to me and embraced me tightly around the neck. They had taken her phone, but she appeared to be unharmed.

She started to run down everything that happened, and I waved her off to let her know we had to do that on the way. I tried to pull her along, but she wouldn't budge until she got off her question about Antwon.

I confessed that I still didn't know where he was, but I did know where he would be, and when. I also knew enough to believe he was safe. Only for the time being, though. Which is why we had to hurry.

We pulled away from the hotel, and Amelia was in the passenger seat, trying to tell me all the stuff I'd already knew about her manager wanting Antwon. I'd already guessed that he was the one who'd had her take a keen interest in her son once she found out he was brilliant. The one who had her get him tested then pushed for her to get full custody. It was only in saying the words that I could see it dawn on her how Cameron had been manipulating her every move.

The realization made her tear up, and I placed a consoling arm on her shoulder. She didn't fully know yet what her friend and manager was affiliated with. Manipulation is what they do.

We swung back by my house just to pick up some supplies. It was nearly three a.m.

I went inside to find Kierra gone, along with all her things. No *Fuck you* text. No goodbye letter stuck to the fridge. I guess every down-ass bitch got their breaking point. I checked my stash spot to find that she didn't even hit me for any cash on the way out—I wouldn't have been mad if she did, and had I been there, I would've blessed her with a parting gift.

Amelia wore a look of apology on her face, but I just waved her off like it was nothing. Kierra and I never discussed the future, and neither of us thought it was a Forever thing. I knew I wasn't the easiest person to get along with. Definitely not the most communicative.

It was the best thing for her, getting the fuck away from me. Especially after what happened to Lexy. I knew my life would always be crazy as long as I was involved in this game. I'm built for war, but I couldn't stand the civilians around me having to get caught in the line of fire.

In the basement, I grabbed a few more pistols and a few more clips before I hit the side door. While locking the gate at the side entrance, I glanced towards the kitchen, thinking it would feel a little less than cozy without her strutting around half-naked with those long legs and pretty toes. Kierra would always have my gratitude for turning something I'd built strictly as a defensive stronghold and making it feel like a home.

We was back in the Benz, blowing through post-midnight traffic on the way to the train station. I pulled up while it was still closed. I parked in the empty lot, of course in a space that allowed me to see anybody coming or going, and access to the exit if I needed to dip out quickly. I sat a pistol on each lap and the Sig Sauer on the back seat.

The historic Michigan Central Station had been built in 1914 and stood as a Detroit landmark until its closure in 1988. Decades of abandonment and neglect had left the train station and the eighteen-story office tower as a 500,000-square-foot crumbling eyesore until the previous year, when the cash-strapped city somehow found $740 million for a renovation project.

But with a shifting timeline for the old historic building's reopening, the newer Amtrak train station on Baltimore Street was still the place offering passenger train service for Detroiters. And it was where Terrence had told me he was supposed to meet for a parting moment with his son. I told him he was still free to meet Antwon there after he left the emergency room from getting his fingers reset.

I shared with Amelia my working theory that Zakiya's plan was to take Antwon to the UOTA to give him sanctuary. It was about the only place he would be safe if these people had the type of power that Tuesday claimed. Only there was another three hours before the train station opened, and another forty-five minutes after that until he could board.

"You believe that Antwon and the girl have been working together this entire time?" Amelia asked, with skepticism pinching her face.

I had enough conversations with Zakiya to peep that the UOTA had evolved since I'd left. They were xenophobes. But she knew things about the outside world, had a much broader understanding that would only come if they had access to the internet. But knowing my paranoid father, if they were online, it would only be on the fringes. And according to Terrence, Antwon was active on the dark web.

Antwon figured out who Cameron was and what they planned to do. He reached out to the UOTA, and they dispatched Zakiya to extract him. I told Amelia that it was Antwon who took out the power and cameras at my house. The same thing he'd done for Zakiya back at the condo, because I never could figure out how she'd gotten inside in the first place.

"Listen, I always knew Cameron was well-connected, which is why I got him to represent me. But a member of a secret society out here kidnapping kids? Where is he?"

I raised my right arm to the ceiling, opened up my fingers. Then I brought my hand down and smacked it against the console. She didn't seem to get it.

Amelia frowned. "He trusted his father enough to tell him, but not me."

Antwon might not have told his mother for fear she wouldn't believe him, or out of fear that even having knowledge of this shadow organization might make her a target. To him, allowing Amelia to believe that Zakiya was there to kill her might've been the lesser of two evils.

But I told her the real reason he didn't tell her was the same thing I had briefly thought before I talked to Cameron. Antwon had thought that Amelia was the one trying to sell him to the Kamku.

Amelia looked hurt, shocked, skeptical. "My own son wouldn't think that about me. He knows I love him."

Antwon had been investigating these disappearances, and knew that in many cases, the parents were either responsible, or had been bought off. I had Amelia play a game of connect-the-dots. She hadn't been there for most of his life, then out of the blue, she wants full custody. The diet and constantly being on his case could appear to him like you were grooming him for something. Those threatening calls she kept getting on her phone, even after she changed numbers, was clearly Antwon using a bit of misdirection. Just like that $60,000 she found hidden in his room was what he was taking to run with.

Amelia shook her head. "I can't believe this is the person he thinks I am."

I typed out on my phone that she had an opportunity to explain all of that in the morning. Maybe she could get on that train with him? Or maybe she could just send him off with the knowledge that he actually had a mother who loved him enough to choose his own path?

She leaned over and rested her head on my arm, and even that simple display made me nervous. I had been in constant motion, and it was the first time I had to truly process that two innocent adults and one child were dead for no other reason than their loose association to me. I was already living practically nomadic, but going forward, I couldn't have a semblance of a personal relationship with anyone. Everything will have to be transactional, business only.

Especially with the women: no more baby mommas, girlfriends, or fuck buddies. Just disposable pleasures that I could bust a nut on, then send on their way with a couple of dollars.

Amelia laced her fingers into mine, and it didn't quite feel right to reject her. Her son was in trouble, and she was scared. I held onto her hand, telling myself I was just comforting her.

Chapter Sixty-nine

I woke up to dawn's light gleaming through the streaked windshield of the Benz. I had intended to stay awake, but at some point, my eyelids had won the battle against my will. I nodded off sitting upright in the driver's seat instead of stretching out lengthwise in the back. My neck and shoulder screamed its opinion about me choosing right then to break my Percocet addiction.

I turned over to the passenger seat to find Amelia's eyes awaiting mine. She looked alert, like she either hadn't slept or had been up for an hour.

She must've saw the question on my face. "Dude, I tried to wake you, but you were out like a drunk. I shook you and everything. You were snoring loud enough to rattle the fillings in my teeth." I could tell by the way my body was feeling that I had needed those two hours, and ten more.

I looked down and saw she had my Walther between her tucked thighs. I made the gimme motion for my gun back.

I looked over the train station. She said, "They just now opened." Her dashboard clock read 6:13 a.m. She explained that the few cars that had filtered into the lot while I slept were only employees.

I checked the departure times online and discovered that the only train going towards the northwest, in the general direction of Washington state, would be pulling out at 7:15. That meant a 6:45 boarding call.

We sat there for a few minutes watching passengers slowly start to arrive, probably looking oddly suspicious just sitting here in this expensive car. I was watching for anybody who might match Antwon's height or build. Wouldn't be easy for him to slip past, even with a disguise on.

It was around 6:20 when a black Durango pulled up that gave me a cautious vibe. It pulled in too slow, like someone surveying their surroundings and not like a traveler trying to get to a train. It disgorged two passengers near the entrance, and they walked towards the entrance like they weren't in any particular rush. They were only inside briefly, then stood posted on either side of the entrance. I could tell by the way they moved they both were carrying.

Shit was about to go down. Two standing by the door stared at the big white Mercedes like they were doing more than just admiring it. Amelia had a twenty-five percent tint on her windows, but they knew who was inside. The driver crept past us, then slotted the Durango across the parking lot and three slots left of us.

I checked the clip in my Walther and another S&W .40 that I grabbed from the house. I threw a glance to the back seat at my Sig just to be sure my baby was ready.

I knew the best thing would be to leave her at the house. But she had been adamant about wanting to see her son. I'd given her my warning, and she chose not to listen. Wasn't shit I could do; I wasn't her bodyguard anymore.

I gave Amelia the nod. It was time for her to make that move we'd already discussed. She climbed between the two chairs into the back seat. She kept her hands low when she slipped me the rifle from the back. I slid her the Smith & Wesson.

My first instinct was to just roll out the car and start pumping rounds into the SUV and the two waiting by the door. I just kept the rifle across my lap and waited. Zakiya and Antwon needed to board that train; I couldn't start a shootout in the parking lot before they got here.

But the closer it came to departure time, the more I started to think. Zakiya wouldn't walk into a trap any more than I would.

I glanced back at Amelia and gave her an apologetic look. I threw the Benz in neutral, got the RPMs up, then launched it forward. I hit the Durango hard enough to buckle the front end and push it back into the iron fence.

The airbag deployed and damn near gave me a concussion. I staggered out the door and pumped two shots into the Dodge's windshield.

One of the clowns over the door had already raised a Glock and was busting at me. I laid the Sig over the top of the roof, and hit him three times in the chest. Just the sight of this bitch seemed to be enough to send his boy scrambling inside the train station.

I waved for Amelia to follow me, then gave chase into the building. I went into the waiting area and saw attendants ducked down behind the ticket counters. I found the men's bathroom and started kicking in stall doors. And found Antwon in the third stall, perched on the toilet.

Antwon was sat holding a duffel bag and holding his phone, looking at me like he was in trouble. I had to motion three times for him to move his ass.

We left the bathroom, hurried through the lobby, and out to the open-air platform. The 412 to Seattle had already started its boarding call, although there were only a few passengers. Antwon and Zakiya had a fifty-six-hour train ride ahead of them, and then another two and a half hours by car.

I was halfway across the platform when one of the shooters appeared behind in the doorway to the station building. I had the Sig, but he was at my back, and I had no time to spin and fire. Muthafucka had the drop on me.

He took aim at me, but the shot went wide, pinged off the side of the train. In that same moment, his head exploded.

I didn't see Zakiya until she rose from her sniper's nest on the roof of the station building. It wasn't a long shot, but she was pretty accurate with that AXMC.

Amelia had come in from outside by the time Zakiya climbed down from the one-story height. I saw the tentative expression Antwon gave his mother, and I motioned to let him know it was cool. I thought it would be better if Amelia explained that for herself.

Now the fact that his father wasn't here to see him was on me.

When Zakiya walked up to me, I punched her in the throat.

She didn't play me as much as I'd played myself. I had mistakenly assumed Amelia's political views had triggered a Black nationalistic group, and she had simply acted on the narrative that I conveniently set up for her. And all that Sun Tzu and Machiavelli shit that I thought I was running on her, turns out the whole time I was putting her next to Antwon just like she wanted.

Amelia embraced her son like she hadn't seen him in years. "Baby, I'm so sorry that you felt like you couldn't trust me. But where in the hell do you think you're going? I'm supposed to just let you run off and join some cult?"

Zakiya said, "These people won't stop coming for your son. The Universal Orthodox Temple of Alkebulan is *thee* only place they won't dare try. And we are not a cult."

"This is a fifteen-year-old boy, and I am his legal guardian."

What Amelia didn't understand was that either Antwon was going with her or the other people, but either way, he couldn't stay here. I don't know what type of sales pitch they gave, but I used my phone to warn Antwon that life in the church was hard, could be downright brutal. He will be protected, but he might come to realize that he hadn't chosen the lesser of two evils.

Antwon said to his mother, "I know what these people will do, know what they're capable of. You can come with me. So can Dad. The temple would accept us, and we could be a family."

Whatever the hell they were going to do, they needed to do it now. If the police arrived and found a crime scene, they would stop the train from leaving port. Luckily, the conductor was unaware, or he might abort the departure himself.

I had made a quick stop at the store on the way there. I tossed Zakiya a small pack of Lorna Doone shortbread cookies that had gotten crushed in my pocket. She knew who they were for. Then I motioned that they had to go.

The train blast its whistle. Of course I couldn't hear it, but I felt the vibrations.

Antwon was still trying to plead with Amelia when I just pushing all of them towards the boarding ramp. If she didn't want to go all the way with her son, then she was free to get off at some stop along the way, but they had to go.

I was still pushing them to the door when I saw Zakiya's face brighten with surprise. I knew what was happening behind me before she made her move.

The AXMC was too long and cumbersome to raise it in time. I saw a bullet tear into her chest just as I spun and raised the Sig. Firing even before I saw Muuaji dart across the platform.

Chapter Seventy

I missed him wide and high. He was moving to the right, concealed himself behind one of the brick beams for cover.

Zakiya was down on the platform, bleeding from a wound in the chest. I made one final motion for Antwon and Amelia to get onboard. They finally listened just as the train was pulling away from the platform.

I traded a few more shots with Muuaji but didn't have the benefit of cover. I dragged Zakiya away from the tracks next to a row of seats used for waiting passengers. I kneeled with her there.

I grabbed her hand, made her keep pressure on the wound.

I traded a few more rounds with Muuaji until the Sig was spent. I dropped it, pulled my Walther, but only had a few left in the clip.

I couldn't just stay pinned down. So I ran at him hard, busting as I came, and spent those four rounds by the time I got to him.

He tried to bring up his AR-15, but I grabbed hold of it. We wrestled; then I slung it away from both of us.

He said, "All the elders in Alkebulan conspired to conceal what you did, because you were their pride, and Chifu's son. The boy who wasn't even stopped when he lost his ears. Held up before the rest of us as an example of determination.

"Meanwhile, my little cousin didn't get the dignity of a proper burial. Just left him at the bottom of a ditch to be torn apart by animals." My bad. I had thought they were brothers.

Nothing he said was wrong. All the OGs in the church had known what I done and kept it hush. They concocted some story for the family about him losing his footing, and falling into that ravine. The kids who were there were given the new script. And of course, they weren't worried about me saying anything.

"You don't even remember his name, do you?"

I shook my head, concealing any degree of shame. His young brown face would be forever painted behind my closed eyelids. But as far as a name, there were no mental breadcrumbs to lead me through that dark forest. If I ever knew it, I'd forgotten it no sooner than it was told to me.

"Don't worry about it; you're going to learn it today." He began to loosen up, and I did the same.

"It's strange to me that you're a mute, because you weren't actually born deaf. They say you haven't spoken a word since you were seven years old. Well, I'm gonna make you talk today. I'm going to make you say his name."

Did he take the time to learn Lexy's name? Or her daughter's?

We began to circle each other, started our dance. I can't remember the last time I'd went into a fight with this much nervousness.

Muuaji feinted with the left, and I responded by doubling up my right jab and caught nothing but air. He was quick as advertised and very elusive. "His name was Alton Norwood; didn't live long enough to earn a tribal name from the elders. When we were youngsters, before our parents brought us to into this bullshit, they used to call him Li'l Peanut."

His style was some weird fusion of Dambe, Aikido, and traditional boxing. Muuaji danced around on his toes, and used an excess amount of head movement that made him hard to target.

He lunged in with a side kick that I easily avoided. I nearly caught him with a spinning backfist that only grazed his temple.

He stepped back, looked at me stunned, as if that wasn't even supposed to happen. I looked insulted that I'd even come that close to touching him.

I just nodded to let him know I was going to do that and more.

He feinted again, trying to get me to reveal something of my defenses. I didn't buy into it, then realized that I actually bought into it by not flinching. That right came faster than I thought anybody capable of throwing a punch. I saw his fist coming for my face, but before my brain could send the message for my neck to respond, he had already made contact with my mouth and nose.

I stumbled back, sucking blood off my bottom lip. I was willing to bet my last dollar that was some lucky shit until I caught shots like that over and over again. His speed was unbelievable. For a big fella, I'd always had pretty quick hands, but Muuaji was like a video game character with a cheat code activated. "Say it. Alton Norwood."

He neutralized many of my attacks by deflecting or just avoiding them. He slipped my punches and caught me at angles I wouldn't think possible. After I missed with a forearm strike, I received a shot to the left kidney. I staggered a foot back and had to take a knee in order to catch my breath.

He continued to dance with those jerky head movements.

I fought to get to my feet, still holding my side. I figured I might piss blood for a week. We squared up, began to circle each other again.

In our next exchange, he caught my shin with a low kick. But I accepted this pain to give some in return. I grabbed the back of his head, and smashed my forearm into his face.

It was his turn to retreat, and he brought his fingers up to his nose to confirm it was bleeding. This was my first decisive blow; up until then, I had been on the receiving end of all the punishment. This muthafucka had been looking a little too pretty. It felt good to make his ass look like he was in a fight, too.

Our next two exchanges favored him, but I was just studying his moves like I usually do. I moved like Zakiya had taught me, incorporated some Capoeira—not full-blown dancing, just the fluidity of it.

But more important than my body was what I did with my mind. I was present without thought of the past or the outcome, of winning or losing. So as hard as it was, I put the image of Lexy and Kiyuana out my mind. And any feelings of remorse and revenge got pushed aside. And when I found that place in my mind, I actually felt lighter, faster.

After that, our exchanges were fifty-fifty, with me giving as well as I got. At one point, he caught a hold of my wrist and tried to snap it, but I reversed the hold and dislocated the thumb on his left hand.

Muuaji paused for a moment, grunted as he snapped his thumb back into place.

We engaged again and pretty much had fifty-fifty exchanges. But I soon began to make order of the chaos.

I slipped another punch, elbowed his nose, and slipped around his back at the same time my arms coiled around his neck. I twisted hard until I felt the bones in his neck snap. Then I let his body drop down on the tracks, just like I'd done his cousin.

I scooped Zakiya into my arms just as I saw squad cars pulling to the parking lot of the Amtrak station. The way I crashed the Benz into the Durango partially blocked the entrance.

I jumped down to the tracks, landed not far from Muuaji's body, and took off running.

Chapter Seventy-one

I ran for about a quarter mile up those railroad tracks with Zakiya in my arms before I realized she was gone. At some point, her arm stopped cradling my shoulder and merely hung limp around it. Her eyes had closed, and her chin had tucked down to her chest.

I couldn't walk the streets at seven a.m. carrying a dead body, and I hated to have to do her like this. I rolled her up in an old blanket I found and temporarily stashed her in an abandoned garage. I came back for her later that night. Concealed by darkness, I drove to Palmer Park and carried her into the untamed forest far from the bike trails. I dug a grave that wasn't quite six feet, but deep enough that she shouldn't be disturbed for decades.

I placed a knife inside, along with her Hecklar. She had died in combat with a weapon in her hand. The Thunder God would smile at her.

I know that burying Zakiya didn't absolve me of killing Alton back in the day and leaving his body to be devoured by coyotes. But I did feel that it helped to bring the scales closer to being balanced. Muuaji had won, in a sense, because he promised to make sure I never forgot the name, and I never did. Alton Norwood, aka Li'l Peanut.

I could kill Muuaji a thousand more times for what he did, but there was some microscopic portion of me that felt sorry. This man had spent the better part of his life obsessed with me. He let the hate drive him, let it consume him, and in the end, let it destroy him. But at the same time, I didn't even know, or care, that he existed. There's a lesson in that somewhere.

The hardest lesson was for me, and it came about thirty-six hours after Antwon's train left the station. News outlets all over the TV and web got flooded with the same breaking story: *Terror on the Tracks*—but of course, each different source had its own adaptation of that same theme.

According to reports, Amtrak passenger train 412 from Detroit to Seattle had suffered an accident that caused it to derail somewhere in Montana. Rescue workers were going through the wreckage looking for survivors but weren't optimistic. Early indications were that it was a bomb.

A few hours later, the news reported that a radical hate group had taken credit for the bombing. The Universal Orthodox Temple of Alkebulan, or UOTA. A Black-nationalistic, militarized force who wants nothing less than the elimination of all non-Blacks. I watched the report with my mouth hanging open.

I don't doubt that Muuaji could've planted a bomb on that train; I just don't think that he would've. Big and messy is not how the church does things. And they definitely wouldn't do anything that would put a spotlight on their clandestine operations.

I thought back on what Zakiya said, about this war between good and evil. There weren't any white hats on either side, but this damn sure felt to me like the opening salvo.

Chapter Seventy-two

It was three days after and another unseasonably warm spring day in mid-April that felt like early August.

I crossed the Belle Isle Bridge in another one of my low-key stash cars—a twenty-year-old Mercury Marauder that had no other distinguishing feature than tinted windows. It didn't get any attention from the ladies in their floral-printed sundresses or the jack boys looking for a lick.

I drove along the strip, saw a few families out there barbecuing. Saw a lot more people just out there chilling in smaller groups, seated on lawn chairs or blankets, shaded by trees as they looked out over the water. I parked towards the middle of the island in a spot that attracted few picnickers because the trees were scarce. I knew it didn't really matter where I parked, because they would find me.

I had been summoned again. But because I threw away the Big Phone, they had went old school. I checked my mailbox this morning to find a note with no envelope. This was at my new house that I had paid cash for and bought through a dummy corporation that Tuesday had helped me set up. By reaching me there, they were sending two messages at once.

I left the chill of my air-conditioned vehicle and took a seat at the picnic table and looked out over the water. The river was widest at this point. Huge cargo ships cruised the waterway that separated the Canadian skyline. I was approached by the occasional seagull, because so many had made a pastime of coming to feed the birds.

The sun beat mercilessly down on the back of my neck. The only things I had chosen to combat it were a wifebeater and a jumbo raspberry slush.

It didn't take long for him to find me. Never did. Two Range Rovers slotted themselves on the right side of my Marauder. Both black and both with a zero-percent tint all the way around—illegal in Michigan, but I doubted if any state trooper would stop them.

The passenger door opened on one, and he climbed out, looking like himself again. For our last meeting, he'd been casual in a Polo shirt and Levi's. This time it was a royal-blue suit that probably cost twenty bands, pinstriped with a gold-colored tie. He was forced to walk over the grass in those expensive brown oxfords, but his steps weren't tentative like he was worried over staining them. I expected this meeting to be different from the last in more than just the way he dressed, in tone more than anything.

He joined me on the same side of the picnic table. As usual, he looked healthy, but fatigued around the eyes.

He signed to me: "Secluded. About a quarter mile between witnesses from the right or left, but still not too deep into the island. Three different streets converge here, so you would have multiple routes back to the bridge. Tactical."

I used my hands to respond that I wasn't the only one thinking tactically. I didn't need to see in the second Range Rover to know that there was somebody in there watching me through a scope. One aggressive move and a high-velocity bullet was going come through that windshield and split my melon.

"We seem to keep placing yourself as a stumbling block to my objectives."

I responded, "You seem to keep trying to manipulate and control me."

"I never made you take this job. You had a choice."

He didn't make me take it, just made it too sweet for me to pass up.

This slick muthafucka knew that Antwon had figured out that they were coming for him and found a way to get in touch with the UOTA for help. The reason he had wanted me was because he knew the only thing that could beat a Shango warrior was a better one. Caine was easily the most cunning man I'd ever known, but I doubted that even he could predict that a second one would come who just happened to have a personal grudge with me.

I looked at his hands. There was a Greubel Forsey on his wrist, the type of watch that cost a million dollars and you only depreciated by adding diamonds. His only other jewelry was a simple wedding band that was most likely a remnant from his life with Tuesday. I signed to ask why he doesn't wear the ring.

He squinted hard against the afternoon glare. "It's an antiquated and self-defeating idea, one that I hope to do away with. They're elitist, and people wear them to feel superior. You can't have true anonymity while wearing a trinket that screams, 'I'm anonymous'!"

I thought they wore them so the members in secret could recognize each other. He read that off my hands. "But you aren't a member, and now you can recognize us, as well." I nodded, conceding that point to him.

"Very few people will have the vision to see what we are doing here. Secret societies laid the foundation of this very country. You think that it's a coincidence that so many of the founding fathers are Freemasons? But the foundation that they laid is steeped in institutional racism. A system to keep themselves at the top, while promoting few if any of us from the bottom.

"Men like your father think they can fight an operating system that has been in place for four centuries, when the best course is to infiltrate it. We take our talented tenth and strategically place them as agents within their four major pillars: Government, Finance, Education, and Media. We don't just play spooks who sit by the door. We take over the whole damn house, just like they do, and call it Manifest Destiny."

Being my father's son, I'd heard crazy conspiracy shit my whole life. He sounded insane, but it was plausible insanity. I had to ask him with my hands if this was just a polished sales pitch, or did he truly believe they could pull this off.

"Of course not in our lifetime. But I believe it so deeply that I sacrificed my own daughter for it." And I saw in his dark brown eyes there wasn't an ounce of regret in that decision.

He switched topics. "I understand that you got personally attached to Antwon, and as a show of good faith, I'll personally absorb the cost of losing him."

I gave him a *Nigga, please* look. We both know the UOTA didn't bomb that train, and I wasn't convinced that Antwon was even dead. The crash could've been a way for them to snatch their prize and silence any potential witnesses. For appearances, they'd probably planted the remains of someone matching Antwon's description at the scene, while the real one was somewhere on a private island, being indoctrinated.

He saw the question in my eyes and gave me nothing either way. This dude had a hell of a poker face.

"You will have to answer for Cameron, though. I never met him personally, but I was told he was kind of an asshole, and I can imagine some of the things he might've said to provoke you."

He stood up and straightened his jacket, brushed any dust from the back of his pants. "However, he was a Brother in Good Standing, and under our protection." He turned to me. "You should expect punitive repercussions."

He glared at me long and hard, in a way that used to make the hairs on my arms stand up back when I looked at Sebastian Caine as some ubiquitous force, and not just a man who could bleed just like me.

He knew that I had a one-year-old child and a second baby momma that I was purposely steering clear of. I signed to let his ass know that if anything happened to Quianna and my son, whether it be death or sickness, malicious or accidental, the act of a drunk driver, or an act of God himself, I was going to burn down the Great House of Kamku. I'm killing everybody from top to bottom: partners, associates, subsidiaries; debtors, creditors, sponsors; parents, friends, kids; even the nigga who mop the floor in the secret room where they have their meetings.

I stood chest-to-chest with him and returned the glare that he had given me. I knew the sight caused the snipers in the Range Rover to tighten their fingers on the trigger.

I signed, "They might call you The Invisible Man, but I see you. Anything that can be seen can be hit, and if it can be hit, it can be killed."

I had hoped my threat would invoke some emotion, but he was too much of a pro to fall for that. The man remained stoic.

He merely extended his hand to me. "As we now find ourselves at cross purposes, this concludes our relationship."

I shook it. It wasn't as slick as the shit I said to him, but it was still a threat.

Epilogue

I sat a block away from the target house, in another nondescript stash car I bought at auction for $3,800. I kept the brick Colonial in my sight as my mind went down a rabbit hole constructed of memories and imagination.

Renovations on my second home were coming along slowly. I had an actual castle to defend this time, but my contractors were running into unexpected problems. This was an older house, and I was trying to repeat what I did at the last one, which was recently built. I was still who I was, and because of who I'd pissed off, it was even more critical that I had bulletproof walls and secondary barriers at the points of entry. The bills were sky-high, and without Dirty Red's heroin business to help feed my bag, I was feeling the pinch. But it will get done eventually. And I while it might be nice to have somebody there to make it feel like a home, I wouldn't subject them to dealing with everything that came along with me.

I saw Kierra a few weeks ago, totally on some random shit. I had business on the eastside near Mound Road and 6 Mile. I just happened to get caught at a red light, peeked into the red Challenger next to me, and found her eyes awaiting mine. Still sexy as ever, still grown as fuck and rocking her hair in twin ponytails, still had the lips that caused a thousand cum stains. She looked less stressed, and I chalked that up to being away from me. She was in the car with some older-looking dude with a bald head; I didn't know if he was a brother, a friend, or her new man. Our only exchange was to acknowledge each other with slight head nods. The light turned green, and she sped away into her life. I returned to the constant warzone that was mine.

After three months in hiding God-knows-where, Amelia started popping up on television again. Overnight, the narrative about her seemed to change as she went from radical, right-wing antisemite to innocent victim of cancel culture. Like a thrown switch, everybody just stopped being mad at her, and her career rose from the ashes. She started out as a panel guest on a few of the local shows; then her face started popping up on CNN. Amelia worked her way into their rotation, first as a regular guest, then as a guest host. Not soon after that, I saw a promo for her own nationally syndicated show.

The part I found interesting was that Amelia is no longer a hardline Republican. All the conservative, pro-gun, pro-life, America-is-the-land-of-milk-and-honey bullshit that had made her name before had changed. Her political views had shifted closer to moderate: advocating for women's rights, gun control, and equal opportunity. I occasionally watched her on some debate program, trying to determine if she was acting then, or acting now. It was suspicious as hell to me that no one, not the moderator or her rival, ever mentioned or called Amelia out on this sudden pivot. It was like she was totally rebranded, and that other Amelia never existed.

It was the same for her son. I scoured the newspapers and internet, but there was never any story about a local Detroit boy named Antwon Jenkins being killed in the train crash. The story itself only had legs for a day or two and was then rinsed from the media cycle. It was just like Tuesday had said: a Google search turned up plenty of Antwon Jenkinses in Detroit, but not the fat-faced boy with the box fade. No Twitter, no Facebook, no Tik-Tok. Antwon had already moved like a ghost in that cyberworld, but now there was no trace of him in this physical one. I had played with the idea of breaking into his old school on the off chance they had some hard copies of his records, but didn't waste my time. These Kamku muthafuckas were so good that even the footage of Antwon recorded at the house by my personal security cameras had been corrupted and turned to static.

Two months back, my daily scan of the obituaries page did turn up one for a Terrence Jenkins. An old photo came up on my screen of him ten years younger, wearing a smile like he'd cracked a particularly good joke. A westside man, thirty-eight, was found dead in his own home of an apparent heart attack. His job called in a welfare check to the police when he missed four consecutive days at work.

There were no signs of forced entry or foul play, but thirty-eight is kind of young for your pump to just quit on you. I wondered if it was just poor diet, or had Terrence started asking too many questions about his son.

I had one I wanted to ask myself, but had to wait another six weeks after Terrence passed for the opportunity. She was currently stationed out of Atlanta, but I learned that she had returned to Detroit for a press junket to promote her new show. A small group of fans waited for her outside the television studio in Southfield, 9 Mile Road, where Detroit's own Fox 2 News was broadcast.

Amelia stepped out of the building dressed in a cream Chanel pantsuit. She was rocking her hair shorter, but still with natural curls. She looked ethereally beautiful, a face the cameras loved and the people trusted. She smiled, happy to sign a few autographs on the way to a black Escalade. She was only ten feet from the rear door when I moved to intercept her.

But she was being escorted by a two-man security detail. They were Black, both in suits similar to the one she'd bought for me, looking professional, the way she liked. I could tell just by the way they moved, they were armed, highly trained, and didn't always play fair. These weren't just bodyguards. They were killers like me.

They cut me off before I could get within five feet of Amelia. Pistols appeared as if by magic, and they pressed me back to a safe distance.

I had figured I wouldn't get close enough to use my phone, so I had prepared a sign on a seventeen-by-twenty-four-inch sheet on orange construction paper. I pulled it out and held it up for her to see.

I didn't want my sloppy handwriting to be an issue, so I used big three-inch stenciled block letters to pose my questions: *When did you get off that train?* And *No funeral for Antwon?*

For a second Amelia looked at me like I was some homeless stranger; then I saw recognition widen those pretty brown eyes. She scanned my sign again, then shrugged innocently. Her lips formed the words, "I'm sorry, sir, but who's Antwon?"

And that's when I spotted it, pinky finger of her right hand. A small, bronze, triangle-shaped ring.

The last few months were hectic, but movement down the block snapped me back to the present. The Tahoe backed out the driveway and turned into the street. The interior of my car was briefly swept up in the glow of its headlights as the SUV cruised past me.

This was something that had been fucking with me for a while. Something that I just had to do.

I went into my gym bag on my passenger seat and did a final check of my supplies. Bolt-cutters, zip ties, a sandwich bag full of rib bones for the puppies, and an extra T-shirt and jeans just in case she needed clothes. And of course, a Walther P99 with a full clip. I pushed out the driver's door and headed for the house.

I didn't know if the same girl was still there after all this time, but I hoped for her sake that she didn't meet the likely end for discarded sex slaves. I didn't care if it were her, or a totally different girl being kept chained up in there.

Today she was going home, whether she wanted to or not.